Evelyn's Promise

A More Perfect Union Series Book 4

Betty Bolté

www.MysticOwlPublishing.com

Copyright © 2020 by Betty Bolté.
First edition published 2016
www.bettybolte.com

Ebook ISBN-13: 978-1-7354669-1-0
Paperback ISBN-13: 978-1-7354669-0-3
Audiobook ISBN-13: 978-1-7354669-9-5

Also by Betty Bolté

Becoming Lady Washington: A Novel
Notes of Love and War

FURY FALLS INN
The Haunting of Fury Falls Inn
Under Lock and Key

A MORE PERFECT UNION SERIES
Elizabeth's Hope
Emily's Vow
Amy's Choice
Samantha's Secret
Evelyn's Promise

SECRETS OF ROSEVILLE SERIES
Undying Love
Haunted Melody
The Touchstone of Raven Hollow
Veiled Visions of Love
Charmed Against All Odds

Preface

Evelyn's Promise is the fourth historical romance I ever published and as such it was written many years ago as I was a new author. It's amazing how much my storytelling skills have improved over the past four years since this book was originally published. The core of the story remains the same, but hopefully with more skilled telling. This edition is a revised version of the fourth book in the A More Perfect union historical romance series. I have corrected and revised the text throughout the story.

Thanks for reading!

Chapter One

Charles Town, South Carolina – 1783

*P*leasure and grief battled in Evelyn Hamilton's chest. She cast a sidelong glance at the lean man standing beside her.

"Looks like the entire town turned out for the triple wedding and the festivities afterward." He glanced at her and then returned his gaze to the room at large.

"Yes, food tends to lure people out of their homes." She kept a smile on her face as she observed the multitude of people milling about in the candlelit and lavishly decorated home.

Her pulse throbbed in her ears at Nathaniel Williams' proximity, a sensation she'd only experienced when in fear of her late husband's next actions. She held still, though actively attempting to calm the alarm inside her chest. Not only had Nathaniel stolen food from her pantry but his height and breadth rivaled that of her dead husband. She'd learned to mask her inner strength, what she possessed, by bowing her head, studying her hands or even her feet if necessary.

In her experience, men could be cruel without a second thought, and she wouldn't give them a reason to inflict said cruelty upon her person.

She surveyed the happy gathering, the friendly mood of the group working its magic as she held her murmuring infant son. She relaxed a bit, though having the tall, powerful man standing so close caused a fine tremor in her gut. He wouldn't harm her, not in the present situation. Nathaniel's attention lingered on the three happy couples as they received congratulations from the guests snaking past the newly married. She was exhausted and longed for a quiet room, but remained amidst the jocular gathering. "I understand you are to thank for the handsome decorations?" He lifted a brow and folded his arms across his chest, shifting his weight to rest on the hip closer to her.

"Thank you." She'd enjoyed applying her talents to making the house reflect the importance of the day's event. In truth, the triple wedding made Twelfth Night a livelier and more joyful occasion than in previous years, especially those under British occupation. "I enjoyed dressing the house for the happy occasion."

Nathaniel regarded her with a gentle smile. "After all the horrors of war, the opportunity to enjoy such merriments is a delight to the senses."

She shifted the bundle in her arms. "Even during the war, life has a way of pushing through to keep hope alive."

She looked down as her son squirmed in her embrace. A white cap, made with her own hands from fine linen, covered his wispy red-brown hair. His eyelashes fanned on his cheeks as the little mouth pursed in his sleep. The white dress he wore had been handed down from his cousin when he'd outgrown the garment. Even Walter, her deceased husband, had expressed pride in Jim. She'd promised herself that she'd do all in her power to ensure Master James Christopher

Hamilton grew up to honor his name. No matter what she must do, she'd prepare Jim for whatever opportunities life brought his way.

She and Nathaniel, a virtual stranger to her up until the reverend performed the weddings a few minutes ago, had already paid their compliments to the three pairs of smiling husbands and wives. Her new friends and her sister stood together. Each bride shone with happiness, their smiles vying with the candles for lighting the room. The happy couples made a striking and impressive group.

Candles flickered throughout the newly redecorated house, illuminating bouquets of flowers tied with long curling ribbon secured to the banister and resting on tables. In the parlor, a string quartet played softly. The feeling in the home seemed magical and dreamy, like something out of a play. Even her old gown of silk and taffeta, with its embroidered stomacher and flowing cerulean skirts, appeared revitalized and beautiful. She'd been relieved when the dress fit upon her matronly figure after birthing the baby a mere two months previous.

Nathaniel caught her attention with a tilt of his head and wave of his hand. "Do you know all of these people?"

"On Twelfth Night, everyone is invited. I hope we don't run out of the rum punch and egg nog."

"Would you care for a cup of either, before such a tragic event occurs?" He winked at her, an impish grin teasing her. "I'm happy to oblige, if so."

"No, but thank you. My hands are already full." She tucked the light blanket around her son's sleeping face.

"I imagine they will remain so until your child is grown." He stepped closer to her as guests pushed behind him on their way to the virtually groaning table of refreshments. "It appears the party is just beginning."

"Yes, it should last for several days as long as the food and drink hold out."

Nathaniel towered over her petite frame, a giant dressed in fine clothes. She lifted her chin, despite her unease, and studied the stranger's scarred yet striking features. His luxurious chestnut brown hair, shot through with gold, tempted her touch, but she resisted the urge. His earlier brief conversation with Benjamin, her sister's new husband, revealed he had fought in the state militia. He had come to town at Benjamin's express invitation. What kind of business could he possibly have with the major? And, more urgent, why did he need to stand so close?

His steel gray eyes searched her face, his gaze flitting from mouth to nose and finally resting upon her eyes. "Unfortunately, I don't expect to stay for the duration."

"You'll miss the celebration of the end of the holidays." She drew a slow, unsteady breath as he continued to study her with the ghost of a smile. She lowered her eyes, smoothing the baby blanket as an excuse for looking away.

"I'll miss more than that, I imagine." He lifted the edge of Jim's blanket, peered at the sleeping infant before he speared her with his black-rimmed eyes. "He has your nose."

She giggled, then sobered, annoyed with her school girl reaction to the man. What was it about him that provoked such a reflex? She pressed her lips together but a smile forced its way through. "Perhaps he should give it back to me, do you suppose?"

Nathaniel's smile widened to reveal his teeth. "Mayhap you can share it."

Laughter bubbled out of her mouth and she quickly stopped it. "That would prove unsatisfactory."

He chuckled, eyes twinkling. He glanced away and then back. "Looks like we're about to have some company."

Evelyn followed his gaze. Her sister Amy and Benjamin led the others to where Evelyn stood with Nathaniel by the cold fireplace, its firebox laid with kindling and tinder for later in the evening. With the press of so many bodies during the middle of the day, Evelyn had decreed no additional heat necessary. She'd been right, too. The doors and windows stood open to let in the cold January air, helping to mitigate the warmth created by the crush of guests.

The ladies had chosen beautiful gowns of their own for this special day. Cousin Emily's pale yellow gown suited her to perfection, with white roses embroidered around the scooped neck of the bodice and then reaching out in rays down the skirts. She wore her blonde curls in an smooth bun beneath a matching pale yellow hat made from lace and decorated with real white roses. Amy wore a midnight blue dress overlaid with lavender netting. Her dark locks had been tamed into an intricate hairdo, a few curls left to hang beside her rosy cheeks. Samantha, her new friend and adopted sister, had boldly chosen an emerald velvet gown, with a deep plunge of the neck and scattering of rhinestones across the bodice, which suited her coloring and green eyes. Her ebony hair had been fashioned into an elegant braid for the occasion, with wisps of curls left to dance about her face. Gold bobs hung on her earlobes and a matching chain graced her neck. A lovely trio indeed.

"Evelyn, I cannot thank you enough for your efforts to make the house so beautiful and welcoming." Emily drew her husband Frank Thomson closer to stand with her at Evelyn's side. "Everyone is talking about the beautiful flowers and ribbons, oh, and the array of branched candlesticks."

"You created a beautiful and romantic setting for our special day." Amy lightly hugged Evelyn, careful to not wake the baby. "A simple thank you cannot convey the depth of my gratitude. Especially after the terrible losses you've endured over the past month or so."

Amy's comment raised the memory of the gun shots, the violence, and the violations Evelyn had experienced. Her late husband Walter had been a difficult man to please. When she had not produced an heir within a few months of their marriage, he'd turned violent. Fortunately, she conceived a baby and his tirades abated. Until the renegades and scouts took turns scavenging the property. He held his tongue while the invaders took all they wanted, but then he had unleashed his anger upon her. She sniffed and shook off the misery threatening to dampen her spirits. She wouldn't permit anything to interfere with her happiness on her sister's wedding day.

"One must look to the future and move on when adversity strikes." Evelyn joggled Jim as he began to stir. Soon he'd be wide awake and hungry. He must be her focus, not the death of her abusive husband, nor the conflagration that consumed their manor house. Looking forward meant figuring out how she'd provide for her own household.

"I'm pleased you chose to accept our parents' offer. Since I'm moving out soon, they would be lonely without having one of us with them." Amy clasped her hands before her as she nodded. "It's some form of a miracle our father's finances are sound after all of the trials he's been through over the course of the war."

"Indeed. I'm fortunate they do not mind my return to their house." But Evelyn minded, more than she'd shared with any one. Her first task was to find her own place to live and raise her son. But how could she afford a house? The money Walter had set aside would last a few months with the current rate of inflation and the devaluation of paper money. Then what?

"At least you have a roof over your head." Nathaniel shifted his weight, closing the distance between them so his hip nearly touched hers. "I've just arrived in town and must find lodgings until I can locate a suitable domicile."

"I'm certain someone will open their home to you." His

nearness sent shivers through Evelyn's midriff. He exuded a force she sensed but couldn't define, one tempting her to touch him. What was wrong with her? She barely knew him. She took a half step away, covering her movement with a peek at Jim.

"We're a friendly city, now that the bloody Britons have departed." Frank slipped his arm around Emily's waist. "What do you think of having a guest?"

Emily glanced at Evelyn and then back to Frank. "If he'd like to stay with us, I'm sure we can make him comfortable."

Nathaniel inclined his head in thanks. "Very kind of you. But, what about your honeymoon?"

Frank shook his head, his blond hair neatly held in a queue for the occasion. "We've decided to remain at home and enjoy our newly refurbished abode instead of traveling at this time of year. But in a little while, we will make a journey."

"All the more reason for me to decline your generous offer." Nathaniel shrugged as he glanced at Emily. "I wouldn't wish to interfere with a newly married couple."

Trent raised both brows and shook his head. "Do not worry. We'll help you find lodgings. Perhaps Captain Sullivan will have a place, like he did for Benjamin."

"Nonsense, my friend. What of southern hospitality? Mr. Williams, you are welcome to stay with us. Isn't he, dear?" Benjamin peered at Amy. He was tall, dark haired, and handsome in an elaborately embroidered waistcoat peeking out from under a bright blue coat and trousers. Amy slowly nodded, doubt in her eyes. "See? We'd be pleased for you to share our house as long as you might need."

A host of conflicting emotions flashed across Nathaniel's face before he shook his head. "I appreciate the offer, but I simply cannot believe the newly married would wish a stranger in their midst. I'm sure if I were in your shoes I'd be reluctant to entertain guests."

Evelyn avoided meeting Nathaniel's eyes as he contemplated her with his last words. She hugged Jim close, her cheeks warming under his regard, and looked anywhere but in his direction. He seemed to hint at the underlying meaning of his words to her, provoking the tumult raging in her mind. She needed to remove herself from his presence and soon.

"That is a valid point." Benjamin grinned at Nathaniel. "It may be hard to sleep nights."

Amy swatted Benjamin's arm, blushing as his meaning spread through the group. "Mind your manners."

"Where will you stay then? If you won't stay with any of us, I mean." Samantha clasped her husband Trent Cunningham's arm as her gaze shifted from one to another of the group.

Evelyn liked Dr. Trent, and rejoiced that her dear friend had found the love of her life in the sandy haired handsome man. Like the others, Trent had donned his finest suit, the dark blue setting off his crystal blue eyes and a discreetly patterned waistcoat, both of which showed his strength and elegant carriage.

The rustle of taffeta and thump of leather shoes on the wood floor drew Evelyn's attention to the elderly couple approaching. Her parents, Richard and Lucille Abernathy, had aged gracefully, though her mother's ramrod straight back had bowed a little more each year. Their love revealed itself through the angling of their bodies toward each other as well as the looks they shared. Evelyn quickly made the appropriate introductions once they came to a halt.

If she could one day find a man who would treat her with the same respect and concern as her father shared with her mother, she'd be content. But the pickings proved slim after so many men had lost their lives securing the independence of America from British tyranny. Societal expectations weighed on her mind. She should find another husband, one to provide for her two-month-old son. If she only had herself to support, she'd manage with sewing or perhaps by being a governess. Jim, her mother had reminded her, needed a father to teach the boy how to be a man, and to ensure he received the requisite care and education to grow to his full maturity. Yet part of her wished to remain unmarried, independent of the needs and demands of a husband. But even knowing of the dearth of eligible bachelors, the next time she accepted a man's attentions, she'd be very careful and certain of his personality. She'd promised herself no one would hurt her ever again.

"I couldn't help but overhear. We have room for you and no recently wed occupants to worry about." Richard Abernathy slapped Nathaniel on the back. "Interested?"

Nathaniel smiled, his attention flicking her way and then back to her father. Evelyn held her breath, squeezing Jim until his murmur of protest made her relax her grip. Would this man be staying under the same roof? She desired distance between them, and suddenly the absolute opposite results hovered in the air. Definitely time for her to find another place to reside.

Nathaniel studied her for two beats of her heart before turning and stretching out his hand to shake with her father. "I'd be honored to accept, as long as it does not inconvenience any one."

"Not at all. If you'd like, you can ride in the carriage with us back to the house." Richard rested his large hand at the small of Lucille's back. "We intend to leave in a little while. We tire easily as the years go by, so we're off to say our farewells and then we can depart."

"Very good." Nathaniel nodded to Richard as he led his wife away, then fixed his attention on Evelyn. "Do you mind that I accepted your father's offer? I have no wish to make you uncomfortable in your own home."

"Why would I mind?" Evelyn kept her eyes on the handsome yet dangerous man regarding her with a serious expression. Dangerous first with regard to the scars he'd suffered during the fighting, indicating he resorted to aggressive behavior when pressed. Dangerous in that he'd also been a party to the raid on her house, a violent invasion of her home by the American militia in search of sustenance for the soldiers. Finally, dangerous to her equilibrium by his presence and his belief that fate had brought them together that scary day last fall during the raid on her home. She straightened her back, stiffening her resolve at the same time. Handsome is as handsome does, after all. "As long as you keep to yourself, we shall get along."

He nodded slowly but his charming smile slipped back into place. "I shall endeavor to honor your request."

"See that you do." A flicker of humor flashed in his eyes and she drew in a breath. "I'm in mourning, so your attentions would be, if not welcome, at best inappropriate."

The sparkle in his eyes went out. "I see."

Amy took Benjamin's hand in hers as she addressed Evelyn. "My dear sister, you, of all people, know how fearful it is to be without a home to live in. Now that your worries are behind you, please don't begrudge the young man shelter from the elements for a short stay while he makes other arrangements."

Evelyn angled her head and frowned at her sister. "What do you mean, my worries are behind me?"

"Why, you have a home and the security of our father's fortune to provide for you and your son." Amy waved a hand in the space between them. "You need not trouble your head about where and how you'll live. It's been decided."

Surprise swept through Evelyn. "No, it has not been decided." She espied doubt on the faces of her friends. "I have no intention of living with my parents for long."

Nathaniel nodded at her. "Looks like we have something in common."

Evelyn opened her mouth to contradict his claim, but Amy cut into the conversation.

"Look, Benjamin, Mr. and Mrs. Walters are preparing to leave. We must go thank them for their wedding gifts." Amy tugged on Benjamin's arm, drawing him away from the cluster of friends.

"Will you excuse us?" Benjamin addressed the group at large as he allowed Amy to pull him along behind her.

"Be off with you." Evelyn waved the three couples on their way. "We'll catch up with you later."

"Thanks again for all your help, Evelyn," Samantha said as Trent proffered his arm.

"My pleasure." Evelyn shooed them with a happy chuckle. "Go. See to your guests."

After the chattering friends had blended into the surrounding crowd, Evelyn turned back to Nathaniel. "So, Mr. Williams, will you be staying in town long?"

"I'm not sure. It depends on what Major Hanson has to say to-morrow when we meet." He peered at her, and a gentle smile emerged on his lips. "And what a certain recent widow might have to say as well. She may wish for me to dawdle in procuring my own residence."

Evelyn raised one brow at the provocative suggestion and then shook her head. She had absolutely no intention of beginning her husband hunt so soon after becoming widowed. "Do not depend on such an unlikely occurrence, Mr. Williams."

"Please, my friends all call me Nat. And I shall call you Lyn." He chuckled and folded his arms. "Since we'll be living under the same roof for a time, we may as well be friends."

Evelyn blinked at the man, astonished at the level of his audacity and yet drawn to him like the tide by the moon. Yes, he was definitely a dangerous man. No one had ever shortened her given name into a nickname. Especially not a pet name that sounded so divine on his lips. She couldn't let him use the nickname if she had any hope of keeping him at a distance. "Please, call me Mrs. Hamilton, and I will call you Mr. Williams."

He shook his head, as though sad to correct her. "I think not. Lyn suits you exquisitely better."

Clearly, he couldn't be reasoned with, intent on having his way, much like Walter, who had cowed her into doing everything to please him. But no matter what she did or how she behaved, she had never really satisfied her husband. Except maybe in having a son. A son she'd do everything in her power to protect. Squaring her shoulders, she blinked at Nathaniel. She would not travel the path of subjugation ever again.

"I have never answered to a nickname, so if you intend to be friendly, you'll respect my wishes." She snugged Jim closer to her, preparing to walk away from the charged space suddenly stretching between them.

Nathaniel smiled at her, and made the beginning of a bow before straightening, glee in his eyes. "If you insist."

"I do." The mischievous smirk on his lips did not bode well. She'd seen his type before. She would make certain he behaved properly toward her.

Her young maid appeared out of the crowd. Dressed in her best frock, the black slave soon reached Evelyn's side and reached out to take Jim into her arms. "Want me to carry him? Your arms must be tiring."

"Yes, thank you, Jemma." Evelyn gladly transferred the weight of her son to the girl. "He may need a clean napkin, as well."

"I'll take good care of the young'un." Jemma rearranged the blanket over the wide awake boy. "You enjoy yourself, you here?"

Evelyn huffed a laugh as she fingered her skirts. "I have been, but now it's time we depart."

"Yes, miss." Jemma peered at the man beside Evelyn. "Is he coming with us?"

"It appears so. This is Nathaniel Williams." Evelyn glanced between the maid and the man. "My father invited him to stay with us for as long as he'd enjoy visiting."

"Pleased to meet you, Jemma." Nathaniel offered his bent arm to Evelyn, an invitation to his escort, but also the dubious invitation to touch him. "Shall we join your parents?"

His nearness set her heart racing. To lay her hand on his muscular arm would invite an undesired response. As much as she wanted to touch him, she could not permit herself to indulge the desire. She must tread carefully, and see he did as well. "As long as you remember you are a guest in our house, I will treat you with respect and deference." She had promises to keep, ones made to herself and to her son. Nothing would sway her from her mission. Not even tempting lips and an endearing smile. "I ask you to do the same."

"You have nothing to fear from me." He inclined his head and grinned at her when she gingerly rested the tips of her fingers on his coat sleeve.

The light yet electric touch of his arm, even through the sleeve, evoked a tiny gasp from deep inside her. Propriety kept her hand in place as they stepped off, making a path through the crowded rooms. They paused in an antechamber to don their warm cloaks and hats, avoiding further contact until he again crooked his arm. After pulling on her gloves, she reluctantly accepted.

As they approached her parents at the open front door, he glanced down at her. "I shall be on my very best behavior, Lyn."

She gaped at him. The challenge in his expression made her snap her mouth closed as they passed through the door and out onto the street. He dared her to accept his flirtation, a dare tempting and intriguing if worrisome. Her parents climbed into the conveyance as Nathaniel escorted her toward the vehicle. The corded muscles in his arm flexed beneath her tense fingers before he took her hand and helped her up into the waiting carriage.

She gathered her long skirts close as she sat on the cushioned bench seat, and then stifled a gasp when Nathaniel squeezed in beside her, Jemma and Jim on his other side. His leg rested against hers, hidden beneath the flap of his coat and her own voluminous skirts. With her parents sitting directly in front of her, calmly smiling and chatting with Nathaniel, she dared not draw attention to his impropriety. She pressed her lips together to keep from chastising him. Oh, she wished she'd been wrong, but she'd been so very right. He was indeed dangerous on all counts.

Spirits flowed freely, both the ale and the mood, in McCrady's Tavern the next day. Nathaniel perused the men and ladies crowded into the popular gathering spot, before returning his gaze to rest on his companions. Benjamin and Frank conversed with easy familiarity, the result no doubt of a long friendship. They'd agreed to join him for a drink and a discussion regarding his troublingly uncertain future.

"I'm sorry to hear of the loss of your family and property." Frank dragged his chin side to side, a slow acknowledgement of what Nathaniel had come to think of as his personal tragedy. "My sympathies to you."

"I appreciate it." Nathaniel's grief over losing his wife during the bloody war echoed in his chest, a throbbing underlying each beat of his heart.

He'd returned home the November past only to find the house charred ruins, his pretty but sometimes bitter wife buried nearby beneath a crude wooden cross. A neighbor had relayed to him the horrible details of the devastating attack by loyalists six months before the war ended. The neighbor hadn't known where Nathaniel was, so stepped in to handle matters in his stead. He'd thanked the man for his efforts but found he couldn't stay on the property. He decided to take the major up on his offer to help him after the war ended. He'd find work and a new place to start over. He turned over the deed to the property in exchange for the little gold specie his helpful neighbor possessed and rode away.

"I must forge ahead. Start anew somewhere." He toyed with the blue glass bottle he clasped with both hands.

"Why not in Charlestown?" Benjamin tapped his bottle of ale to Nathaniel's. "The new and improved city of Charlestown would welcome an industrious man such as you."

"Yes, we've much to offer and more to come." Frank also touched his bottle to Nathaniel's. "What did you have in mind?"

The question of the year. He'd pondered possibilities with no resolution. "I'm open to suggestions, though I've considered perhaps a surveying job."

"Dangerous work, that." Benjamin savored several long swallows, then wiped his mouth with the back of his hand. "Out in the wilderness with the bears and wolves to contend with."

"I enjoyed being away from town while in the militia, sleeping under the stars." The diversity of the others eating and drinking at the many tables suggested a lively and varied population. Could he live in a city, even an interesting and bustling port city such as Charlestown? He'd never done so, or at least not for more than a few days. Adapting to the inherent sights and smells proved challenging.

Frank snorted and tapped a finger against his bottle. "Not something I can relate to. I'd much rather be in a comfortable home or, even better, on a ship sailing to distant lands."

"My precise meaning, Frank." Nathaniel spun the bottle with deliberate movements. "The frontier is one option. I'm waiting for the payment from Congress before I can truly decide my future."

"The debt may not be paid, from the rumors I've heard." Benjamin's gaze put truth to the gossip. "Congress lacks the funds to make good on their promise to the soldiers."

"Damnation. I'd counted on the payment." Nathaniel drank from the glass bottle, fighting a sinking of his spirits along with his prospects. Congress had enlisted thousands of men on the promise of a yearly salary until the war ended, and then a pension for life of half the annual salary. Such funds served as the mythical foundation of his future, one he couldn't see clearly and now had no means with which to pursue. "I suppose I'll need to find work, if that's the case. Any ideas?"

"You and every other soldier returning home are seeking employment. With so many men flooding back into town, work is hard to come by." Frank looked around the room, his gaze lighting briefly on the other patrons before returning to rest on Nathaniel. "I could use some help at the print shop running the press, if you're so inclined."

A printing press? Could anything be less interesting? Still, he'd not turn away any opportunity, however tedious. "Doing what precisely?"

"Setting the type for various printed materials." Frank grimaced with each word spoken. "A task I'd readily hand over to someone more adept."

"For how long?" Did he say tedious? Setting type seemed like a monotony of a kind most appalling. Simple enough work, though. He'd do anything to fund his most beloved dream of moving away from the painful memories he associated with the coast. "What about payment?"

"I'm thinking six months, while Emily and I take the journey I'd promised her. We've been talking of going to France in the next few months. As for payment…" Frank waggled a hand in the air above the scarred wood table. "We can work out an appropriate wage if you're interested."

Six months of his life spent in a shop. He sipped his drink, contemplating the ramifications of agreeing with the offer. One advantage would be the accumulation of money toward purchasing his own property wherever he chose to settle. Perhaps the most tempting reason to accept was proximity to Evelyn, the enchantress who soothed the grief thrumming inside with a gentle smile and a lighthearted laugh. She attracted him with her beauty, her wit, and her intelligence. And something else, something…more he couldn't describe. With time he hoped to discover the enthralling attribute.

"Take it, man." Benjamin punched Frank on the shoulder. "He's earned the reward of a trip abroad after all his sacrifices during the revolution."

Nathaniel lifted his ale and drank, delaying a response. If the work enabled him to follow his dream, then the time would be well spent. He envisioned a fine home and perhaps an orchard, acres and acres of fruit trees to harvest and sell. He imagined Evelyn tending his hearth and garden, while young Jim grew into a fine lad to help him run the place. A dream, surely, but one he felt certain he could bring to pass.

"Very well, I accept." Nathaniel shrugged and tapped a finger against the glass vessel. "Tell me more about what you'd expect me to do while you're traveling with your wife."

Nathaniel listened to Frank's description of the work involved. Since the British had embarked their troop ships for England the month previous, Frank had received more and more business in the forms of pamphlets, announcements, even books of poetry and romances. He asked a few questions now and again, but mostly listened. The more Frank talked, the more he wondered why exactly he'd agreed.

The door opened, sunlight and fresh air filtering into the dimly lit interior. Glancing up, he grinned as Evelyn and Amy crossed the threshold and paused. He smiled even more broadly when Evelyn's gaze met his. He rose, knocking lightly on the table as he did. "We have company, gentlemen."

Benjamin and Frank also stood to drag two more chairs over to the table. Nathaniel motioned for the ladies to join them. The graceful sway of Evelyn's hips as she approached distracted him until he forced his gaze up to her regard. Flustered by her smirk, he busied himself with pulling out the chair and assisting her to settle onto the hard surface.

"I'm glad to be indoors again." Amy shivered in her seat beside Benjamin, her gaze bouncing from one face to another.

"The wind picked up so that it howls down the street." Evelyn relaxed against the chair back. "Though even that didn't deter folks from crowding the lanes and alleys."

Benjamin chuckled as he attracted the barkeeper's attention with a wave of his hand. "The relief in town is keen. I imagine some time will pass before the celebrations subside."

"Where is Emily?" Frank cocked his head at Amy, his brow furrowed. "I thought she'd be with you."

"She stopped at her shop to check on its progress." Amy shrugged. "Tom Elfe was having some difficulty with the design of the cabinetry. He's not as talented as his pa used to be, but he'll manage. She'll be along."

Frank nodded and lifted his bottle. Nathaniel mimicked his movements while tracking Evelyn's. She watched her companions with a puzzled expression, as though not quite understanding their conversation or actions but amused in spite of her confusion. He recalled that she had been isolated in the country for several years, kept away from her family and friends by her deceased husband. Why the man hid his wife from everyone remained a mystery.

Her beauty and social graces made her special. More than the superficial aspects, though, her quiet intellect spoke to Nathaniel in ways unlike any one else. Despite the reality that they'd formally met a few days before, he wanted to protect her, prevent any harm or hurt. There was only one problem with his intent. He couldn't pursue his desire to court her until he established his plan and a means to support a new wife. Until then, he'd not entangle their futures in any way. It simply wouldn't be fair to her. He studied her for several moments until she aimed her gaze at him. He blinked and sipped his drink, the pungent hops sweetly bitter on his tongue. But damn, he'd love to pursue her as a real contender to be her beau.

A precocious waitress sashayed over with a tray bearing crystal glasses of sherry for the girls. She set them before Amy and then Evelyn, then spun away with a toss of her head.

"Nathaniel, my mother asked me to inquire whether you will need a personal servant while you're staying with us." Evelyn sat up straight and clasped her hands in her lap.

"No, I can manage on my own." He detected uncertainty in her steady gaze and smiled to reassure her. He was rewarded with the gentle lift of her tempting lips, the smile he ill-advisedly loved to distraction. "But please convey my appreciation for her thoughtfulness when you see her next."

"I will. I believe she'll be relieved, to be honest." Evelyn wrapped her fingers around the stem of the crystal glass, lifting the red wine toward her enticing mouth.

Nathaniel looked away from Evelyn to calm the reaction in his midriff. Every act and smile evoked pleasure in his chest. Such a lovely woman. He could gaze upon her features forever, but the timing of his infatuation proved inconvenient for them both.

"Because of the want of slaves in town?" Amy asked.

"We lost several to the departing British ships and haven't yet been able to replace them from the plantation." Evelyn sipped the garnet fluid and then set her glass on the table.

"Your family is not the only one facing such a problem." Frank nodded slowly as he glanced around the group. "I understand a ship is due soon which brings hundreds of indentured servants and slaves."

Benjamin set his drink on the white linen dressed table. "A temporary solution but at least some help is on the way."

"Why not hire some of the returning militia to work instead of buying a person, indentured or slave?" Nathaniel had never liked the idea of buying servants.

He only hired those who had the right to choose where they worked and for whom. But his needs were small. He appreciated the dilemma planters faced. The thousands of acres of crops to be sowed and harvested each year required many hands. Far cheaper to buy the slave than to pay wages, thus making the crops vastly more profitable. But at what cost in humanity?

"Many of the men seek employment, while others have elected to be an artisan or tradesman." Amy tapped a manicured finger on the tablecloth. "My cousins, for example, are considering their options as well."

"The Sullivan brothers could turn water into wine with their talents." Frank gripped his bottle with one hand, sliding it closer to him. "When they team together, they can do most anything."

"You're correct, my friend." Benjamin huffed a laugh. "It's best to keep an eye on them and invest in whatever they do."

"Of whom do you speak?" Nathaniel asked.

"My apologies." Benjamin lifted his shoulders and let them fall back into place. "Emily's brothers, Ethan, Luke, and Bill."

Evelyn bobbed her head, one brow raised as she laid a hand on the tabletop. "They have King Midas' touch. Everything they try, even if it appears it will fail, turns into a profitable endeavor."

Nathaniel contemplated Evelyn, awed by her animated features, her elegant hand laying so close to his, as well as her allusion to the ancient king. Midas had been able to turn anything into gold by a simple touch. Unfortunately, his talent applied to his food as well, which must have made eating problematic. Evelyn's fingers rested inches from where he held his blue bottle, tempting in their undeniable attraction. He shouldn't indulge in his desire, but the temptation proved more powerful than his will. He released his grip, moving his hand toward hers. Would she permit him to clasp her hand?

Closer, ever closer his fingers moved toward hers, until she glanced at him and lowered her hand into her lap. Denying him the delight of making contact. He inclined his head in brief acknowledgement of her opinion of his action. He swallowed a gulp of ale, determined to assume an aloof and disinterested demeanor.

"I look forward to making their acquaintance." Nathaniel gripped his bottle with both hands, ensuring he couldn't indulge his whims.

"I understand Luke is thinking of starting a stable from a pair of my father's horses." Amy made circles with one finger on the tablecloth. "They've chosen well, I believe."

"What is their aim?" Benjamin asked. "A racing stable or something else?"

"Yes, racing. He's chosen a proven blooded stallion and a

refined mare to begin a new line." Amy folded her hands together in her lap. "I'm sure he'll bring his brothers into the endeavor over time."

"He'll need money to build a new stable, so I'm sure they'll be looking for employment as well." Benjamin glanced at Frank and then to Nathaniel.

"So it's a good thing I took your offer when I did." Nathaniel grinned in Frank's direction. "With so few opportunities in town, I mean."

A fiddler struck up a tune in the far corner of the tavern, his bow flashing in the glow from the lamps placed around the walls. The jig soon had several couples up and dancing to the lively music. Spectators clapped along to the beat as the couples formed circles.

"What offer?" Evelyn regarded him with raised brows.

Frank slapped Nathaniel on the back. "He's going to take over setting the type for the press."

"So you will be staying in town for a while." Evelyn nodded to herself and sipped her wine.

What was she thinking behind her shuttered expression? Did she approve his choice? Nathaniel couldn't tell. Why should it matter whether she approved or not? He didn't want to seek the answer to his own question. "For six months as things stand now."

"What then?" Amy leaned forward to pluck a roasted pecan from the bowl in the center of the table.

Nathaniel shrugged, reaching for a nut as well. "I don't know yet. But by the passage of six months, I intend to have a plan for my future."

"I'd expect you could establish a path forward by then without fail." Evelyn sipped her wine, her gaze drifting over the group.

"In fact, I have the glimmerings of one in mind already." Nathaniel aimed a smile in her direction. His heart raced as a sudden idea entered his thoughts. "Perhaps you'd help me sort out my options?"

She inclined her head with a smile. "I'd be honored to assist any way I can if it shall hasten you on your way."

He guffawed, attracting the attention of the tavern's patrons. Swiping tears from his eyes, he shook his head. "My dear Lyn, you have no idea how much I enjoy your wit."

She quirked a brow and lifted her chin. "It is my pleasure to help you succeed in your quest."

Benjamin slapped a hand to the table and laughed. "You two make such a charming couple, especially with your jesting of each other."

"Who is joking?" Evelyn shot a look at Benjamin with a lift of one brow and laughter in her eyes.

Amy chuckled as she placed a hand to her chest. "You're slaying me. Stop so I can breathe."

Nathaniel glanced from one to another and then finally considered Evelyn's mirthful countenance for several seconds. He'd gladly take her up on the offer of assistance in order to enjoy her company and convince her to enjoy his. All while maintaining his distance, of course. "Your help will indeed be appreciated, likely more than you can fathom."

After supper at McCrady's, Nathaniel elected to walk back to the Abernathy town home. Evelyn, Emily, and Amy had climbed into the open carriage with Benjamin and Frank for the drive back to their respective houses. His friends had protested, of course, but he'd held firm. After all, if he permitted himself to be confined so close to the woman, his will would break down and he'd do or say something they would both regret. With every move, utterance, and most definitely her smile, he'd been drawn to her like a moth attracted by the heat and light of a candle flame. What would she feel like when he touched her? He huffed. He would not touch her. That path led to his ultimate destruction. No, far better for him to keep his own company, let his desires for her cool with each stride along the dirt and sand street on a cold winter evening.

The windows of the houses he passed glowed with the soft flickering light of candles. Smoke drifted up from the chimneys to mix in the darkening sky. Stars sparkled above, their silent observation comforting and familiar. He pondered the people inside, wondering about their lives and their hopes. Each must have some path they expected to walk in life. But what obstacles would they face and how well might they meet the challenges? How would he?

He'd become maudlin and shook his head, chuckling at his wayward imaginings. Evelyn would never fall into such musings and probably would not approve of him doing so either. He tripped on a tree root, regaining his balance through a series of stumbles and hops, arms outstretched to either side. When he came to a halt, he laughed at himself. So much for his serious thoughts.

He resumed his stroll, hands clasped behind his back. An elderly couple made their way toward him, arms intertwined as they walked side by side. Her dark bonnet and long cloak shielded her from the wintery night, a smile on her weathered face. Her escort likewise had dressed to face the cold air of their evening amble, a tricorne hat pulled down over his gray hair. Would he ever again have a wife, one to grow old with and cherish? Nathaniel had once hoped to do so with his deceased wife, but what now? He tipped his hat as they caught up to him and then passed.

Evelyn's pretty smile and engaging laugh came to his mind. As much as he enjoyed her company, he did not fathom where his future might take him. Would it be wrong to wish to explore whether he might have a future with

Evelyn? Given his attraction to her, every aspect of the woman, wouldn't he be doing himself a disservice to not find out?

His steps died as the realization struck. Other residents passed by him, on their way to their homes for the night. Still, he stood in one place, blinking as his thoughts spun. Perhaps his future had slapped him on the forehead. Wiggling into his heart with the ease of a worm in soil. An idea worth considering as a minimum. Humming, he continued at a trot in the direction of his lodgings, eager to discover the truth.

A house slave admitted him into the home with a brief exchange of pleasantries, resplendent in the Abernathy livery. Chatter echoed down the main hall from the parlor, where the family had apparently gathered for an after dinner beverage. Evelyn's laughter had him hurrying toward the sound. A few strides from the open door, he slowed to a halt.

Torn between an urgent longing and an iron will, he concentrated on dragging in a deep breath and easing it out over several beatings of his heart. He needed to contemplate his next move. Needed to consider what his heart desired from all angles before he embarked on attempting to engage in any type of romantic relationship with the woman chuckling on the other side of the wall where he stood in a quandary.

He spun on his heel and went to the library at the other end of the passage. He closed the door to the room, and perused the contents. Floor-to-ceiling bookcases were spaced along three of the four walls, each packed with books with titles on their rigid spines. Between the cases on the outside wall, two windows overlooked the dormant garden. A crackling fire, with wisps of red and yellow flame, popped and snapped in the brick firebox, sparks drifting up the chimney. The fourth wall served as a frame for a collection of comfortable chairs and a cheery wood table in the center.

A pleasant space in which to while away time reading from the many fascinating tomes, not that he expected to have time to read all of them. Or even many.

He removed his cloak and draped it over one of the chairs, thoughts whirling and spinning in his mind. One lingered for several breaths, and he tried it on much like a new shirt. Slipping into it and tugging it in place, wrapping himself in the possibility. He smiled to himself when he realized it suited, as though made for him by an expert tailor.

Chapter Two

$\mathcal{B}$olts and swatches of sumptuous fabrics tempted Evelyn's fingers. Her mother's upstairs parlor teemed with women discussing the merits and uses of each. Several tables had been brought in and topped with the array of choices. She'd not had a new gown in several years, between the constraints of her miserly husband and the ravages of the war. But now, mayhap she'd indulge in the luxury of a beautiful dress. Anticipation thrilled through her, making her hands tremble with eagerness.

Across the room, a debate escalated in volume as to which laces and ribbons to purchase and from where. Some argued for ordering them from Philadelphia or New York, others from distant countries. Evelyn preferred to buy from American merchants, but the latest fashions could only be obtained from overseas countries. How long would it take for American fashions to overtake those from France and England? She grimaced. Probably not in her lifetime.

Amy strolled up and stopped beside her, reaching out to finger an azure silk with silver threads woven through at intervals. "Gorgeous, isn't it?"

"Dare I dream of a gown in such a sumptuous color?" Evelyn sidled away from the table burdened with bolts of cloth.

"Of course. Mother ordered these from France and China months ago in anticipation of needing to freshen our dresses." Amy tugged Evelyn closer to the table and handed her the bolt of fabric in question. "You'll be beautiful wearing this."

Evelyn hugged the cloth close to her chest and studied her sister's beaming visage. "I do love it. Perhaps with a lemon yellow skirt? What do you think?"

Amy squeezed Evelyn's shoulders. "I think no matter what you wear, you'll please Nathaniel."

Startled, Evelyn gaped at her. "What do you mean?"

Had she given the man the wrong impression? She didn't want to mislead him, to cause him to think he had any possibility of succeeding in his pursuit. She'd grown accustomed to hiding her truth, as well as the strength of will she managed to contain in order to survive a brutal marriage. Since death had freed her from the marriage contract, she'd begun to permit herself to be strong for her son and herself. The relief at no longer having to subdue her responses to ameliorate a volatile situation made her realize how oppressed she'd been. Never again.

Amy chuckled. "I have eyes, my dear. He's besotted, acting as though he'd like nothing more than to observe your every movement."

"You're mistaken, surely." But was she? Nathaniel had seemed to be looking at her each time she glanced at him at McCrady's. She'd thought he was merely being considerate, but Amy's revelation made her rethink her supposition. "He's only recently arrived in town."

"Love at first sight does not take long." Amy folded her arms and continued to smile at Evelyn as she slowly tilted her head. "Do you like him?"

"He's a polite gentleman." Evelyn didn't want to love any one. Not yet. But if she were to change her mind, she could envision falling for someone like Nathaniel. "I'm not interested. It's too soon, and I have to support my son."

Amy frowned. "Marrying would help in that regard."

"I know, but I want time to find the right man." Evelyn sighed and squared her shoulders, shifting the bolt of cloth to angle across her body. In truth, if her inappropriate and undesired reaction to him meant anything, her body seemed to think she may have already found him, but the timing proved sorely inconvenient. "In the meanspace, I think I have struck upon a prospect of providing for myself and my son without needing a husband."

"How do you plan to do that?" Amy's raised brows signaled her curiosity.

Dare she speak aloud her idea? "What if I rebuild the manor house but add on several dedicated rooms for a boarding school?"

Amy took a step back, and peered at Evelyn. "That's brilliant. You'd make an excellent teacher."

Evelyn grinned as she rocked side to side. Her sister's enthusiasm bolstered her confidence in the spontaneous idea. "I've spent years reading all of the books in Walter's library. Everything from history to government to famous artists."

Emily strode into the room and hurried over to where Evelyn and Amy stood chatting. She seemed frazzled and out of breath, but a happy demeanor suggested she'd been having a fine day.

"There you are." Emily sidled up to join their conversation with a long sigh. "Young Mr. Elfe continues to vex me with his lack of understanding of my intent. I'm beginning to think he is working for my father to prevent me from opening my shop."

"Uncle Joshua isn't very supportive of your desire to run

a business, is he?" Amy shook her head slowly. "At least Frank doesn't mind. And he continues to publish your essays."

Emily shuffled through the bolts of fabric. "Frank's most definitely on my side in this debate."

"I'm glad to hear your husband supports your endeavors." Evelyn laid the blue silk among the others on the table. "By the way, your last essay proved highly controversial at our dinner table."

"Which one? The need for education for every child?" Emily fingered a gold taffeta with reverence. "Or the one suggesting that men should be more involved in their children's lives?"

Evelyn shook her head, glancing at Amy before focusing on Emily. "Let's see, I think it was 'Reasons for Women to Speak Their Minds.'"

Amy chortled and clapped her hands twice. "Father nearly had an apoplexy."

The three women laughed together, finally subduing their merriment after the other women all turned to stare at them.

"What were you speaking about when I walked up?" Emily tilted her head and regarded Evelyn, turning away from the tempting silks and brocades. "You seemed pretty intense."

"Speaking of education, guess what my sister has decided to do." Amy fairly hopped in her eagerness. "Evelyn is going to open a boarding school."

Emily turned shocked eyes to regard Evelyn. "Where? In town?"

Evelyn lifted the blue silk again to hold in front of her stomach, reluctant to risk another woman choosing it before she laid claim. Having only minutes ago chosen to start a school, the details evaded her. She hesitated to collect her scattered thoughts. "I'll rebuild my estate. I already own the property, and there is plenty of space to enlarge the building to include room for, say, ten girls."

Emily hugged Evelyn, squashing the cloth between them. "I love your idea. If I can assist in any way, please let me know."

"I suppose the first step is to sketch out a design for the house." Evelyn let her gaze drift over the gathering of women bedecked in a variety of colorful gowns. Being with her friends and family again filled her heart with pleasure. But her future surely lay in the country on the property she'd come to think of as her real home. In spite of the unsettling memories of Walter, she'd make the attempt to turn the place into a fine abode. She and Jim would be happy there. "Then I'll need to find men to build the house."

"Oh! My brothers might be able to help with the construction." Emily ran her fingers over a bolt of brocade. "They said they were looking for something to do to earn a bit of money for their next joint venture."

"Do you think they'd be interested in building a manor house, though?" Evelyn peered at Emily, hope surging in her breast. Now that she'd struck upon a viable course of action, she saw no need to delay making her vision a reality. "I can pay them a little bit, but I don't have much myself."

"Perhaps we can barter part of the costs," Amy suggested.

Evelyn, once again shocked into silence, gazed upon her sister for several moments. Had she heard correctly? "We?"

"You don't think you're going into this venture alone, do you?" Amy chuckled and refolded her arms. "I want to help, too."

Evelyn dropped the bolt of cloth onto the table and hugged first her sister and then her cousin. Stepping back, she grinned at them both. "Well, what are we waiting for?"

❧

Rays of sunlight shafted onto the oriental carpet in the sitting room. Evelyn held a sketch book on her lap, a pencil poised above the drawing of the house she worked to design. The mingled sound of birds singing, men shouting, and conveyances rumbling past the house floated through the partially open window. Enough of a gap to help her breathe more easily. A day like any other, and yet an urgency compelled Evelyn's focus on her personal mission. Studying the picture, she pondered what was lacking.

The shape and size of the building pleased her: two stories with tall rectangular windows flanking the front door. The vision of the interior came into her mind, with rooms designated for music and dining below as well as several bedchambers on the upper floor. She'd add a stone or brick kitchen out the back door to reduce the chance of fire destroying the house again. Doodling, she drew in some bushes and flowers, then erased them as she'd done an imperfect job. She pondered the page for several seconds before she knew what she'd forgotten.

"A veranda!" She scratched the pencil over the paper, pushing the tip of her tongue between her lips as she worked, and soon sat back to judge the result. "Perfect."

Footsteps echoed in the passage. Nathaniel strode into the room. Her breath hitched and she mentally chastised herself for the visceral reaction she experienced every time the man neared. Closing the sketch book, she laid it on the settee beside her. She composed herself as he approached to sit in a chair next to where she worked. He need not know how he affected her, for such knowledge would serve to encourage him.

"Good day, Lyn."

Goodness, how she loved her pet name said in his baritone voice. Too much, in fact. "My name is Evelyn, and good day to you."

"I am well aware of your name, my dear." Chuckling, he unbuttoned his coat as he adjusted his position on the hard seat. "Is this a good time for me to discuss my options with you?"

"Yes, I've finished my project." She laid the pencil on top of the book with trembling fingers. "Where do you wish to start?"

He hesitated for the time it took to draw in a long breath and release it. "I cannot help myself. I've tried, but all I can think of is…you."

"Excuse me?" Such a startling beginning to the conversation. She swallowed, striving to maintain her recently restored comportment. "What, pray tell, is your meaning?"

"I do not know what will happen in my future, but I do know what I'd like to have happen in my present." Nathaniel grinned at her. "I wish to wait upon you."

"But—"

He held up a hand to stop her protest. "I understand you are technically in mourning, but I also know you didn't love the man."

She frowned as she blinked at Nathaniel. "How do you know that?"

"Amy informed me of your relationship with your husband. How he treated you and that he was suspected of poisoning you." He rested his elbows on his knees, his hands clasped together. "The way I see it, you should be celebrating your widowhood."

"Celebrate?" Shock ricocheted in her chest. He spoke of her marriage in terms she'd never employed. Coupled with the blatant desire to woo her, his speech crashed against her sensibilities, upsetting her so her hands trembled more.

"You're free from him, and that means…" His gaze flicked from hers to rest on her mouth as lightly as a butterfly before returning to delve into her astonished gaze. "That means, you are also able to accept me waiting upon you with the intent of discovering if we are a happy match."

"Your reasoning defies logic." Why was her heart racing at his proposition then? "Only three months have passed since he died."

He bobbed his head several times, his smile growing. "Exactly. Long enough for a decent mourning and short enough to enable us to become better acquainted."

"Why would you know what is proper in terms of mourning?"

His smile tightened but clung to his lips. "Because I lost my wife last year. So I understand. But life goes on, and we must live our lives. Perhaps together, depending on what we discover as we get to know one another."

She stared at him, her thoughts spinning and tumbling as she contemplated exactly what he asked. The temptation to agree surfaced, but she submerged it back into the depths of her soul. She didn't dare to succumb to the wanton urges simmering beneath her calm facade. The inexplicable desire to touch the handsome, fun, dangerous man surged until she was forced to stand and turn away. She studied the pattern of the wallpaper, focusing on the fine detail of the birds of paradise and bouquets of lilies. Slowly, she regained her composure. Taking a deep breath, she pivoted to face her earnest admirer.

"You need one important thing before you can attain your goal." She considered her next words for several slow deep breaths. "My agreement."

He rose and crossed the room to clasp her hands with his larger and stronger ones. "All I ask, Lyn, is for us to have a chance. Please?"

She was so tempted to say yes, but she had to remain firm in her resolve. For her son's sake. And for her heart's.

She swallowed the tears threatening to escape, aware that if they made an appearance she'd seem weak. "I cannot."

"Lyn, reconsider, I beg of you." Nathaniel squeezed her hands, a quick press and relaxation, but held onto them. "You needn't decide in this moment. Take some time to think upon the matter before you deny my plea."

She pulled her hands from his grasp and folded her arms. She couldn't think with him touching her. Couldn't puzzle out an answer to his question with him gazing at her with imploring eyes. "Very well. I'll consider your request, but do not expect me to agree."

"Thank you." He sighed his relief at her words. "I will endeavor to maintain my distance until I have your answer."

"See that you do." She turned to pick up her book. "If you'll excuse me, I have work to do."

"I'll look forward to the pleasure of your company at dinner then." Nathaniel stopped at the open door to wink at her. "See you later, Lyn."

She nodded as he flashed her a grin and then strode out of sight down the hall. She hugged the sketch book to her chest and stared at the empty room. *Goodness.* He held out hope she'd change her mind. She had seen it in his expression, in the swing of his stride. She sank back onto the settee, going over their conversation, his plea, and his intent. She sighed and leaned her head against the tall back of the couch. What had she done?

The early morning sunlight shimmered on the bowed sides of the fish piled on the table. The market was busy on this cold winter day. Evelyn let her gaze drift over the plentiful offerings displayed on tables and hanging from ropes strung between poles. Mingled among the food booths were jewelry, sweetgrass baskets, braided rugs, and more. She needed to replace a damaged basket, but first she must find something for dinner. Not that the cook couldn't have made the trip to the marketplace. Evelyn had wanted an excuse to leave the house for a time, so when the cook had muttered something about having to brave the cold, she'd eagerly volunteered.

She turned back to the fish. The merchant displayed a large variety, including seatrout, red drum, and perch. Evelyn examined a silver seatrout, its distinctive spots marching from nose to dark finned tail. A good weight, about four pounds. She sniffed its aroma and nodded to the seller. "I'll take four."

The seller pulled out a large piece of brown paper and carefully wrapped the fish. While she waited, she surveyed the market area with her gaze. The place resounded with the hawkers' raised voices advertising their wares. Children dashed between the stands, chasing each other with abandon and shouts of laughter. The smell of hot bread battled with the stronger aroma of the fresh fish.

"Quite a gathering today."

She jumped and spun toward the familiar deep voice, her heavy cloak eddying about her legs when she stopped. Her pulse kicked and she swallowed to restore her equilibrium. "Nathaniel, you startled me."

"Please, call me Nat." He inclined his head. "And I am sorry. But I'm surprised to find you among the fish. What are you doing here?"

She wanted to speak his preferred nickname, to lower the barrier she'd erected in a vain attempt to keep him away. Could she risk her heat so soon? She shrugged as she slipped a hand inside her cloak to pull a purse from her skirt pocket. "I offered to save our cook the trouble of venturing out into the cold." She searched inside the cloth bag for the necessary coins.

"Here, allow me." Nathaniel rummaged in his pocket and then dropped several coins onto the man's waiting palm.

"You didn't need to do that." She closed her purse and put it away. She looked up at him, detecting laughter in his expression. He seemed rather jolly for a man who happened to be at the market. "Besides, you're our guest."

"As such, I feel an obligation to contribute to the larder when possible." His smile grew as he pointed to the basket hanging from her arm. "May I?"

"I can manage, but thank you…Nat." She swallowed hard at his delight over her use of his nickname. She let the seller drop the package in the basket. Despite holding the basket with both hands, the sudden weight nearly made the container fall onto the sandy ground. She hadn't done the math to calculate the multiplied weight of the fish. Sixteen pounds proved heavy indeed. "Perhaps I'll take you up on your offer."

Nat grasped the handle and lifted the basket from her hands as though it weighed no more than a hen's egg. "My pleasure."

"Tell me what brings you to the market." She led the way through the booths, dodging behind a gentleman and his hunting dogs. Her senses hummed with awareness of the man close behind her, imagining the gentle breeze of his personality mingling and consorting with her own. She suppressed a shiver. "Somehow, I don't believe it's your usual haunt."

He chuckled as he drew abreast of her. "I came in search of you."

She glanced up, brows raised, her heart in her throat. She hadn't yet decided how to tell him she couldn't give her assent to his proposition. Though she'd tossed in bed the last two nights because of his sincere plea. Unfortunately, her body had not understood the message from her brain. "Why?"

"I believe you know why." He shifted the basket to his other hand. "To be honest, you have weighed on my mind so much I had to find you. To hear your voice."

"So you've found me and heard me speak." She waved him off, unsettled by his words more than she'd say. To be missed and longed for proved a new sensation that rocked her to the core. "You've accomplished your mission."

"In one way, yes." He paused beside her at the array of sweetgrass baskets on and around several tables. "Now I have given myself another mission."

"What, pray tell, might your newly defined mission be?" She inspected a basket designed to carry bottles of wine, its intricate weave a work of art. Anything to not look up into the smiling eyes of the man beside her. She needn't indulge in the temptation. She sensed his every movement, every sound, every breath.

"I will escort you until your shopping is completed and have arrived safely home." He laughed, a rich merry sound reverberating in her chest. "You can't object to that."

"If you insist." She lifted another basket to inspect, a wide deep one with a curved handle. "I shan't be much longer as I need to return to my son."

"He's at the house?" Nathaniel shifted his weight to rest one hip, patiently waiting for her to make a selection.

"Yes, with his nursemaid." She went to set the basket down only to fumble it to the ground.

She reached to retrieve it as Nathaniel bent to do the same. He bumped into her, knocking her sideways. She splayed her hands to catch herself only to have Nat grasp her arms to steady her. A sensation akin to lightning ripping across the sky flashed through her as she locked gazes with him. The shock proved much like the fear when a thunderstorm accosted her home. Time stood still for the span of several breaths. She detected from the startled look in his eyes that he experienced the same reaction. Slowly he released her, as if reluctant to end the contact, and retrieved the basket.

"Th-thank you." She stepped back, trembling and on fire, as he set the container on the table. With shaky hands, she pulled out her purse and handed the money to the woman watching them with intense interest. Time to steer the conversation back to neutral territory so she could restore her composure. On a breath, she pasted a smile on her lips. "Where were we? Oh, yes. I had to hire the woman after my slave ran off with the British last year. Very inconvenient for me, and dangerous for her."

Nat accepted the basket from the seller with a nod. "I do hope the Britons honor their promises. But I have heard the slaves who followed them ended up worse off than before."

"I have heard the same." She slipped her purse into her pocket and gazed up at him, towering over her much like a tall, straight pine tree lording over a sapling. "Have you started your new job yet?"

"Not yet, but soon." He glanced away and then back at her. "It's not what I'd prefer to do, but at least it will afford me income."

She made the mistake of meeting his gaze, an answering smile springing unbidden onto her lips. Lord, he attracted her despite her resolve to remain unmoved and unmarried. His black-rimmed steel gray eyes sparkled with merriment. Nut-brown locks glinted with gold, calling to her fingers with anticipated delight. His classic features, strong chin, and high cheekbones gave him the appearance of a Greek god. Perhaps a brunette Bellerophon, the mythical rider of Pegasus. The more time she spent in his company, the more she contemplated following Amy's advice. She could do worse than to marry Nathaniel Williams. Was she ready to embark on a new relationship?

"My parents are pleased to have you remain with them as long as you need lodgings." Evelyn turned to stroll toward the table filled with candles, contradictorily pleased when Nat fell into step beside her. What was wrong with her? She didn't want his attention but longed to be with him. She mentally shook herself. She had to focus on her plans and leave him to his. "Unless you decide you will stay permanently and want your own home."

"Living within the bounds of a city does not appeal to me." Nathaniel held both baskets, one in each hand, as he stopped beside her. "In fact, my plans remain in a state of flux as I continue to identify my options."

"We didn't get very far in that discussion, did we?" For a very simple reason which she wouldn't raise.

She selected several bayberry candles and paid for them. She placed the candles in the new basket, nearly dropping them when her hand accidentally brushed Nat's where he gripped the handle. She pulled her hand away and flashed a glance at his smiling countenance. *Goodness.* Stepping away, she increased the space between them, only to have him move closer.

"In a hurry?" Nat chuckled as he strode beside her.

"Like I said, I need to return to my son as soon as possible." At least little Jim's need to nurse provided an excuse for her to flee home. But not away from Nat, she realized, as he matched her pace. "Then your mission will be completed as well."

He laughed, the sound echoing in the cold morning air. "Pray don't run away on my account, Lyn. I do not mind escorting you on your errands, no matter how long you are out and about."

Mayhap not, but Evelyn didn't know how long she could resist his attentions, his company, and the compelling desire to touch him. "You may have the leisure to dawdle, but my chores await."

He matched her quick stride with ease and grace. "Anything I can do to help you?"

"Not unless you know how to nurse a baby." She tossed him a glance, a smile springing to her mouth as he shook his head with seeming remorse. "Then you'll have to be content to simply walk me home and then leave me to do your own tasks."

"If you insist." He chuckled as they turned onto Queen Street and strolled east in the direction of the Cooper river, lying beyond their destination. "I would not mind waiting until you have finished."

She laughed at his pleading tone. "You'd be bored sitting idle for so long. Here, let me carry the candles."

He relinquished the basket to her as they strolled toward home. "More than likely, but I'd enjoy your presence as a reward for my patience." He shifted the basket of fish to his other hand and then took her hand in his as they neared their final turn on Meeting.

She wanted to withdraw her hand and yet couldn't make herself pull away from the long-awaited contact. The pressure of his hand wrapped around her fingers soothed the agitation in her chest. "I'm sure you must have better ways to occupy yourself."

"None come to mind when I'm with you, Lyn." He squeezed her hand and swung their joined hands to and fro.

His declaration swept joy through her, and she laughed at the fun she experienced whenever she spent time with Nat. Perhaps she could consider agreeing to his request to see her, to court her, to make love with her. "We'll have to think of something then to distract you while I retire to my room."

"You're my distraction, Lyn." He tugged her to a halt at the bottom of the steps leading into the three-story brick house. "Whether I'm with you or not, I can think of nothing else but how much I enjoy your company and how much I desire to become better acquainted."

She stood on the edge of an emotional cliff. Did she dare to take the next step, the one that would surely send her plummeting into a relationship with the man searching her expression with such hope?

The door opened and Jemma, holding Jim on her hip, grinned at them with a knowing smirk.

Evelyn nodded to her and then looked into Nathaniel's adoring eyes. "We should go in."

Chapter Three

The next afternoon brought a happy respite from the more serious consideration of Nat's proposition. With each pierce and tug of the threaded needle, Evelyn imagined wearing her new gown. Sewing her own dresses, much like tending her garden or cleaning her house, satisfied a bone-deep desire to be self-sufficient. A trait she intended to instill in her son as he grew. The sumptuous fabric, draped across her lap, lingered in her fingers. Because she intended to wear it only for more formal occasions, she had not sewn in openings on each breast to allow for nursing her son, like the one she wore. The flaps required to cover the holes prevented the proper drape of the fabric. Thus, she'd chosen to finish it as a normal costume.

She resisted the urge to hold the nearly finished garment against her chest and dance around the small parlor of Frank and Emily's home. She and Amy had decided an outing would improve their moods, so they had gathered their things and hurried to the three-story brick mansion on King Street. Before long, she'd have her wardrobe expanded with the lovely item.

Amy perched on a chair by the sunlit window. She opened the heavy tome, Homer's *The Odyssey*, and then looked at Evelyn. "Shall I read aloud?"

"It will be diverting to listen to it while we work." Evelyn pulled the through the silk. The subtle vibration as the thread slipped through the fabric pleased her, knowing each stitch brought her closer to wearing the frock.

"Please, Amy." Emily kept her eyes on her work but bobbed her head in encouragement. "I haven't read it in some little while."

Emily worked on some fancy stitching to decorate a gentleman's waistcoat. She'd used too many colors to count on the exquisite pattern. The complicated embroidery was far beyond Evelyn's talents. She predicted her cousin's shop would prove a success with such beautiful work for sale. Tommy, her one-year-old adopted son, busied himself by playing with a leather ball stuffed with cotton. His nursemaid, Jasmine, worked on mending socks, keeping an eye on her young charge.

Evelyn recalled how Tommy became Emily and Frank's responsibility. Emily's twin sister, Elizabeth, became betrothed to Frank's brother, Jedediah, who died in the war. Frank stepped in to marry Elizabeth when she discovered she was with child to ensure the boy wasn't considered a bastard by society. Upon her death, Emily had perforce assumed the infant's care. Then Frank followed his heart to marry Emily. She had wanted a family but feared death during the lying in, as happened to both her sister and mother. After they married, Tommy once more had two parents and they had Tommy. How long would it be before the newly married couple would create a child of their own?

Her thoughts drifted to her son, brought into this world not out of love but obligation. She'd married Walter Hamilton knowing he harbored the potential to become difficult, but didn't anticipate his turning violent toward her. If events went against his expectations, however unreasonable, he inflicted some form of punishment. Perhaps a pinch, or a slap. How she'd begged him to stop, to let her return to her parents. To end their marriage. He'd raped her—she hadn't wanted to lie with him, fearing what abuse he might employ in such a vulnerable position—and then her flux stopped and she carried his child.

Despite all the terrible actions Walter had taken against her, she could not blame the wee babe. She'd loved the child the moment she discovered its existence. She would always love him. A vital promise she'd made to her son and would never break. Every decision she faced would be based on his best interests. Like the decision to leave him behind with Jemma while he napped, rather than disturb him with the noise and activity of the friends as they chatted and sewed. Still, she missed his little smile, his pale green eyes watching her. The pressure building along with the tingling of her breasts reminded her that she'd soon need to return home to feed him.

Amy theatrically cleared her throat. "*The Odyssey*. 'Tell me, O muse, of that ingenious hero who travelled far and wide after he had sacked the famous town of Troy. Many cities did he visit, and many were the nations with whose manners and customs he was acquainted; moreover he suffered much by sea while trying to save his own life and bring his men safely home.'"

"I'd forgotten the opening," Emily interjected with umbrage in her tone. "Frank may as well be Odysseus, traveling about by boat and hoping to arrive in strange places safely."

"What do you mean?" Evelyn peered at the frowning woman.

"He wants me to go with him on a trip abroad, to France

and England." She shook her head, the frown deepening. "I don't know what to do."

"But I thought your shop is due to open soon." Amy fingered the page of the book as she studied Emily's tense posture.

"Next week, in fact." Emily gazed at Evelyn and then Amy. "How can I satisfy my husband's desires as well as my own?"

"You can't be in two places at the same time." Evelyn resumed her stitching, her eagerness to finish outweighing the import of the conversation.

"Exactly why I'm struggling to find a resolution to the dilemma." Emily stuck her needle into the waistcoat with more force than strictly necessary. "He's longed to travel for years and had been denied the possibility because of the war."

"So now he's anxious, I'm certain." Amy rested her hand on the pages of the book. "Can you delay the opening until your return?"

"I could, but I do not wish to." Emily's hand stilled as her attention turned inward. "My dreams or his. That's what it boils down to."

"I suppose I should be glad my choice of opening a girls' school isn't subject to the same debate." Evelyn shook her head, her long tresses brushing her shoulders. The enormity of her decision weighed upon her with its suddenness and importance. A daunting task lay ahead, one requiring perhaps more abilities than she possessed. Even so, she enjoyed a challenge. "I've been contemplating the curriculum as well as the design of the building."

The change in topic smoothed the worry from Emily's brow. "My brothers said they'd speak with you soon about how they can help you. Ethan seemed most enthusiastic."

"With the racing stable on the horizon, they need money to bring it to fruition." Amy shifted in her seat and grabbed the book as it slid precariously on her skirt.

"I'll be glad of their efforts." Evelyn detected curiosity in Emily's expression. "As for what I'll teach, I'm thinking the usual history, literature, needlework, and music and dance, but adding in mathematics, natural science, and astronomy. Do you think it's too much?"

Emily shook her head as she kept her focus on the needle moving through the fabric in her hand. "Impressive. You'll need to find someone to teach the sciences, won't you?"

"I can manage an introduction on each subject to begin. I'll keep learning myself and then share what I've learned." A vision of studying by candlelight after the household quieted each evening flashed through her mind. Long days and nights loomed in her not too distant future.

Emily chuckled, drawing Evelyn's attention. "You sound like Samantha. She told me something very similar only a few months ago."

Evelyn drew her needle through the silk as an answering smile grew on her lips. "I always thought she was a smart lady."

A few more stitches and she had finished sewing her dress. She cut the thread and tied it off, and then stuck the needle into the pincushion on the table. Standing, she held the frock by the shoulders and shook out the long blue skirts with a flourish. "What do you think?"

"What a gorgeous dress!" Amy flowed to her feet, dropping the book onto her abandoned seat. "I love the scalloped bodice, too."

Evelyn turned to show Emily. "Does it need some decoration on the bodice?"

Emily tilted her head to one side then the other, contemplating the gown with her artistic eyes. "Some sequins and seed pearls in a scatter pattern would enhance the fine work you've done. Would you like me to do it for you?"

Evelyn raised a brow as she regarded her eager friend. "If you have time, I'd appreciate your talents."

Amy crossed her arms. "Wait until Nathaniel sees you wearing it."

"Whatever do you mean?" Warmth spread up Evelyn's neck as she imagined the man's reaction. She hadn't seen him all day, what with his starting work at the print shop. She found herself dwelling on him when she should be concentrating on the task at hand. Waiting to hear his voice or, better, his laugh. His opinion had grown to matter despite her protests. Would he like it? Or think it too much? "Why should I care about his opinion?"

Amy lifted her elegant brows with a shrug. "Only because he is enthralled by your every movement and word each time you are in the same room with him."

As she felt when in the same space as him, but she had to remember her promise to her son. She'd make a good life for him, take care of him, and see him grow into a fine man. Maybe one day she'd find a man to be a father to him. First, she wanted to establish her own future, not be beholden to any man. Ever. Not even Nat. She silenced the inner voice suggesting she hid from the truth of the matter.

"Nathaniel Williams is mistaken if he believes I care for his attentions." Evelyn hugged her gown to her stomach, trying to quell the tumult rolling inside. "When I wear my dress, it will be for my pleasure, not for his."

Amy chuckled. "Maybe so, but see if you can stop blushing when you do."

Pungent. That was the word for the sharp odor of the ink. Frank used two wool-stuffed leather beaters to apply the black fluid to the rows of metal letters in the galley. Nathaniel had traded fresh air for ink. Not a fair trade either. The press filled the center of the room, massive posts spanning floor to ceiling to brace the heavy equipment. Large rectangular sheets of damp paper waited in the tympan, a leather-covered frame holding the pages to be lowered onto the inked tiles. He had begun to understand the methods and processes but would the time ever arrive for him to truly begin his new life?

"Make sure to evenly coat the plate." Frank, performing the role of beater, glanced up at Nathaniel, one brow raised.

Nathaniel nodded once in reply. He waited for Frank to continue but after a moment realized he desired for him to ask. "What's next?"

Confined in the print shop for the third day, Nathaniel longed to flee the pounding vibrations of applying the ink as well as the tedious nature of the printing business. His honor anchored him to his commitment, attention fixed upon his employer's demonstration. Once he gave his word, only the person he'd promised could release his obligation. He'd adjust in time to the smells and tasks. He hoped.

"I'll have Sawyer show you the rest." Frank wiped his hands on a rag and dropped it on the table beside the press. "I'm to meet Emily in a few minutes at the shop."

"Ready to open the doors?" Nathaniel stepped to one side as Sawyer moved in to replace Frank. Though younger, Sawyer's height and breadth suggested he was a man to avoid bringing to anger.

"Almost." Frank sighed and shook his head. "She's adamant about not traveling yet."

Sawyer laid the paper on the galley, then slid the bed under the platen, a large wood block whose job was to make the impression on the paper. Pulling on the bar, Sawyer lowered the weight for the count of five. Raising the bar, he lifted the platen and slid the bed out and opened it.

"You can lift the paper off now." Sawyer waved at the still wet broadside. "Lay it over the drying rods."

Nathaniel did as instructed, hauling up the paper carriage to its open position. Then he lifted the large sheet of paper by the corners and draped it over one of several horizontal rods. One down, two hundred forty-nine to go. He turned back to face Frank. "You need a compromise."

Frank barked a resigned laugh. "I'm open to ideas. I've run out of my own."

Chuckling, Nathaniel propped his fists on his hips. Not that he'd suggest any only to find himself in hot water when it didn't work. "Next question."

Sawyer guffawed, the sound like gravel hitting a wooden dock. "Nice maneuver, Mr. Williams."

"I've a learned a lesson or two while in the militia." Nathaniel grinned at the freckle-faced youth. "How fast can you print the required sheets?"

"It would go faster with another man to help, especially with business increasing daily." Sawyer shrugged. "If you'll help me with these we'll be free in an hour to start laying the type for the booklet. The pages are on the table over there."

"I'll see about finding another man to fill the role of beater. That booklet is going to raise a lot of eyebrows in town." Frank crossed to the table to peruse the contents. "The farmers up north don't understand the importance of slaves to our economy. Calling for an end to the practice in the states responsible for the raising and harvesting of cotton would devastate the area."

Nathaniel shook his head before he'd consciously considered his response. Taking a deep breath, he regarded Frank for several moments, pondering his view of the matter. "You're right. At the same time, I've heard even General Washington has quietly expressed a desire to see the end of slavery."

"It's a matter of time," Sawyer said. "The manumission of the slaves in the northern states, like Pennsylvania and more recently in Maryland, will eventually lead to all the states following suit. At least, that's what my father and I believe."

"I do not see the end of slavery in my lifetime." Frank gazed at the two men, concern clouding his expression. "We'll print the booklet, but I wonder about the reaction of the town leaders."

"You're going to be late to meet your wife." Nathaniel confiscated the pages from Frank, and indicated with his head for the man to leave. "We'll take care of things here."

"Blast it, you're right." Frank flung his cloak around his shoulders and crammed his Monmouth hat on his head. He rushed out the door into the pouring rain, a refreshing blast of air ushering him from the room.

"If Frank follows through on hiring another lad to help, we might stay abreast of the work we're facing." Sawyer picked up the beaters and regarded Frank. "You be pressman, and I'll be the beater."

Nathaniel took his position, while Sawyer used the beaters to ink the galley. When he finished pounding, Nathaniel went into action with the paper and platen. "What else is in the queue, other than the booklet?"

"An almanac, some business forms, and the most time consuming, a map of the area." Sawyer finished his task and paused. "Frank is willing to add on more staff now that the war is over and his mission complete. A new book binder is due to start to-morrow to handle the orders for blank leather bound books for the planters to track their crop rotations and business transactions."

"Good news indeed." Frank released the platen and removed the paper, hanging it on a nearby rod. "The more hands the lighter the work."

His comment brought the memory of his wife's desire to have children as soon as possible in order to have helping hands around the house and garden. He'd agreed with pleasure, sharing the desire to surround them with little ones to love and raise. They'd tried to conceive a child but had failed. Patsy grew more and more shrewish toward him, blaming him for everything. Especially the fact she remained childless after years of marriage. He still had no idea whether she had been right or not. Perhaps if he took another wife, he'd find the answer.

The door opened, jangling the bell above. Nathaniel turned toward the customer but held back. Sawyer moved to the high table dividing the entrance from the work area and nodded a greeting to Dr. Trent. Better for the experienced apprentice to handle the business.

"Good day, gentlemen." Trent laid his tricorne hat on the wooden surface, droplets running down the sides. The shoulders of his cloak glistened with rain. "I'd like to place a notice in the next paper."

"The next edition won't be released for two days," Sawyer said. "Will that suffice?"

Trent nodded as he unfolded a piece of paper and smoothed it onto the table. "I suppose it must. In the event, it's not a significant delay."

Nathaniel moved to read the notice with a quick skim. "A new hospital?"

"Yes, I've been working on preparing the facility and locating qualified doctors to add to my staff." Trent smiled, a huge grin revealing his pride and pleasure. "Something I've envisioned doing for years."

"You fancied building a hospital? That's quite an ambition." One Nathaniel could never imagine for himself. Such a project would tie one not only to a certain place, but also to a community and an immense responsibility.

"And it's going to be a reality. In only a week, I'll open the doors to our first patients. Thus my notice to the townsfolk."

"Will your wife be working with you?" Sawyer transferred

the page to the side table with the other projects waiting their turn to be set into type for the next paper. His glance toward Trent contained a question as well as humor.

"Absolutely." Trent laid a few coins on the table. "I've learned the value of her experience both as a healer and as a midwife."

"I'm sure she's pleased." Sawyer glanced at Trent, his grin matching the doctor's. He deposited the payment into the cash box in the drawer of the table. "After all the trouble you two had last year over whose methods proved reliable."

Nathaniel sensed an underlying joke in the exchange but didn't pry. If they wished him to be in on it, they'd share the secret. Still, he suddenly felt like the outsider he was.

"Yes, well…" Trent slipped his hat back onto his head with a small shrug. "Good day to you."

Trent turned and hurried out the door, his cloak billowing about him. Nathaniel glanced at Sawyer, one brow lifted in question.

Sawyer chuckled and shook his head. "You weren't here last year when Miss Samantha and Dr. Trent struggled to work together without becoming involved, even though it was obvious to everyone around them that they belonged together. Trent had wanted to put her out of business, but she prevailed. Now they're married, just to prove the point."

"That explains his reaction to your comment." Nathaniel moved back to take up his position. "I suppose we should finish this job, since more work awaits."

Sawyer stepped back to pick up the beaters. "One thing for certain. The women in this town have their own views and expectations now that the war is over."

"What do you mean?" Nathaniel prepared to put the paper on the plate, but paused to wait for the man's response.

"Each of the women in town have spunk." Sawyer looked at Nathaniel for a long moment. "Even Miss Evelyn, if I'm not mistaken. Despite her husband's attempt to quell her spirit."

Nathaniel studied Sawyer while he set to work beating the ink onto the plate. Why had the younger man included Evelyn in his observation? Was Nathaniel being too obvious in his affection for Evelyn? Did he care if others knew? Something to contemplate.

They worked in companionable silence for the next hour, exchanging a word or two only as needed to accomplish their task. Nathaniel ignored the growling in his belly. His thoughts strayed to Evelyn time and again. How was she occupying her time? Thinking of the woman in question proved more enjoyable than focusing upon the task at hand. Her pretty face appeared to his mind's eye, with lips forming a soft smile and gray-green eyes framed by red hair pulled up into a soft bun. The way she held her son and gazed at him with love shining in her expression. The graceful sway of her hips when she sauntered across the room toward where he waited, hungry for her touch and longing to taste her mouth. Everything about her commanded his attention and piqued his interest. What would he do if she denied him? He couldn't think about such a dreary prospect.

He started enjoying the rhythm of the press, of working with his hands and seeing the fruit of his labor. Similar to his satisfaction in producing a hearty stew from a variety of foods when he'd served as cook during the war. In both instances, the finished product became something more—better—than the individual ingredients. When they'd finished printing the broadsides, they paused to catch their breath.

"You've got the hang of it." Sawyer drank from a dark green bottle then wiped his sleeve across his mouth. "I'm pleased you're working here."

"As am I." For a time, Nathaniel would submit to the employment. He'd started to enjoy the work and hoped for a relationship with Evelyn, if she'd consent. But for how long would he stay in Charlestown, or even South Carolina? How long before his desire to move on had him packing his few belongings? And how would his departure fit with his growing need to be with Evelyn?

With every bounce of the single-seated phaeton, Evelyn's reluctance to return to the burned shell of a home intensified. Amy handled the reins with confidence, the pair of matched bay horses trotting at a good clip, their black manes and tails flying in the wind of their own making. Evelyn clutched the small quilt draped over their legs to ward off the cold as well as to hide her trembling. Before long, she'd be back where violence had been a dominating aspect of her life. Did she really want to return to the place so much evil had lurked?

"Not too much farther." Samantha leaned forward from where she sat on the other side of Amy, catching Evelyn's eye. "How are you doing?"

"I'm fine." The doubt in Samantha's expression made Evelyn squirm. "It's not easy, that's all."

Samantha relaxed against the seat back, gazing at the road ahead. "That I believe."

"It's why we all came." Amy glanced at Evelyn, then back at the horses and the stretch of road they traveled. "We want to stand with you."

Evelyn glanced behind the carriage where her three cousins, Ethan, Bill, and Luke Sullivan, rode on horses. They'd elected to venture out with the ladies to judge the scope of the effort. Nobody would mistake them as anything but brothers. Tall with black hair and piercing blue eyes, they sat in their saddles with fluid grace. Their black leather boots shone while their breeches strained over powerful thighs.

Riding coats of vibrant colors and beaver tricornes declared them gentlemen with strength and power. Yet the hands on the reins seemed gentle and kind to the horses' mouths. Their familiar presence reassured Evelyn, calming her agitation.

Ethan, the oldest, rode a rangy chestnut gelding with a white star in the center of its forehead and four white stockings. Bill, the middle brother, had chosen a sorrel mare with an attitude, tossing her mane as if to say "Look at me; I'm a princess." The youngest brother, Luke, sat on a coal black stallion with a hint of a white snip on its nose as relief to the dark color. Ethan nodded at her, a smile in his eyes, while the other two continually searched the surrounding landscape for potential trouble. Beautiful animals, each of them in their own way. The men and the horses. She grinned to herself as she turned back around.

Too soon, they arrived at the circular lane with its statue of Pegasus forlornly welcoming visitors to the blackened remains of the manor. The circle of flowers around the base of the marble statue had withered and died over the winter, adding to the beleaguered appearance of her home. She stared at the rearing winged horse, recalling the reason for its presence. The Greek symbol of wisdom, Pegasus also was a friend of the Muses. He had been ridden by the Greek hero Bellerophon to defeat the Chimera monster. Walter had admired all things Greek, and Bellerophon in particular, for his ability to defend against evil. She admired the horse and its ability to fly, to be free to live as one chose. To escape from an undesirable situation. She was pleased her favorite statue had survived.

"What a terrible day when the fire destroyed the house." Amy halted the horses, their harnesses jangling sharply in the sudden quiet.

"At least he died before seeing all his work burned to the ground." Evelyn removed the quilt from across their laps and folded it over one arm. From her seat, she could see the forest which once had been hidden from view by the house. Goodness but she was glad to have escaped with her son from what would have been a death trap. "Come on."

The three men dismounted and tied their horses to the hitching rail set a distance from the remains of the house. Ethan stopped to study the situation, slowly trailing his gaze from left to right. Luke and Bill, voices lowered in seeming respect for the disaster, joined the ladies heading for the ruins.

"That must have been quite an inferno." Ethan strode to catch up to the group, a ground covering stride as fluid as a panther.

"It was." On a sigh, Evelyn strolled toward the wreckage, grief over the destruction and a foreboding sense of unease creating a knot in her chest.

The stone foundation remained, black and charred from the heat of the wood sides that had been engulfed in flames. Three chimneys poked upward, each column of blackened stones reaching for the blue sky as silent testimony to the ravages of the conflagration. She closed her eyes, remembering the last view of their home as the wagon carried her and the others farther and farther away. She'd prayed for Walter then, hoping he'd survive the fight with the vengeful renegades. But the prayer for his survival ultimately went unanswered. He'd died during the gunfight that preceded the fire, defending his home as best he could. Exactly the way he'd wanted.

Opening her eyes, she inspected the remains of their home. In truth, it had not been a happy place. She'd not cry for the loss, nor for the remembered pain and fear her marriage had instilled in her heart. She'd been trapped in an abusive relationship, one which only death could have ended. As a widow, she possessed the power to choose the path to a better life, for her and little Jim. A power she had earned with her tears and submission.

"Where to begin, that's the question." Samantha joined Evelyn in her perusal of the blackened piles and mounds where the impressive house once stood.

"First, the debris needs to be hauled away." Ethan's deep bass voice reverberated in the chilly air. "We'll come out with a large wagon in a few days and begin on that part."

"So it's worth salvaging?" Evelyn glanced at Ethan, then to the blackened mess.

"The property, certainly." Ethan clutched his waist and considered the task. "It'll take some work, but we can rebuild a better house for you if that's what you want."

"It is. Let's see if anything inside is salvageable."

Ethan helped Evelyn pick her way up the ash-covered brick steps, his massive hand warm and steady under hers. He released her hand when they halted at the top, standing side by side as they surveyed the scene. Evelyn's thoughts tumbled upon themselves at the extent of the damage. Perhaps the silver service had survived, but locating any intact items would be perilous work.

"I doubt anything could be used in the new house." Evelyn sighed, letting all of her worry and fear escape to mingle with the breeze. "If it's not burned, surely it would reek of smoke. Definitely I plan on separating the kitchen from the main house."

"Most everyone has done so to protect the residence." Ethan held out his hand, palm up. "Here. Give me your hand."

Evelyn did as instructed and let her cousin lead her closer to the burned threshold. The wreckage up close seemed worse than she'd imagined possible. Some hope had lodged in her chest prior to witnessing the reality of the devastation. A sharp pain ricocheted through her as unwanted tears burned her eyes. Could she find any hope of happiness where so much ill had occurred?

Amy soon made her way up the steps to pause beside Evelyn. "I'm sorry about all the pretty furnishings lost."

"I'm not." Evelyn rested her fists on each hip as she surveyed the charred lumps of debris covered by soot and ash. "Nothing but bad memories are associated with every single thing in the house."

"I wonder how usable the outbuildings might be, given the ferocity of the fire." Samantha shaded her eyes, gazing at the ruins from where she stood at the bottom of the steps.

"You were fortunate to have escaped." Bill's firm voice stated the cold hard truth.

"Yes, indeed." Evelyn pivoted to descend the brick steps. "Let's see how the other structures fared."

Evelyn let the others surround her as they made their way back to the safety of the open yard. Ethan and Bill walked with the ladies, while Luke climbed onto the phaeton and drove the team around the side of the house. Nobody joked as they chatted, as though they attended the funeral of the building itself. After all, Walter had died and, thanks to Benjamin, lay six feet under the ground in the small family cemetery at the edge of the woods. She'd not had the courage to face the place until now.

Only two months had passed since the gunfight between Walter, Benjamin, and the desperate men who had kidnapped Amy and Samantha as war booty. Two months which saw terror transformed into love. As she made her way to the side of the building, the barn came into view.

The doors stood open, hanging to either side of the central aisle. She quickened her pace, striding into the dim interior with purpose. Could the barn be converted into a place to live? She had pondered the question for several weeks as she began to think about the design of the new house. After all, she'd need to be close by during the construction to make sure it met her standards. With her away from the city,

Nathaniel wouldn't be quite so near to disrupt her composure and cause wanton thoughts, another benefit. A quick perusal of the half-walled stalls and the small windows answered her question in the negative. She sighed and spun on her heel, hurrying back out into the sunlight where the others waited for her.

"Maybe the carriage house?" Evelyn strode to the smaller building situated beside the barn.

Samantha trailed after her, matching her pace. "For what?"

Tugging the double doors open, Evelyn walked inside and smiled. The building consisted of two large alcoves flanking the doors, where two small carriages and a wagon were parked, with a central area leading up to an immense fireplace and chimney. Large glassless windows with wooden hinged doors invited the winter chill to fill the space.

"Much better lighting from the windows. And see, there's already a fireplace the smithy used to make horse shoes and tools, and rims for the wagon wheels."

"So?" Ethan studied her, one brow lifted. "What are you thinking?"

"I'll convert it into a temporary house for me and Jim. It's big enough to divide so my servants have a place as well." Evelyn slowly pivoted in the center, nodding as she inspected the area. She'd espied a new appreciation in Ethan's steady regard, an awareness of her as a female. He was her cousin and friend, nothing more. "We can park the vehicles in the barn and then put up some slats between the spaces, glass in the windows, build a new wood floor, and we'll be comfortable enough."

Amy sauntered in to stare at Evelyn. "Comfortable enough for what exactly?"

"To live in, of course." Evelyn studied her sister as she crossed her arms. "I have a plan."

Chapter Four

The warehouse had seen better days. Ignored and neglected during the war, the brick building hunkered at the dark end of the alley between two much larger buildings. Nathaniel approached it with due caution, inspecting the surroundings with each step. If Benjamin had not invited him to meet at the shuttered place, he'd never have ventured down the suspect alley.

Pushing the heavy wood door open, he entered the storage facility. A lantern hung on a hook by the door, shedding much welcome light. Barrels and crates filled the space, some with their lids pried up and left askew. Others stood against the wall, covered with markings from distant ports. Given the quantity of crates, the collection must be immense. Nathaniel moved among the containers, taken aback by several of the more life-like exhibits. Several shelves stretched across the back of the building and boasted a group of straw-stuffed birds and liquid-filled glass jars in an assortment of sizes displaying a montage of specimens. He steered clear of the two-foot-tall jar displaying a black python in a contorted position.

The whole situation brought to mind his experience

during the war. Of the lifeless eyes of his enemy as well as compatriots. Death marches into the fight with every army, often proving to be the only victor to the clash. He'd seen enough of the results of men in hand-to-hand contest to never desire to engage in another argument, let alone combat.

"Hello?" He sidled around a large barrel, noting the high shrouded windows. "Benjamin?"

A rustle preceded the sound of boots on the floor. Nathaniel turned toward the noise, relieved when he spied Benjamin's head and shoulders swaggering closer to where he stood. He'd prefer to not venture any farther into the warehouse. In fact, he'd rather be outside, away from the cold stares of the creatures.

"Finally. Come with me!" Benjamin turned midstride and retreated into the depths of the warehouse.

Wrong direction. Nathaniel sighed and followed Benjamin. He edged past the python and then around an orangutan, his long orange-haired arms raised as if he wanted to attack whoever ventured near. Why would any one want such a monstrosity? To terrify small children? Or mayhap to warn away potential thieves? He shuddered. With a last glance at the ape, he hurried to catch up.

"Wait until you see this." Benjamin bent over a low box, rummaging in the straw before lifting a mask from its depths.

He straightened and tilted it so Nathaniel could see the red and white painted stripes stretching from below the eye holes to the bottom edge. Long black hair hung from the top, apparently to be worn over the head as further disguise. The resulting expression proved monstrous to the extreme. Yet another object intended to frighten.

"Fabulous, isn't it?" Benjamin held the object of his delight in both hands. "It's a war mask from Africa. One of the slavers managed to locate it on one of his voyages and thought we'd like to include it in the museum."

Nathaniel didn't want to contemplate what else the man had brought from Africa. A tremor snaked down his back. "I'd hate to see a person wearing such a hideous mask coming at me."

Benjamin chuckled and replaced the item in its nest of straw and settled the lid into place. "Indeed."

"Why did you want me to come here?" Nathaniel gestured to the room at large, encompassing the many crates and barrels. By doing so, he attempted to replace the image of the mask with a more pleasing one. "What is all this?"

"Frank and I would like to enlist your help." Benjamin crossed his arms and regarded Nathaniel for a long moment. "If you're so inclined?"

Nathaniel shrugged. "What form of help?"

"We've located a better place to house the museum collection and we need to move everything from here to there."

Which translated into handling the creatures, too. Nathaniel suppressed a shudder with an effort. Animals should be alive, not stuffed and put out for all to gawk at. On the other hand, how would people learn about them if they never had chance to see them? "I don't know…"

The door swung open, admitting both a blast of cool air and Frank. Dust motes floated on the air and settled as he made his way through the cluttered room. His Monmouth hat and the shoulders of his matching cloak glistened with rain, his tall black boots leaving wet prints on the grimy floor. The weather had apparently deteriorated in the minutes he'd stood within the warehouse. Distant thunder announced the approach of a storm, confirming his supposition.

"The man for the job." Frank halted in front of Nathaniel to shake hands with him. "Has Benjamin shared our proposition with you?"

"I started to before you interrupted." Benjamin shook

hands with Frank and then focused on Nathaniel. "Three days and a wagon would see the work done."

"It's not that I don't appreciate your offer." How could he explain without his new friends thinking ill of his reason? "I do."

"We realize you're in some financial straits." Frank laid an arm around Nathaniel's shoulders. "Let us help you at the same time you help us."

The weight of Frank's arm reassured Nathaniel of the man's intent and sincerity. "Would the stuffed creatures need to go as well?"

Benjamin raised a brow as a knowing grin appeared on his mouth. "Definitely. Is there a problem?"

Frank removed his arm and stepped to one side, peering at Nathaniel. "Do they perturb you?"

Nathaniel swallowed, fighting the urge to vomit. "I can't touch them."

The very idea raised horrific images in his mind. When he was six or seven, his family had gone to visit his uncle Jack in Virginia. The huge man scared him into silence with his gargantuan frame and snarling features. Added to his appearance, which surely Nathaniel would have grown accustomed to provided they had remained longer, his uncle delighted in capturing animals and then killing and stuffing them to set out in his house. Indeed, the entire abode seemed to overflow with creatures—foxes, squirrels, rabbits, raccoons, coyotes, bear cubs, and even a mountain lion—on most every horizontal surface, shocking him at each turn. When Jack had tried to force him to play with them, he'd run screaming from the house and refused his parents' attempts to make him go back inside. The memory evoked a shudder of loathing.

Benjamin folded his arms across his chest. "We can manage those. What do you say?"

Hesitating, Nathaniel considered his response. On one hand, he sorely could use the income. On the other, the very idea of returning to move among the stuffed and preserved animals made him quake in his boots. Yet, he had no other plans at the present to conflict with their request. But those eyes…

"We'd pay you, of course." Frank rested his fists on his hips. "Twenty dollars specie."

"That would give you the wherewithal to court Evelyn." Benjamin dropped his hands to his side, and rested one hip against a barrel. "With some left over for your pocket."

"Court Evelyn?" They knew he wanted to make love to the beautiful widow? To see her and hold her hand? When he first laid eyes on her, the day of the army's foraging raid on the Hamilton estate, she'd seemed so frail and pathetic he'd taken pity on her. Then when he met her at the wedding, she had changed enough he almost didn't recognize her. She'd bloomed as a result of her widowhood.

"You'll need to make your intentions known soon. You have some competition in that arena, if my eyes didn't fail me." Benjamin straightened up, planting his feet as though standing on a moving deck. "Ethan Sullivan seemed to find her equally intriguing."

Startled by the observation, Nathaniel straightened his shoulders as he studied his friends' smirks. Competition indeed. He recalled the brawny specimen of a man, and settled on his answer. "Then I suppose I should accept your offer so I can do something about this situation."

"Good man." Frank shook his hand. "What else do you need to know?"

Despite his objections and disgust at the prospect, the fact remained he needed the money. More urgently now than mere moments ago if he had any hopes of wooing his love. To make his personal dreams a reality, he'd do whatever necessary.

Including moving dead animals. He swallowed the rising bile in his throat.

"When do we start?"

The aroma of pan sausage and coffee drew Evelyn down the stairs as surely as the echo of her parents' banter. She followed the scent of cloves and spices and the sound of laughter into the dining room. Richard and Lucille glanced up from their discussion at the rectangular table in the center of the room. Crystal candlesticks stood at each end of the white clothed surface, surrounded by platters of steaming corn cakes and sausage.

"Running a bit late this morning, aren't you?" Richard lifted his cup and saluted Evelyn.

Chuckling, Evelyn strode farther into the room. Her father always said the same thing when she appeared for the morning meal. A question started when she was a child and overslept one morning. On her sixth birthday, no less. She'd never lived down the lapse.

"Did you leave me some coffee?" Evelyn grinned as she went to retrieve a cup of hot brew.

Taking her seat, Evelyn swallowed a sip. The liquid burned the tip of her tongue, but the pleasure of the taste overrode the discomfort. She caught her mother's eye as she lowered her cup to the table. "What's the occasion?"

"Nothing really. I merely decided to use the ingredients on hand rather than having to go to the market." Lucille picked up the platter holding the finger-sized rolls of browned sausage. "I think they turned out the best I've ever made."

"They certainly smell divine." Evelyn took the platter and speared two rolls onto her plate.

Her mother was an unusual mistress of the household, insisting on preparing part of each of the meals enjoyed by her family. The elderly black slave who assisted in the kitchen prepared dishes to complete the menu which her mother had chosen. Most likely, her mother made the sausages while the other woman whipped up the flapjacks and set out the honey and butter. Tea and coffee also were the slave's domain. Lucille relied on teaching others by her example and wouldn't ask any household servant to perform a task she couldn't do herself as well. A trait which endeared her mother to her servants, eliciting their loyalty and respect.

"Have some corn cakes with that." Richard passed the plate of golden flapjacks.

"You'll spoil me with such fine eating." Evelyn added a pair of cakes to her plate, then reached for the crystal bowl of honey resting on a silver plate. She removed the lid and lifted the small spoon to dip into the amber fluid. "I'll need to hire a cook when I move to my own lodgings."

Richard paused in putting a bite into his mouth. He swallowed and peered at her. "You have no need to leave. You're welcome to stay as long as you'd like."

"I appreciate your hospitality more than I could ever repay." Evelyn drizzled honey across her corn cakes. She hadn't planned to blurt out her desire to move out of her parents' home. But she'd resolved over the days staying with them on her course of action. "I have to think about my son's future as well as my own. I do not wish to burden you any longer than necessary."

"You're never a burden to us, dear." Lucille caught Evelyn's attention with a wave of her hand. "We shall always support you when you have need."

"I appreciate your concern." Evelyn cut into the flapjack and lifted a bite to her mouth. How should she relay to them her plan? She swallowed and laid her fork on the plate. "I rode out to the manor the other day, to see what is left of my home."

"What did you find?" Richard gripped the fragile handle of the porcelain cup, hesitating in the act of drinking its steaming contents.

The scene appeared in her mind, the charred remains and desolate chimneys, causing a knot in her throat. The shadow of disquiet she'd felt passed over her, making her shiver. She rested against the chair back and sighed. "The fire destroyed everything except the stones and bricks. Those were covered in soot and practically unusable."

"You didn't go alone, did you?" Lucille regarded her with a frown and a troubled gaze. "It's not safe for a young woman to venture out of town without an escort."

"Amy and Samantha went with me, along with Ethan, Bill, and Luke." She recalled how attentive her cousin had been, wondering about his intentions. She had no interest in him as anything more than a relative, but he did not know that. She hoped his feelings proved not to be what she imagined, especially since she refused to consider remarrying until more time passed. "We went to determine what I could do with the property."

"Without a house to live in, you may as well try to sell it and stay here with us." Richard sipped his coffee, returning the cup to the saucer. "There's plenty of room."

"I enjoy having a baby in the house again." Lucille leveled a gentle smile at Evelyn. "I could help you raise him."

"You have plenty of experience with babies and children." Tears smarted Evelyn's eyes at the gentle kindness in her mother's voice. Her mother adored children of all ages, but especially infants she could cuddle in her arms. Evelyn blinked away the lingering tears. Her intent would cause no little consternation for her parents. "The property is part of my son's inheritance, so I'd hesitate to sell it. But I do plan to rebuild the manor house."

Richard studied her in the time required for three breaths,

fingers gripping the fragile porcelain handle of his cup so hard she feared he'd snap it off. Her mother added more honey to her cakes then cut into them with her fork. Evelyn waited for her father's reaction, which she sensed was imminent.

"You intend to move out there by yourself? With just your wee son and a servant?" He blinked as he shook his head. "Not a wise move, to my mind."

She'd marshalled her arguments and reasons the night before while lying in bed. Or rather tossing and turning in a vain attempt to find sleep. Her father's objection came as no surprise. Indeed, she'd have been surprised if he hadn't objected. Neither of her parents had approved of Walter's decision to live so far from Charlestown. As much as she'd prefer to live in town, she desperately needed to prove to herself she could survive on her own terms. Through her own initiative and efforts. To make decisions for herself to the benefit of both her and her son. The years of her marriage to an abusive husband, trapped by the circumstance with no easy way out, made her appreciate the independence widowhood granted. She could choose for herself if and whom she married. She could sign contracts, and buy and sell her property. Actions forbidden to married women under the archaic coverture laws. With good fortune, those would be changed in the new America.

"I won't be alone as I intend to expand the building to add several rooms." Her father's curiosity was plain in his expression as he lifted a brow and waited for her to continue. She gulped as she picked up her fork to occupy her hands. "I'm going to start a girls' boarding school."

Her father put down his cup with a clatter, tea sloshing onto the white cloth. "A school? Who will teach the girls what they must learn?"

Obviously, he didn't think her capable, which only made her more determined to overcome her own doubts to achieve the goal. "I will, to begin with. I've studied Walter's books for the last several years."

"Reading novels does not make one a teacher." Richard tapped a finger on the table to emphasize each word.

"Not novels, Father, but books on history, philosophy, geography." She regarded the stern face. His tapping finger, visual evidence of losing control, revealed the degree of his distress. She had to make him understand. She'd thought through the entire proposition and decided she would do everything in her power to succeed in conveying the proper education to her students. After all, no other viable options had presented themselves to her. She may as well follow through on the school. "I will hire another teacher to assist me, naturally, when I have enough students to afford to, but I believe I have the ability to teach."

Lucille put her fork on her plate and then laid her hands in her lap. "Since Walter's library was destroyed in the fire, you'll need to buy new books, which is not a minor expense."

"I'm aware of the cost of replacing the books, but they will be needed for certain subject matter." The memory of seeing the burned pages of the many volumes among the ashes made her wince. So much lost in the conflagration. She had to start over from the beginning to put together a new household. "I never said any of what I'm about to do will be easy."

"Then why do it?" Lucille tilted her head to one side for a second before straightening her neck. "You know you don't need to subject yourself to such a strain, do you not?"

How could she make her parents comprehend? "All I know is that I want the best for my son. I believe I'll be better able to teach him as a result of teaching others. Does that make sense?"

"I suppose there is some logic in what you say." Richard shook his head and picked up his fork. "Do girls need to know about math?"

She stared at her father, unsure how to respond without offending him. Many sharp retorts struggled to spring from her lips, but she wrestled them back. A simple, straightforward answer would serve the purpose. "Yes."

He raised a brow as he speared a bite of sausage, holding it aloft. "For what reason would a girl need to understand formulas and calculations?"

"Every time she goes to the market or the milliner's." Evelyn snared a bite of corn cake with her fork, dredging it through the honey pooled on her plate. "So she can determine the correct price and total of money she spends."

"You have a point, but the fundamentals are all that is necessary for any woman to understand."

The exact attitude she intended to defy with her course of instruction. Emily's advocacy for equal education informed Evelyn's approach and expectations. Her effort may be only one small step. To her mind, if she taught her students to believe learning about the world around them would help them be better people, then perhaps they'd teach others to respect the concept of education for all.

"Don't neglect the girls' domestic education." Lucille lifted her fork again, poised to spear a piece of sausage. "They must know how to manage a house no matter what else they learn."

"They will receive a comprehensive grounding." Evelyn sipped her coffee, swallowing the last drop. Setting her cup on its matching saucer, she sat back in her chair. "The Sullivan brothers will start to clean up the debris in a couple days. I've nearly finalized the sketch of my idea for the new house."

"You're serious?" Richard switched from tapping to drumming his fingers on the tablecloth. "You're going to move back to that place? After all that happened there?"

"Yes." Short and to the point seemed to work best when

dealing with her father. Especially when she had one more subject to discuss with him.

Richard shook his head, disappointment etched into the lines pulling down around his mouth. "Very well. I cannot stop you from acting on your desires, though I do question your decision. But as your mother said, we shall always support you."

"Which is why I'd like to request your help." Evelyn glanced at each parent in turn. The next words proved the hardest for her to say. But say them she must. She swallowed the fear of refusal. "Will you loan me the money I need to start the school?"

After a miserable day of aligning letters and hanging pages, Nathaniel needed to wash before enjoying a before-dinner cocktail. A double quantity of whatever hard liquor Mr. Abernathy had on hand. He'd started at dawn, not even taking time to enjoy breakfast with the family. And Evelyn in particular. He considered his absence from her company a dear sacrifice indeed. But his employment demanded his presence. He and Sawyer worked hard throughout the entire day, striving to meet the burdens of the growing number of customers. The increase in clientele reflected the rebound of the entire city, a positive turn indeed. He slipped into the house and hurried up to his room, avoiding meeting any others in the state of his attire. He poured water from the pitcher into the basin and quickly scrubbed his hands clean with a bit of soap.

He changed from work clothes into proper dinner garments: dark pants with a precise crease, white silk shirt and cravat, completed with a jacket embroidered with flowers, vines, and birds on a ruby background. He'd been especially pleased with the beautiful coat given to him by his wife, who had made it in honor of his twenty-fifth birthday three years ago. One of the few reminders of her left to him. He trailed a hand over the stitching, imagining Patsy's hands creating the elaborate design. Drawing in a deep breath, he released it in one long sigh. She might not have been the most loving woman, but they'd had a satisfactory life together. He missed the companionship and someone to share his day.

His thoughts naturally drifted to Evelyn and his hope for a future with the tantalizing woman. The biggest problem he faced was how to provide for her and her son. No woman with any sense married solely for love and companionship, especially one with a child to consider. He grabbed a brush and stroked it through his hair, detangling it so he could tie it back with a length of black ribbon. With each pass, he tried to decide his next steps. Two came easily to mind. First, make enough money to fund his ultimate plan. Second, convince Evelyn to permit him to court her in earnest. But the first one should precede the second, in a perfect world. He released an impatient breath. He didn't live in a perfect world, not by far. He laid down the brush and straightened his jacket with a sharp tug.

Feeling refreshed and presentable, he sauntered down the stairs, heading toward what he hoped would be a relaxing dinner and conversation. Mayhap Amy would tell a story, or Evelyn would sing a song later. He smiled as he strode into the parlor where the family gathered before the evening meal.

Richard stood near the fireplace, holding a crystal glass containing amber liquid. "Evening, Mr. Williams. Would you care for a splash of whiskey, to whet your appetite?"

Nathaniel acknowledged the sentiment as he strode across the oriental carpet and paused in front of the high-backed stuffed chair standing to one side of the fire. A vague disappointment settled on his shoulders. Evelyn had not made an appearance yet. "A double, if you have some to spare."

Lucille spoke from her seat on the gold brocade sofa facing the fireplace. "I hope your day did not prove too fatiguing."

Accepting the glass from Richard, Nathaniel sank onto the cushioned seat. "Fatiguing indeed. I am grateful for the position, but am glad I won't remain in it forever."

"We each must do what is necessary to survive." Richard crossed to sit beside Lucille, his easy grace and fluid movements belying his advanced age.

In some ways, Evelyn's parents reminded him of his own. Their easy companionship flowed between them, binding them together. One could tell they cared deeply about the other, and the example they set for their daughters proved instructional to the maximum. He envisioned Evelyn, the care and adoration of young James evident each time she gazed upon the boy. Oh, to have her express such a feeling for him…

He sipped the fire water, the whiskey living up to its name as it coursed down his throat. Burning the dust from his tongue and the smell of ink from his nose. While he found some measure of enjoyment in working with his hands so he could see tangible progress in the form of printed materials, the repetition of the required actions aggravated his equanimity. He'd prefer to be out of doors, hunting or farming.

"I've agreed to work for Frank for six months, and I'll keep my word." He sipped and cradled the glass between both hands. "By then I will have decided what I will do."

Female laughter made him turn toward the open door, anticipation sharp on his tongue. The rustle of skirts and the patter of slippers on the wood floor announced Amy and Evelyn, walking side by side with arms interlocked. Benjamin strolled into the room behind them, a bemused expression on his face. Nathaniel met Evelyn's gaze and smiled in welcome. When she smiled back, his heart filled with an abiding sense of pleasure. After everyone had settled onto a seat, with a glass of whisky or sherry in hand, he indulged in simply observing her.

She had certainly changed over the last several months. No longer did she hunch her shoulders or look at her feet while she conversed. She held her head up, eyes alive with an inner fire as she spoke. Her shoulders squared, her back straight as an arrow, her comportment rivaled that of a queen. Her hands featured long, tapering fingers clasped around the glass of sherry. A longing to hold her hand, to touch some part of her, stole his breath and made his heart pound. Racing with the desire surging through him.

"Dinner is served, Miss Lucille." Sally, the dark-skinned cook, dipped into a brief curtsey in the open door and then pivoted on one foot and hurried out of sight.

The group rose as one and followed the cook's retreating figure down the hall and into the dining room. Nathaniel trailed the exodus, lagging behind so he could calm his racing heart. What was wrong with him? Too much liquor? Or too much wishful ponderings? He tried to shake the sensation away with a toss of his head. Took a few deep breaths, letting them each out over several moments. Better.

Evelyn and Amy skirted the long table with its array of platters of meat and bowls of winter vegetables and condiments. Silver candlesticks and crystal glinted against the dark blue cloth covering the table. An elegant presentation, one befitting the status of Richard Abernathy. Nathaniel moved to pull out Evelyn's chair, but Benjamin had anticipated the need after seating Amy at her place.

Nathaniel settled onto his seat while Richard assisted his wife. He felt like the odd man out, which wasn't technically possible in a room with three men and three women. Oh, and of course, the two waiters standing at opposite ends of the room, biding their time until everyone had taken their places. They wore the green and gold livery Miss Lucille had ordered from Philadelphia. She'd seemed rather proud of the appearance of the two slaves as they attended to the needs of the family and their guests. Still, their stoic presence proved disquieting.

As soon as Richard sat at the head of the table, the two men began to hold the various platters for each person to select from the duck, venison, chicken, and fish. The smaller bowls of chutney and relish along with steaming bowls of stewed apples, boiled carrots, and seasoned beans passed from hand to hand around the table.

"Nathaniel, you were saying your plans are in flux?" Richard stabbed a piece of meat and popped it into his mouth.

"For the next few months, I'll be at the printing office as agreed." Nathaniel lifted his fork. "After that time has passed, I'm not certain what my future holds."

"Is anybody?" Benjamin chuckled. "Especially at this moment in history."

Nathaniel nodded as he chewed the roasted duck, detecting rosemary and garlic among the savory flavors exploding on his tongue. His stint as cook made him appreciate the nuances of various herbs and spices in ways he'd previously never noticed.

"I know what my future holds." Evelyn laid her knife on her plate and then speared a piece of cooked apple, cinnamon and nutmeg spices speckling the surface and perfuming the air. She smiled as she glanced at each person at the table. "I'm going to start a school for girls."

Gasps of surprise and murmurs of approval followed her announcement. Nathaniel remained silent, observing the happy responses at the surprising news. He laid his fork down, the ring of metal on porcelain drawing attention to him.

"Are you qualified to teach?" Nathaniel studied Evelyn's demeanor as she ate her meal.

How could she think to engage in such an endeavor? While he appreciated the sentiment, the desire to further others knowledge, she didn't seem suited for teaching. She possessed the knowledge and aptitude, certainly. But why would she want to lower her station in society from lady of the manor to tutor to young girls? If she were his wife, he'd not permit her to denigrate herself in such a manner.

She met his gaze and nodded once. "I plan to hire someone to assist with those subject areas I'm weakest in. But yes, I have much to share with the girls to prepare them for their futures."

Benjamin cast a doubtful look around the room, encompassing the entire structure of the house, then focused on Evelyn. "Is there enough space for a school?"

"Not here." Evelyn laid down her fork and peered at Benjamin. "I've hired the Sullivan brothers to rebuild my home with a few additions."

She planned to move back out into the countryside? Where the law barely reached to keep order? Nathaniel frowned, worried for her safety. Sure, she had an inner strength and courage enough to teach a thousand girls. But surviving on her own with merely servants to aid her endeavors? No husband looking out for her? Protecting her? What about her son?

"How can you afford to start over out there?" Nathaniel searched for viable reasons to prevent her from making what he considered to be a huge mistake. "Inflation is out of control."

Evelyn glanced at her father. "Father has generously agreed to finance the building."

Nathaniel had hoped to find some barrier to her intentions, but they melted away under the endorsement by her parents. After all, he had no say in the matter. He wasn't family, nor even a beau. Though he longed for the latter, to investigate and determine if they could have a companionable relationship. He sensed he already knew the result of the exploration, but only time, and her agreement, would reveal the answer.

Richard cleared his throat, drawing everyone's attention. "I did say I'd fund your school, and I'm happy to do so."

"Thank you, Father." Evelyn beamed and saluted him with her glass of wine. "You are making my heart's greatest desire a reality through your support and kindness."

If Evelyn thought running a school equaled the best yearnings of her heart, then he'd dearly love to show her even stronger emotions to entertain and enjoy. With him by her side, instructing her on the finer points of companionship and even more on loving another.

"There are a couple of conditions." Richard lifted one brow as he regarded his daughter. "If you do not accept them, then I cannot, in good conscience, keep my promise."

Tension sizzled in the air between father and daughter. Nathaniel's very skin tingled as they stared at each other for the span of five ticks of the windup clock standing against the wall.

"You did not express a need for conditions this morning at breakfast." Evelyn inhaled and let her breath out on a sigh. "What changed?"

"I insisted upon them." Lucille sat with her hands in her lap, calmly watching the interplay between her husband and daughter. "It's our way of looking out for you, so we require you to adhere to them."

Evelyn's brows rose so high that if she had hair fringing her forehead they would have been hidden. In the event, since she'd pulled her hair up into a bun, the extent of her surprise was clearly visible. Nathaniel suppressed a chuckle, an inappropriate response to the drama playing out at the table. He couldn't help his musings about Evelyn any more than he could make his opinion matter in the current conversation.

"What conditions?" Evelyn tapped her index finger on the blue cloth in a steady tempo.

Richard drew a breath and pressed his lips into a line for a moment. "Two conditions. First, you'll take several of the slaves from the plantation to help you."

"Slaves?" Evelyn frowned and her finger's tempo increased. "I had planned to hire the help I need. Or perhaps an indentured servant so I'm giving someone a chance at a better life."

"You need qualified help, not someone off the streets of London or Dublin." Lucille shook her head. "Our slaves are trained in their jobs and content in their lot."

Nathaniel doubted the last statement, but kept mum. How could any one be content to do someone else's bidding day and night forever? Especially when one had no hope of ever living the life of their choosing? One day, if the trend set by Pennsylvania and Maryland continued to gradually free the slaves, America would have no people in bondage, only independent citizens. Would he see that day? With luck, perhaps.

"You have a point." Evelyn shook her head and sighed, but when she raised her eyes to look at her father her gaze held a hint of reproach. "Very well. What's your second?"

Richard swallowed, glanced at his wife, and then shrugged, barely a lift and fall of his shoulders. "You must take a new husband within one year."

Evelyn sat back against the chair with a thud. She blinked rapidly as a frown descended between her eyes. "Why?"

Lucille squared her shoulders as if preparing to do battle. "Because, my dear, our grandson deserves a father, a man to teach him how to grow into a proper gentleman. Would you deny him his future?"

"Jim is too young to need such an example for some time." Evelyn's gaze drifted to meet Nathaniel's, then flicked to Amy before landing on her mother. "I expect to remarry at some point, but why one year? I'll barely have the school operational."

"Plenty of time to seek and find a fitting husband." Richard picked up his fork and pierced a chunk of meat. "You're a beautiful woman of childbearing age with property, a fine combination for a man seeking a wife."

No doubt existed in Nathaniel's mind as to Evelyn's qualifications for life companion. He'd not viewed them from the eyes of any other eligible bachelor. Not even when Benjamin had mentioned Ethan's interest in her had he truly considered why he might pursue the woman. As long as Ethan expressed appreciation for her as a person and not merely her property, which was surely enough for the stable he and his brothers planned to build. He'd best keep watch over Evelyn to protect her from such a maneuver.

"Especially with so many men returning home to start building a new life." Benjamin glanced from one to the other. "Evelyn shouldn't have any problem meeting your conditions."

"Hush." Amy punched him on the arm. "Mayhap she doesn't want to find a husband."

Struggling to find a compromise, Nathaniel remained silent. Outsider that he was, they wouldn't listen to his ideas. Hope had sprung into his heart at the prospect of helping her meet the second condition. Only to have it dashed when she objected.

Evelyn laid her napkin beside her plate and rose to her

feet. She stood there, a silent statue, for several seconds. Her shoulders drooped as she contemplated her father. On a sigh, she straightened her spine. "I accept your conditions. I'm afraid my appetite has fled, and so I shall ask your permission to be excused."

"Wonderful." Lucille's smile was the only one at the table.

Richard inclined his head. "I'll make the arrangements at the bank to-morrow."

Evelyn glanced at Nathaniel on her way out of the room, the echo of her steps fading as she climbed the stairs to her bedchamber.

Why had she agreed when she obviously did not wish to adhere to either requirement? Should he go after her? Comfort her? Would she let him?

Chapter Five

*B*lankets, bed frames, bed linens, a table—make that two tables—barrels to catch rain water. Evelyn relaxed in her seat at the writing desk, tapping the feather of the quill pen against her cheek. What else? She looked around the room for inspiration. Flames—red, yellow, white, and blue—popped and snapped in the open fireplace. Gold and red brocade drapes hung at the windows. Elegant chairs, featuring cushioned seats and curved legs with claw feet, stood at intervals on the oriental carpet. *Of course.* She dipped the quill and added chairs to the list of items necessary for the interim lodgings in the renovated carriage house.

On the morrow, she'd visit her uncle to ask him to acquire the furniture for the finished house. Uncle Joshua, Emily's father, operated an importing business. The first list included many more items than the one before her. She glanced at the page pushed to the right side of the desk, ready to hand off. Bedsteads, armoires, tables, chairs, carpets, wallpaper, candlesticks, and on and on. She also need a quantity of smaller bits and pieces such as urns and basins, chamber pots, candles, kitchen wares, and a myriad of other necessities. She grinned at the challenge laid before her.

She'd create a welcoming home and worth while school.

The back door thudded closed, followed by the sound of footsteps in the hall. She paused, the quill poised to continue with writing down additions. She listened for Amy's voice but only silence met her ears. Evelyn perused the short list again. Cleaning supplies, cookery, utensils, baskets and bowls, cooking tools. The list seemed to have no end.

"Miss Evelyn."

Startled by the deep voice, Evelyn dropped the quill, knocking over the ink stand in the process. A river of black flowed onto the page, obliterating several of her entries. "Goodness!"

"My apologies." Nathaniel grabbed a stained rag from a wooden bowl on the desk and blottedg the paper. "What is this?"

"A list." After he lifted the rag away, Evelyn fanned the page, hurrying the drying process. "Must you sneak around so?"

"I had not intended to startle you." He dropped the rag back into the porcelain bowl sitting on the wood surface.

"What did you intend?" Evelyn glanced up at him, but the intensity of his expression had her dropping her gaze back to the list. A deep yearning flashed through her, lightning across a stormy sky.

"To talk with you." He offered a hand, waiting with his palm up in invitation.

His hand had fresh ink over the stains from his current occupation. She picked up the rag and rubbed the dabs of wet from his fingers, careful not to make direct contact with his skin or risk upsetting her composure. Restoring the rag to its home, she contemplated his request. "We can talk here."

"Sit with me on the sofa. We'll be more comfortable." He wiggled his fingers until she reluctantly placed her hand in his and stood. "Come."

Evelyn sucked in air in response to his touch, but allowed

him to lead her over to the high-backed garnet sofa and settled on the firm seat. He sat beside her, his breech-covered thigh nearly touching hers. If her skirts had less bulk, she'd probably feel the heat from his leg. Fortunately, she'd donned her thickest petticoat to ward off the winter chill. Little had she considered the garment also would fend off a man.

She clasped her hands together in her lap, then endured his quiet contemplation. The scars on his face twitched as she studied him. Was he nervous? "What did you wish to discuss?"

His smile lit his eyes and revealed his teeth. "Your girls' school."

"I'm sorry. I don't understand." Her mind raced with questions. Why did he care? What aspect of the scheme? Why was her heart pounding so in her breast?

He pointed at the page on the desk. "Your list. Items needed to start over?" He shifted his position, closing the gap between them. "Quite a lot of things."

"Yes." Should she trust him? She knew he wanted to become better acquainted. Her parents' conditions preyed in her mind, rattling her composure. Her hands trembled. "I have my work cut out for me."

"Riding to and from the estate will be quite tiring, I'd venture." Nathaniel laid a hand over hers, his thumb brushing across her skin in a steady rhythm. "You'll want an escort."

Warmth threaded through her body, finding purchase in her cheeks. A current of electricity rushed through her with each tender stroke of his thumb. "I won't need one as I'll be living on the property to oversee the progress."

"Living there? Where?" His thumb stilled and his eyes raised to look into hers.

Detecting concern mixed with something more worrisome to her equilibrium in his steady gaze, she swallowed.

"In the carriage house, after it's been made comfortable." Her heart competed with her thoughts. Which could race faster? "It's only a couple months until the temperatures will rise and it won't be quite so bitter outside."

"You can't live in a carriage house without making significant changes to it." He resumed caressing her hand with his calloused thumb, a faint rasp filling the silence. "Who will make it habitable for you?"

"Ethan has offered to start work next week." Was he suggesting she shouldn't pursue her intent? She lifted her chin and captured his gaze. "Within a few weeks, I should be quite at home, he said."

"I don't like the idea of you being alone with Ethan."

"Why ever not?" She blinked at him, amazed by the vehemence in his tone. "He's my cousin. I have nothing to fear from him."

"He desires your companionship too much, from the gossip I've heard." He shook his head and then peered at her. "I'd prefer for you to not accept his help."

"You do not have a say in the matter." Though she understood from her own exchanges with her cousin that he did indeed display a level of interest she found disconcerting. Still, she harbored no doubt in her ability to squash any unwanted attentions. "What do you suggest I do instead?"

He regarded her for a long moment. "I'd be honored to assist you, if you'd permit me."

"I don't believe it's necessary for you to take time away from your work, but I appreciate the overture." Distance. That's what she needed. To put distance between them so he couldn't distract her. Couldn't make her out of kilter and on edge, as though waiting for something she couldn't define to occur.

"It's not inconvenient for me to take a few days to help."

"I'll not be alone, as I'll have Jemma and Jim with me."

She paused, seeing surprise lift his brows. "And the Sullivan brothers will start working in a short time, as I said. I'll be perfectly safe, I assure you."

"I cannot help but be alarmed for your well-being. Your safety and comfort are my utmost concern." He gripped her hands, his sincerity reflected in both his gaze and his tone. "Lyn, please, let me complete the renovations."

She'd longed to put distance between them, and then he suggested infiltrating her temporary quarters? While holding her hands, which completely set her senses on fire. But then to have the man in yet another of her abodes? An inner voice whispered *yes, yes, yes*. She shivered though no chill swept through her. Instead, desire replaced the denial. She liked him on a deeper level than she'd previously admitted to herself. Must be that second condition her mother insisted upon making her weak. But the temptation remained, and as long as she was being honest, had begun the moment she'd met the man.

"Please?" Nathaniel squeezed her fingers, a persuasive grin aimed her way. "You know I'll take care of it without any delay. You'll be able to move in sooner."

"What of your printing work? Can Frank spare you?" What was she doing? She swallowed a huff rather than venting her inner turmoil. She didn't want his help, did she?

"Yes." He leaned closer as he tugged on her hands, turning her to angle toward him. "I have two days free after to-morrow."

"Free?" She moistened dry lips, enthralled by his eyes, his mouth as he drew steadily closer to hers.

"Yes. We can start for the property in a couple days." He reduced the space between them to a kiss.

Her senses spun, leaving her breathless and off balance. Her racing thoughts crashed to a complete stop. She closed her eyes, relishing the exquisite experience of bussing with a man, this man. Dear heavens above. He slipped inside her mouth, teasing the tip of his tongue against hers. A moan reverberated in her throat when he embraced her, pulling her to him. No longer could she deny her feelings about Nathaniel. She held onto him, an anchor in the maelstrom unleashed by his touch, his kiss, his very breath.

He eased away, slowly and tenderly breaking the contact between them. She just as slowly opened her eyes as she attempted to restore her composure and calm her heart. She blinked, amazed. The room had not changed. Everything still stood where it had been before her world turned upside down. She blinked again when he captured her hands, bringing them up to his mouth.

"We can leave after we break the fast in two days." He kissed her fingers, one by one, his gaze dwelling on her features. "Will that be enough time?"

"That would be perfect." Her voice sounded strange, rough and low. She cleared her throat, feeling awkward and dizzy. "I-I have much to prepare before our departure."

He nodded and helped her stand. "As do I." He pressed his lips to hers, stirring her calming senses. "See you at supper."

He departed, glancing back at her with a grin before disappearing down the hall. She remained still, several realizations descending upon her. Not least of which was, she could fall in love with him.

Charlestown rebounded from its occupation by the Britons with the grit and spirit inherent in the people. The lane teemed with wagons hauling merchandise to and from the docks as well as men riding and walking, conducting their business. Nathaniel sat his roan gelding, Jingo, the creak of leather a soft undertone adding to the commotion on the busy street.

He followed Frank, driving a team of horses transporting the last wagonload of the museum contents on the now familiar route down Tradd to King and then a left onto Queen. After the items were safely inside the brick building, he'd be free to help Evelyn move out of town. Away from him. Unless he could change her mind about her plan.

Benjamin and Captain Joshua Sullivan waited by the rear doors while Frank slowed the team of horses to a halt. Nathaniel dismounted and tied the reins to the hitching post. With a quick pat on Jingo's neck, he strode to the wagon.

"Let's get this job done." Lowering the rear gate, he hopped up onto the wagon.

"In a hurry?" Benjamin moved to receive the box from Nathaniel.

Handing off the light container, Nathaniel nodded. "I have promised to help Lyn ready the carriage house to live in."

Benjamin stopped in the middle of turning to carry the box inside and peered at Nathaniel, one brow lifted in question. "But?"

Choosing the next box, he hefted it and lowered it into Frank's waiting hands. "She doesn't seem to realize the fallacy of her intent."

Frank chuckled as he rested the edge of the box on the wagon. "You're going to try to interfere, aren't you?"

"No, I'm going to attempt to make her see reason." Nathaniel looked at his two friends as they smirked at him, then exchanged a knowing look before finally guffawing in unison. "Why are you laughing?"

Frank and Benjamin exchanged another glance and then shook their heads to dismiss his question as unworthy of an answer. They turned and carried their treasures inside the dim building, trailing the sound of their mirth. Nathaniel stiffened, their censure irritating every fiber in his body.

After all, he had some experience with making a reasoned argument.

Joshua snorted a laugh as he joined Nathaniel by the wagon. "You don't seem to know your way around women, son."

Nathaniel shifted an oak barrel closer to the rear of the conveyance. Leaning on it, he studied the captain. "Why do you say that?"

Joshua folded his arms and propped them on the side of the wagon. "Evelyn's mind won't be changed by making her see reason, first off. She won't listen until her heart does."

"You think you know her better?"

"I've known her since the day her mother welcomed her into this world." Joshua dropped his hands to fist on his hips. "You'd do well to listen to me."

"Perhaps so, sir." Straightening, Nathaniel rested his hands on the barrel and considered his plan. "I've done my best to learn how to reconnoiter for a mission, but my current objective seems somewhat murky." Such as it was.

Joshua's gaze sharpened as he peered up at Nathaniel. "Sounds like you surveyed for the army? I thought Benjamin said you were the cook."

"I was, but only after Smitty fled his responsibilities." A movement to his left drew his attention. Frank and Benjamin emerged from the interior and strode to the wagon. "Prior to that, yes, I reconnoitered the surroundings as the brigade moved."

"Well, then if you're still looking for long-term employment, I know they'll be needing surveyors after the peace treaty is signed. New lands to the west will change hands as a result, lands needing to be appropriately divided and allocated."

Talk about a temptation. The news of the opportunity lifted a weight from his shoulders. Surveying the new frontier lands would give him the adventure of a lifetime. Wilderness to explore as well as wild animals to learn about. Living animals as opposed to the preserved specimens in the building behind him. He'd locate a pretty piece of land to build his own home with a pleasing view of the mountains. Or maybe of a lake or river. The greater the extent of the new lands, the greater the money he'd earn as a surveyor and the more foundation he'd build for his future.

Evelyn's image floated into his memory. He'd only begun to test the waters with her. She didn't fear moving out to the country estate. Perhaps he could convince her to give him a chance as her husband, but would she consider moving away from family? Would she ever love him enough to make such a sacrifice?

"I'd like to learn more about the prospect when the time comes."

Benjamin gripped the side of the wagon and frowned up at Nathaniel. "What of Evelyn?"

"What about her?" The question tumbled out of his mouth before he could think through his response. Nathaniel paused in the act of dragging a barrel from the front of the wagon bed toward the rear. He really needed to think before speaking.

"You seemed to be interested in the lady, yet now you're talking about leaving town?" Benjamin lowered his hands to prop them on his hips. "I won't allow you to do anything that will break my sister-in-law's heart."

"I have no intention of doing so." Nathaniel shoved the barrel a bit closer to its destination while frantically marshalling his thoughts into some kind of rational order. "Especially since she hasn't agreed to permit me to wait upon her. Yet."

"And if she were to permit you? What then?" Frank reached up to help slide the barrel.

"I hope she will." Nathaniel gave another shove and the barrel sat at the edge of the gate. "Then with good fortune, marry me and go with me." Damnation, he hadn't meant to say that either.

Frank and Benjamin gaped at him while Joshua barked a disbelieving laugh. Then all three men started talking at once.

"You can't possibly mean to take her away!"

"What about Amy? She'll lose her sister."

"The frontier is no place for a delicate lady and a young child."

Nathaniel wasn't surprised by their agitation. He'd react the same way to his ill-timed idea. He waved his hands until they stopped speaking. "Hold on! One step at a time."

Joshua frowned at him, hands on his hips and feet apart as though bracing onboard a storm-tossed ship. "You can't mean to drag a lady and child so far from family and friends."

Nathaniel nodded, understanding how bereft the three must feel at the mere idea of their circle being broken by an outsider. But he rather liked what his heart had blurted without his brain's approval. "If she'll have me, then yes."

"Her sister will be devastated if Evelyn does go with you." Benjamin shook his head, a slow movement weighted with reproach. "Such a distance as you're contemplating would make it impossible for them to see each other again."

"Not impossible, but you're correct they wouldn't visit often." A definite obstacle he'd need to contemplate.

"I think it's important for quality folks to make the effort to settle the new lands." Frank grinned up at him, nodding his approval. "Adventurous folks are the ones who establish towns and cities, all of which will help our fledgling country thrive."

He nodded in appreciation of Frank's support, and then absorbed the censure on the other men's faces. "I understand your consternation, gentlemen. But let's not get ahead of ourselves. Evelyn is safe from my scheme." He grinned at the three worried faces. "For now, let's finish the job we started."

"Just tell me you won't spring the idea upon her." Benjamin stepped aside to let Frank take a better grip on the barrel. "And don't breathe a word of the possibility to my wife."

"Agreed." Nathaniel shoved on the container while Frank grabbed the bottom edge. "Catch that other side, Ben."

Benjamin and Frank wrestled the barrel to the ground and walked it into the building, their grunts and curses fading as they disappeared inside. Nathaniel handed down the next container to Joshua. They continued until the wagon stood empty and Nathaniel shut the gate with a bang.

"Thanks for your help." Frank clapped Nathaniel on the back. "I'll add the agreed amount to your pay this week."

"Much appreciated. If you'll excuse me, I have some errands to run."

Benjamin crossed his arms over his expansive chest. "I wish you good fortune in your aims. Despite my misgivings, I respect your ambition."

"Thank you, I think." Nathaniel chuckled, a mirthless laugh. "I will need all the luck available."

No matter what the three sniggering men might think, Nathaniel had every intention of winning his lady's hand. But how?

The last piece of cylinder glass rested against the wall, waiting for Nat to return. Evelyn dipped a rag into the bucket of water, wrung it out, then rubbed the most recently set pane in the carriage house window. Fortunately, the latest method for creating glass panes for the windows had lowered the cost as well as made the pieces easier to install. However, the less expensive process introduced blisters and tool marks which decreased the lucidity of the glass. The result of glassing in the windows would be a warmer and brighter place to live. Well worth the sacrifice of being able to see clearly through the glass.

Using a clean rag, she started drying the pane as her helper strode back into the room carrying a pail of white goo. The door banged closed, startling the baby and Jemma, who tended to him by the fireplace. The merry blaze warmed them despite one remaining open window frame.

Jemma soothed Jim, cradling him in her arms as she rocked him on the hard chair. Evelyn liked the petite girl well enough, but she'd soon replace her with a more competent nursemaid. She wore a pale blue quilted skirt and tan blouse, holding the child in his long baby dress and white cap. Her brown leather-clad feet propelled the chair in a steady beat. They made a pretty picture in the rustic room. But Jemma had other talents Evelyn intended to encourage.

"Ready to put this one in?" Nat pulled work gloves onto his capable hands.

"Certainly." Dropping her rags on the table in the center of the room, Evelyn crossed to help him lift the glass into place.

She held it steady while he applied caulking to seal the gap between the glass and the wood. Using a small putty knife, he filled the crevice an inch at a time, starting on the left side, moving down and across to secure the bottom. Evelyn stood on his right until he reached the middle of the pane, then stepped back to allow him to sidle in front of her as he continued across.

She sucked in her breath when his back barely cleared her chest as he concentrated on his task. Her breasts throbbed, needing to nurse her son. They also ached to be touched by a man. She'd not anticipated having him so close, so often. So much for putting distance between them. Each time they'd placed a window, she'd endured the same intoxicating proximity of the tempting man. But when he finished in a few more minutes, the temptation would end. She hoped.

Nat shoved more of the white rubbery substance into place, finally reaching the corner and starting upward. "Almost done. Just hold it until I reach the top corner, then you can let go."

"The room feels warmer already." She repositioned her hands to allow him access to the upper part of the window.

"Have you done this before?" He glanced at her, a flash of steely eyes that sparked something hot and needy inside her.

"No, but it's not complicated after the first time." Unlike their relationship, which seemed to grow more and more thorny with each passing hour.

They'd worked together all day to make the rustic building comfortable to occupy for several weeks. While spring loomed, the cold temperatures and inclement weather would not end for several months. He had appeared the day prior at the town home with a wagon, its bed covered with a tarpaulin. She'd had the slaves load onto the wagon the items from her short list which she'd gathered over the previous days. Once everything had been tucked into the remaining gaps between the other tools and supplies, they again covered everything with tarpaulins.

They'd driven out early in the morning with the load of glass and wood planks, along with mysterious boxes and small barrels. She soon learned he'd thought of every need for transforming the carriage house into a home. Her appreciation for his thoughtfulness and abilities increased with every item he revealed in his wagon filled with surprises.

The first thing they had done was to remove the vehicles from the carriage house, working together to pull them outside while Jemma kept watch over Jim. Then Nat used one of the handcarts to transfer smaller tools and parts into the neighboring barn. While he worked on clearing the heavier items, she swept out the cobwebs clinging to the corners and in the open windows. Some of the shutters remained, but he'd had to fashion several to replace the ones missing.

The next step had been inserting the glass panes so they would have a safe place to stay the night. In one large room. Together.

With each step they made toward that goal, her awareness of him had intensified until all he had to do was look at her to make her innards sparkle like fireworks on the Fourth of July. While she looked forward to the first ever display in Charlestown later in the year, she truly didn't need to feel all bright and on fire with every chance encounter. At the present moment, however, it proved a good thing the mulatto could serve as chaperone and thus mitigate any further temptation.

"You are quite an amazing woman, Lyn." Nat threw a grin her way. "I think you'll be fine out here, as long as you have someone to protect you from harm, that is."

"I agree, and I will once the slaves arrive in a couple days." She stepped back as he turned the upper corner and sighed, releasing frustration at her parents' condition to use slave labor and its implications. "Father said they had to do some shuffling of duties before he could spare the three he's sending."

"Only three?" He continued to work across the top of the pane. "What will they do?"

"One to cook, one to handle the grounds, and one to work with the animals." She studied his shirt-clad muscled back as he worked, then trailed her gaze up to the collar length brown hair caught by a length of ribbon. A quick tug would free the tresses, a further temptation for her fidgety fingers. She stayed still with a force of will.

A horse whinnied from where the team had been turned out into the pasture behind the barn. Big, strong horses borrowed from her parents in order to pull the heavy wagon. Her lighter horses remained in town during the current trip, but would return with her when she moved her remaining belongings in her own carriage.

Whatever happened to the hunting dogs? They'd been left behind during the flight to town back in November. At least they could fend for themselves, hunting for their food. Maybe they'd see and hear the activity and come home. She'd be glad of the watchful company.

"What about Jim's nursemaid?" Nat shook his head to ward off an inquisitive fly, his hair flowing back and forth with the movement.

She stopped her hand from lifting, reaching for him. She spun away, denying the persistent urge to touch him, and snared the rags and bucket of water. Better to keep her hands busy with work. She lowered her voice to a whisper. "I've arranged for an indentured servant to care for him. I'd rather not have a slave caring for my son."

He turned to face her, pulling a rag from his pocket to wipe the blade clean. He glanced at Jemma, then whispered, "Why not? I'd think you'd want to follow your family's lead."

She shook her head as she dunked and wrung out a rag. "Belinda, my previous slave, fled at her first opportunity. Not that I blame her for wanting to be free, mind you. But it did leave me in quite a predicament. One I wish to avoid in the future."

"Have you arranged for the indentured servant?" He spoke in his normal deep voice, the one that shivered through her with each word, as he laid the knife on the work table.

"Amy and I went with Benjamin the other day to make

the payment for an Irish girl, Peggy McKinley." She rubbed the newly set pane with her rag, careful to not disturb the caulk with each swipe. Beyond, the sunlight faded as night—and bedtime—approached. She swallowed the nervous dismay as she finished drying the glass. "She should be at the house by now, learning from my mother what we expect her to do."

He grunted his understanding and then looked around the room before returning his gaze to rest upon her. "I'll fetch our bedding since it'll be dark soon."

"I'll see to laying the table for dinner while you…"

She couldn't finish her thought. Couldn't say the words "make our beds." She stared at him, helpless to utter another sound until her mind stopped dwelling on the image of sleeping with the delicious man smiling at her. He knew. A slight lift of a brow and the twitch of his lips showed he'd interpreted her silent struggle. She waved him away, forcing a chuckle to cover her discomfiture.

"I'll be back shortly." He removed his gloves, peeling them off to reveal his capable hands, and laid them on the work table on his way out of the room.

After the door thumped closed, she drew in a shaky breath and considered her next move: clean off the work table and throw a cloth over it to provide a decent place to eat their dinner. She glanced at the hamper she'd left by the door, the corner of a red table cloth peeking out of the wicker lid. Her mouth watered at the thought of its contents: fried chicken, sliced roast beef, cornbread with butter, and apple spice cake. First, though, her aching breasts reminded her that she needed to feed her son.

"Jemma, I'll take him." Evelyn strode over to receive Jim into her arms. Jemma rose and stepped aside, and Evelyn sat in the rocking chair. "Why don't you see if you can help Mr. Williams."

"Yes, Miss." Jemma hurried to the door, where she flung a shawl around her shoulders before slipping outside, the door thumping closed behind her.

Alone with her son, Evelyn opened the flap on the bodice of her dress and then positioned Jim for his dinner. She cast a light blanket over him. No need for exposing herself to Nat, even if feeding her son was a natural act. At home, she retired to her room but here they had only one warm space. The setting sun would permit the cold outside to deepen, so the fire was welcome. With no other place to retire to maintain her privacy, she'd stay by the warmth and light while she nursed.

Several minutes passed with only the sound of the fire and her son's suckling. Time in which her tumbling thoughts quieted and her breathing slowed. She lifted the blanket and peered at her son's face, smiling at the tiny nose, closed eyes, and active mouth. He was her world.

The door opened to let Jemma and Nathaniel enter, the woman laden with quilts and pillows while Nat trundled the handcart filled with pine straw into the far side of the building where a carriage had once been parked. While not as comfortable, mayhap, as regular straw, or a real stuffed mattress, pine straw definitely was plentiful in the woods.

"Hold on." Evelyn rose, snugging Jim close, and went to the table, clearing off the rags and tools with one hand. "Put the linens on the table for now."

Jemma placed the pile on the table and turned to watch Nat as he forked three piles of straw onto the dirt floor. Two close together and one set a ways apart. "Jemma, bring some quilts over."

"Warm, if not comfortable beds, for sure." Jemma selected three blankets, spreading them on the individual piles.

Evelyn returned to her seat, repositioning Jim under the cover to latch onto her other breast. Relief flowed into her at

Nat's consideration, keeping his pile separate from hers and her servant's. She lifted her eyes to ask Jemma to set the table but stopped at Nat's enthralled expression. He stared at her as if trying to memorize every detail. After a moment, he blinked and a slow smile spread onto his face.

"You're beautiful, Lyn." He sauntered toward her, one slow step at a time. "You and your baby."

"What are you doing?" She stopped the rocking chair as the handsome man drew nearer. Expectation replaced the relief, shoving it aside without warning.

"Something I've wanted to do all day."

"What might that be?" But she knew, because it was the same thing she'd wanted all day, too.

"I'm going to kiss you, my sweet Lyn." He leaned down to grip the arms of the chair. "Would you permit me to?"

She sucked in a breath, gazing up at him. A quick glance at Jemma confirmed they had an audience, but the young woman smiled in encouragement. What would it hurt to kiss him? She was a grown woman, a widow who could choose her own path. She peered at him and nodded, words failing her again.

His smile lit his eyes as he leaned closer, his gaze fastening on her waiting lips. When he pressed his to hers, she closed her eyes against the onslaught of sensations rocking her equilibrium. She longed for the buss to continue, but Jim squirmed in her clasp and Nat broke their connection. She gazed at him, fighting the urge to stand and kiss him again when he licked his lower lip, apparently savoring the remains of the kiss.

The baby stirred, interrupting the moment. She shook off the lingering desire before addressing Jemma. "Will you ready him for bed while I set out our dinner?"

Jemma took the babe while Evelyn turned her back to Nat and refastened her clothing under the blanket draped over her shoulder. When she'd finished, she pivoted to face him, tugging off the light covering to drape it over one arm. "I'm sorry we were interrupted."

"You don't need to apologize for caring for your son." He clasped her hands, lifting them to kiss each palm. "Your love for him only makes you more beautiful in my eyes."

A frisson of need quivered down her back. "I wish you wouldn't say such things."

He raised a brow and squeezed her fingers. "You don't want me to speak the truth?"

"Yes, I do, which is why you shouldn't tease me with your compliments."

"You make me happy, Lyn." He chuckled and drew her into an embrace. "Happier than I've been in a long time."

With her head against his shoulder, and her sensitive breasts mashed against his chest, Evelyn had but one thought. It was going to be a very long night.

Chapter Six

S leep evaded Evelyn. Even with her eyes closed, Nat's nearness tickled her senses. The rhythmic sound of his breathing. An occasional rustle of pine needles when he shifted. It didn't help that he'd assigned the farthest bed to Jemma. Not one tiny bit. Mere inches separated her bed from his.

Little Jim slept, swaddled and snuggled into the bed beside her. She had settled him on her left, the side opposite from where Nat lay. The boy made soft sounds in his sleep, perhaps communicating with the forest fairies in his dreams. She smiled to herself at the whimsy, a bit of nonsense to pass the time since she remained wide awake despite the late hour.

Jemma never moved after she'd laid down and covered herself with a blanket. Evelyn propped up on her elbows and sighed. If she rose, she'd wake the others. Moonlight illuminated the night sky beyond the windows, though she couldn't see clearly through the imperfections of the glass. Embers glowed red in the fireplace, failing to warm the room with its waning heat.

A rustle sounded beside her, drawing her attention. He sat up and then yawned as he stretched. The sleeves of his shirt pulled up, exposing muscular forearms. She swallowed, desire washing through her as he lowered his arms and aimed a lopsided grin at her. She smiled back. What was he thinking?

"Couldn't sleep?" He whispered as he moved under the blanket to sit cross-legged, resting his elbows on his knees.

She also kept her voice low. "I didn't mean to disturb you."

He shook his head, his hair brushing his shoulders with the motion. "I only need a few hours."

She'd like a few hours to run her hands through his hair. Better yet, to run her hands over his muscular shoulders. He shifted to a more comfortable spot, dropping his hands into his lap. The movement drew her gaze down, but she lifted it back up before dwelling too long on his very capable fingers. She blinked several times, trying to clear the picture of what she imagined lay beneath the colorful quilt draped across his legs. Not that she'd seen any other man besides her husband. But based on what she could see of Nat, she could guess. Simmering desire increased to a boil, making her flush and hot. She'd never experienced such an intense longing for a man. Not even her husband. What was wrong with her?

She knew it was going to be a long night. Especially since she could not act upon her desire. "I'm going to try to sleep because I know to-morrow will be a busy day."

She flopped down and pulled the quilt up to her chin, shivering from the chill in the air as well as the need to deny her reaction. Turning her head, she gazed at him for a second before closing her eyes. If she didn't look at him, everything would be fine.

The sound of his quilt moving should have alerted her to his actions. Suddenly, her own blanket moved and her eyes flew open as he slipped under her covers. He pulled her toward him, but she resisted.

"What are you doing?" She pushed on his chest.

A mistake. The contact only made it harder for her to deny the need building inside. "You'll wake the others."

"Shhh. Let me keep you warm tonight." He stopped tugging on her arm to peer into her eyes. "Nothing more."

"I'm not cold." Indeed, she was on fire. Burning to do exactly what he suggested. Lie in his arms and feel his heat against her body. But she shouldn't. *Couldn't.* Could she?

"You were shivering." He smiled, a knowing grin. "You want to, don't you?"

"I must not."

"Nobody need know." He lifted a brow, suggestive and sexy. "It will be between us."

So tempting. When his gaze lowered to her lips, her resistance faded away. She leaned toward him, drawn to his mouth and the taste of him. One kiss wouldn't hurt.

When their lips met, it seemed only natural to align their bodies and snuggle beneath the covers together. Sampling and tasting as little moans escaped from her mouth. She'd found her own heaven on earth in Nat's arms. He broke the deep, passionate buss with a series of butterfly pecks to her lips. Wrapped in his warm embrace, sleep stole over her. Her last thought was to deal with the ramifications of her weakness to-morrow.

❧

Evelyn jerked awake, alone under her covers. Jim's cries brought her fully alert. Sitting up, she pulled her hair back by running both hands through the long tresses. A quick glance around the room, lit only by the approaching dawn, confirmed Nat was nowhere in sight. Jemma stirred on her bed, rubbing her eyes and yawning. Jim cried louder, his mouth wide and eyes screwed shut.

"Hush now." She smiled at the vocal demand for breakfast. "I'm here."

Evelyn gained her feet and then lifted her son into a cuddle. She inspected the pilcher, the woolen square of fabric pinned over his soft napkin to absorb whatever the diaper material did not. Finding it damp, she indicated with her head to Jemma.

"Will you change him please? I'll ready myself to nurse him in the meanspace."

"I's coming." Jemma rose from her bed with an ungraceful maneuver and then stretched before walking across the short distance. "You know I love this young'un near as much as you."

"Yes. And thank you." Evelyn handed him off to Jemma to swap out the soiled napkin and strode to the rocking chair to sink onto the seat.

Minutes later, Jemma handed the boy into Evelyn's waiting arms. Loosening the blanket wrapped around him, she put him to her breast. Relief swept through her as the child suckled, a welcome release of the pressure that had built up overnight. Sunlight edged over the window sill and splashed onto the floor. The first song birds made their presence known. The day ahead would be busy and full of decisions, but for the moment she savored the quiet.

Jemma busied herself with lighting the fire in order to start the kettle to boiling. Evelyn contemplated the young woman hurrying to put kindling and sticks in the firebox. Jemma had come to her parents a year ago in a trade her father had made with another plantation owner. Her father had disciplined one particularly aggressive Negro several times for laziness and belligerence. He'd finally determined after his "discipline" became beatings that he would rid himself of the problem slave. Thus the trade with another slave owner on the frontier. Jemma had been a good bargain, since she was amiable and gentle. Evelyn held no grudge against the woman; she was capable and friendly.

Still, Evelyn would prefer her helpers work for her willingly instead of by force.

Jim squirmed and stopped sucking, his eyes open and watching her. "Feeling better now, aren't you my love?" She moved him to her other breast and sighed. Was there anything more peaceful than nursing a baby? Knowing she nourished her son?

Stirring the embers to life, Jemma soon had a small fire lit. She added a few bigger sticks on top before turning to the task of setting water to boil for their morning tea. The last pieces of the spice cake would serve for breakfast before they made the trip back to town later in the morning. In the interim, she had a few final touches to put on the little house to make it a home.

The door opened and Nat strode in, a rush of cold air chilling the already cool interior. He paused in the open door, taking in the sight of Evelyn nursing Jim. His expression revealed he liked what he saw. She'd forgotten the light blanket in her haste to feed her son. Ah well. Nothing to do about it now except finish.

He took her breath, the image of a strong, muscular man with tousled hair from what she assumed was his morning ablution. He carried several sticks of firewood in the crook of one arm. Easing the door closed, he crossed the room to place his load in the bin beside the fireplace. Brushing off his hands, he turned to wink at Evelyn.

"Good morning, Lyn." His smile turned wicked. "I trust your sleep was restful."

It was a curse to blush so readily, the heat blossoming in her chest and rushing up her neck to inflame her cheeks. "Yes, thank you for asking."

"I'm pleased to hear you rested well." He winked and then walked over to the hamper where it remained after dinner at the cloth covered work table the evening before.

Evelyn tracked his moves, recalling the sensuous way he masticated his chicken and cornbread. Did she say sensuous? Goodness, she had longed for him to use those lips on hers and that was exactly what she'd gotten. She had to be careful what wishes she made or her perfect plan would fall apart. Much like her comportment had when he kissed her.

Her thoughts did not help reduce the heat in her cheeks. She forced her gaze away from Nat to check on her son. Looking at him proved safer to her composure, allowing her time to restore her equilibrium.

"Are you expecting any one?" Jemma crossed to the window, the sound of muffled hoof beats drifting into the room. "There's a rider approaching."

Nat stiffened and glanced sharply at Evelyn. Seeing the shake of her head, he strode to the door, picked up the rifle leaning against the wall, and went outside. Evelyn heard the horse stop, followed by the murmur of deep voices. If they had company, she should put herself together.

"Jemma, would you take Jim, please?" Evelyn stood and handed the satiated boy to the nursemaid. "I'll make the tea after I dress."

"Yes, miss." Jemma reached out to take the baby.

After Jim had been transferred, cooing and gurgling, Evelyn turned her back to the door to straighten her shift. She picked up her day dress from where she'd draped it over a chair and pulled it on, shaking the light wrinkles out of the skirts. From a small case containing a few of her personal articles, she retrieved a brush and pulled the tangles from her hair before forming a soft chignon. Slipping on her shoes, she was ready to greet whoever had come visiting.

She spooned tea leaves into the pot and added the hot water. Then she hurried to join Nat and their guest. Grabbing her cloak from a peg, she opened the door.

Nat stood beside her neighbor, Enoch Mercer. She hadn't spoken to him very often over the years she and Walter had lived on the property. Mainly because his estate was not within sight. But he had seemed friendly the few times they'd met. A flash of movement to her left turned out to be Walter's hunting dogs. So that's where they'd been, with their neighbor. The dogs appeared healthy and well fed.

"Good day, Mrs. Hamilton." Enoch doffed his hat and performed a half bow. "I'm relieved to hear you are well."

"Thank you, sir. It's been quite a trial, but I believe everything will be better soon." Evelyn gestured to Belle and Rufus as they checked out the barnyard. "Thanks for caring for them."

"I saw the activity here on my way by yesterday and determined to bring them to you." He glanced at Nat then back at Evelyn. "I understand you are returning to rebuild and live here?"

"We've renovated the carriage house for my temporary lodgings until the manor can be rebuilt." She smiled at Nat, recalling his unease regarding her decision. "My servants and I will be quite comfortable for a time."

"If you need anything, don't hesitate to send word. For now, I must be on my way." Enoch replaced his hat on his head and shook hands with Nathaniel before nodding to Evelyn. "Mr. Williams, rest assured I'll do as you ask and keep an eye on your lady."

Evelyn raised a brow at Nat, but smiled at her neighbor. "Thank you for your concern."

They exchanged farewells and then Enoch swung into his saddle and cantered away. Evelyn called the dogs when they started to follow him, and they gladly came. She'd missed their happy faces and enthusiastic greetings. Not only would they be good company but also would warn of any visitors. Nat's concerns were based on the reality of her situation.

A woman alone, far from town. She'd lived through foraging parties and renegades. She'd survive rebuilding the house, too.

"You asked him to watch me?" She folded her arms over her chest, brows raised.

"Most certainly. I cannot, though I would prefer to stay with you." Nat regarded her with a steady gaze. "Until you have at least your slaves here to protect you, I'll worry over your safety."

"The war is over. The loyalists have fled and people are striving to restore some sense of normal flow to their lives." She dropped her hands to pat her right skirt pocket. "Plus, I have a pistol."

"Do you know how to use it?" He relaxed his pose, enclosing one of her hands with his much bigger one.

She nodded, swallowing the desire rising inside from the gentle caress of her palm. "Father ensured my education while I've been staying with them. Apparently, he had feared for my safety as well, after he heard of Walter's treatment of me. While I was living at home, he decided I should be able to protect myself."

On a cold, clear day in February, her father had taken her out to the forest in his small carriage. Then he showed her how to handle a coat pistol, a flintlock weapon of a size she could fit into her pocket. They'd spent the morning loading, firing, and then cleaning the gun until she grew accustomed to its weight and effective range. She hit the center of each target she aimed at by the end of their time together, adding to her confidence in using the weapon for her own defense.

"I'm pleased to know you're not helpless." He squeezed her hand. When she shivered, he peered closer. "Let's go in. You're cold."

"I'm sure some hot tea will serve the purpose." She spun to go inside, still holding his hand.

Nat matched her pace until they reached the carriage

house. Then he hurried to open the door, retaining his grasp while she stepped past him, barely brushing his arm as she did. Enough, though, to elevate the tension in her midriff. She really needed to take a breath and regain her composure. Be an adult and not some swooning youth.

Over a quick meal, they settled on a plan of action. Jemma would straighten the temporary quarters and dress Jim. Nat would ready the wagon for the return to town. Evelyn gathered her belongings and put them into her travel bag before checking the remaining contents of the picnic hamper.

Suddenly the dogs began barking followed by the sound of horses approaching. Evelyn went out the door and into the barnyard. The dogs faced the road, intent on a low cloud of dust drawing closer. Raising a hand to shade her eyes from the late morning sunshine, she squinted to bring the men into focus. The Sullivans. Two mounted, one driving an immense wagon pulled by four sturdy horses and piled with supplies.

"Looks like we have visitors." Nat strode up to stand at her side while they waited for the men to arrive. "And it seems they've brought what they need to begin work."

A thrill of anticipation and delight bloomed in her midriff. A sensation not related to the man inches from her. "They're starting much earlier than I expected."

"I'm not entirely surprised, but I must admit to some relief." Nat shifted closer, draping an arm around her shoulders. "Their presence will deter any would-be aggression by others."

The men and horses rattled into the yard, halting by the barn. The dogs circled around the group, woofing a warning. Ethan and Luke dismounted and ground-tied their horses. Bill secured the traces to the brake before climbing down from the wagon. They greeted the canines, introducing their scent by extending a hand for the dogs to sniff. Satisfied the invaders were friendly, the dogs trotted off to investigate the wagon wheels. Sauntering over to Evelyn and Nat, the men brushed dust off their breeches and jackets.

"Welcome. I'm glad you're here." Evelyn smiled at her cousins, aware of the pressure of Nat's embrace. An unspoken claim directed at the three handsome bachelors arrayed before her.

Ethan removed his hat and held it in front of his chest. His warm smile held more than a hint of interest. "We thought we might as well start so you can live in comfort as soon as possible."

"Very considerate of you." Nat squeezed her shoulder before easing his arm away. He shook hands with the three men. "Do you want a hand unloading?"

Luke shook his head. "We'll manage. Evelyn, where would you have us set up our sleeping tents?"

"Goodness, I hadn't thought you'd sleep outside." Why would they want to live in tents, what with the uncertainty of the weather during the transition from winter to spring? "Surely we can make room in the carriage house."

Nat stiffened and shot her a look she couldn't interpret. Or didn't want to. After his possessive gesture upon their appearance, he may be feeling threatened by the men's occupation of her lodgings. Especially if Ethan were to set up a bed inside.

"No, we'd prefer to sleep outside." Bill huffed a laugh. "We rather like it better than being within four walls after spending so much time in the field."

"If you change your mind or the weather turns ferocious, you might sleep in the barn." She smiled as Nat relaxed, an inaudible sigh easing the tension in the air. "I'll leave it up to you."

"Very well." Ethan caught Nat's attention with a nod of his head toward the wagon Nat had been loading. "Looks like you're planning a trip of your own."

"I'm needed in town and am taking Lyn back to her parents' house to collect the remaining items there." He glanced at the wagon and then back to Ethan. "I'm grateful you're here to take care of the place in her absence."

"I'm pleased to do so." Ethan nodded, aiming a grin at Evelyn. "When I heard you'd elected to assist my cousin, I decided we should hasten our timing of the rest of the construction."

"Yes, the timing couldn't be better." Evelyn motioned to the carriage house in a vain attempt to mollify the sudden tension between Nat and Ethan. "We'll be leaving in a short while. Would you enjoy some tea?"

Luke shook his head. "We'd rather begin, if you don't mind."

She laughed and waved them away, her own relief at not needing to witness Ethan and Nat in the same room for an extended period sharp on her tongue. Men could act like such boys at times. "Have it your way."

They donned their hats and strode off to address the tasks before them, Ethan glancing back at her several times as he trailed after his brothers. Evelyn smiled after them, happy the next phase of her life was beginning in very capable hands.

Looking up at Nat, she shrugged and smiled. "Shall we go?"

He glanced at the waiting wagon, then at the men busily removing tents, shovels, ladders, and other tools from the larger vehicle. "Almost ready. By the time you retrieve your things, we can start."

"Give me five minutes."

"With pleasure." He smiled, his gaze landing on her mouth before flashing up to meet her regard. "I'll be ready when you are."

She blinked twice, aware of a hidden meaning behind his words. Ready for what exactly?

Two days later, Evelyn drove her covered phaeton carriage, drawn by a matched pair of bay mares, toward home. She'd said a tearful farewell to her parents before she and Peggy McKinley climbed aboard and started for the manor. Jemma held Jim close on the rear seat of the vehicle, keeping him warm and dry. The sound of his cooing and burbling mingled with the patter on the cloth roof. A cold rain shrouded the view of the rough lane snaking between the river on her right and the forest on her left. The laden conveyance slogged through the worsening roads, leaving new ruts behind to add to the difficult track.

"Almost there." Evelyn glanced at Peggy's enrapt expression. "Your first time away from town, is it?"

The thin woman sat up straight, her long black hair beneath a simple white bonnet braided down her back and tied with a festive red bow. Evelyn had been impressed with her assertive yet humble grace and demeanor. Her emerald eyes seemed to miss nothing when she aimed them toward Evelyn upon their first encounter at the Exchange to purchase her indenture. That was one trait Evelyn particularly liked in the twenty-two-year-old servant. The keen eye and sharp mind revealed in their first conversation had sealed the bargain for Evelyn. Intelligence would prove more valuable than obedience with training, so that she would be capable of judging for herself the proper response to situations without having to rely upon direction. Still, her attire had cried out for improvement, which Evelyn's mother had addressed forthwith upon Peggy's arrival at their home on King Street. Even dressed in simple homespun, her new maid and, she hoped, friend employed a regal carriage fit for a queen.

"Yes, miss." Peggy shook her head, eyes wide and a smile splitting her face. "It's so beautiful. Almost like my homeland."

"Do you miss Ireland?" Evelyn slowed the horses to a walk as they approached a bend in the road, one made precarious by the onslaught of water rushing across to join the swollen river.

"Aye. But I'm a-hoping to make a better life, a new one, in this new country." Peggy tucked the carriage blanket more tightly over her lap. "Thank ye for paying my passage. I'll work hard for ye, no doubt."

"We'll set a new schedule after we see how the construction is going." Evelyn clucked and slapped the reins on the horses' reddish-brown haunches. They responded by breaking into a trot, harness jangling with each stride. Their black manes glistened in the gloomy light, lifting and falling as they hastened the carriage toward home. "I expect you to take charge of my son's care and assist me with the school after we open to students."

"What about the girl caring for him? Jemma?" Peggy glanced back at the young woman and child. "I do not feel right taking her responsibilities."

"I have other duties for her to pick up." Evelyn smiled at the Irish woman. "I've learned she's a wizard with a sewing needle."

Peggy bobbed her head twice, gazing at the muddy road ahead. "You'll be wanting something special to wear to the Spring Ball in a few weeks, won't you?"

Evelyn grinned and shook her head. "I have already made my gown, and Emily is working on adding some decoration to the bodice."

"Why are you blushing?" Peggy angled her head to peer at Evelyn. "Is there a beau chasing your skirts?"

Evelyn's first thought was to deny such a likelihood. Her neck and cheeks warmed, belying her inclination. But Nat had made it plain his feelings for her grew with each passing day. "Mayhap."

"Have I met him?"

"Nathaniel Williams seems to find me pleasant company." The heat in her face increased merely contemplating his tender smile, his laughing eyes and, even more, his electrifying kiss.

Peggy guffawed, a most annoying response to Evelyn's comment. "From your expression, methinks you feel much the same in return."

"Do not laugh at me." Evelyn tried to sound haughty, to quell the tone of the other woman's rejoinder. She failed. Laughing, she clucked to the horses. "The sooner we get to the manor, the better."

When she drove into the barnyard, Rufus and Belle barked in greeting. Ethan emerged from within the husk of the destroyed building, wiping his hands on his sooty pants. Luke strode out of the barn, a shovel in hand, and stopped to lean on the tool until the vehicle came to a halt. Sticking the point of the blade into the soft earth, he took hold of the horses. Evelyn tied the reins to the brake and pulled her bonnet up to cover her hair before climbing down from her seat.

"Welcome home." Ethan hurried to help her, holding her hand until she turned to face him. "I'm glad you've returned in safety."

Jemma climbed out of the carriage, lighting without a word and striding into the carriage house to keep the little one out of the rain. Peggy emerged from the other side of the vehicle, carrying a long black object as she moved to stand with Evelyn while Ethan continued to hold her hand.

"What do you have there?" Evelyn peered closer at the unfamiliar thingumbob as she freed her hand.

"You've never seen an umbrella before?" Peggy worked with the device and suddenly she held a wooden stick with a silk canopy over Evelyn's head.

"No, I haven't. Where did you get it?" Evelyn appreciated the protection from the rain the umbrella provided.

"A friend of mine moved to France where they are popular. It's made from oiled silk and is very useful. Though some folks believe them to indicate an inferior person, one who can't afford their own carriage. Like me." With a shrug and a laugh, Peggy spun the handle and water flung in all directions.

Evelyn jumped back a step, running into Ethan's sturdy chest. Luke moved to steady her, but Ethan's hands gripped her upper arms.

Gazing over her shoulder into the robust man's expression, she relaxed. He held no fascination for her. "How are you lads doing on the cleaning out stage of the effort?"

Ethan twitched a brow as merriment appeared in his eyes. He released her. "We *lads* have about finished removing the worst of the debris."

"Good, good." She put some space between them and grinned at him, knowing he understood her subtle meaning. "We'll settle into the little house while you continue your work. I don't wish to detain you."

Bill chuckled as he joined the group. Of the three men, his classic features proved the most expressive. Whatever emotion he felt displayed plainly on his face. "I'll work extra hard now that we've got someone who really knows their way around the kitchen."

"Truer words were never spoken by any man." Peggy nodded to herself as she shot a grin at Bill.

He smiled in return. "I don't believe we've been introduced. I'm William Sullivan, but my friends call me Bill."

Evelyn grinned at the awkward introduction. "Oh, Bill, please permit me to introduce you properly. Margaret McKinley, these men are my cousins." She looked at each of them as she said their names. "Bill, Ethan, and Luke Sullivan."

Peggy kept her gaze on Bill for a long moment and finally shook her head with a smile. "You may call me Peggy."

"It's been tough eating the last few days." Bill folded his arms across his broad chest.

"Aye, I can stir together some vittles for you after you finish your day's labors." Peggy propped her hands on her wide hips. "First you work, then you play, my da always said."

Bill stared, enthralled, at the black-haired beauty. He made to say something, his mouth opening and closing several times before he finally cleared his throat. "Whatever you make will surely taste as delicious as you appear."

Then he blushed crimson as his double entendre hung in the drizzly air.

"Be watching yourself, mister." Peggy's smile stiffened, kept there by an apparent force of will. "I'll not be taking insults to my person."

"I didn't mean—"

"I think you meant exactly what you said." Luke punched him affectionately on the shoulder. "Or you wouldn't be so red in the face."

"Enough teasing." Evelyn stroked the neck of one of the mares, laughing at the brothers' unapologetic grins. "How long do you think the building will take?"

Ethan shuffled his weight from one foot to another, his gaze intent upon her face. "How long do you want it to take? We could drag it out, so we stay nearby longer. Just say the word, my lady."

The blatant attempt to woo her made her smile. Ethan's confident smirk revealed an expectation of winning her permission to court her. Tall with impressively muscular shoulders that tapered to a trim waist and then to powerful thighs, he rode a horse as though sitting in a comfortable rocking chair, each movement fluid and sure. A fine man. One pleasant to admire. Just not for her.

She shook her head, pretending to show sorrow for what she prepared to say. "In the event, I'd prefer to move in before summer if possible." She gazed up at him, blinking slowly.

He guffawed, a wide smile lighting his eyes. "Point taken."

"We've worked out a plan to accelerate the rebuild, Evelyn." Bill tossed a glare at his provocative sibling. "Don't let Ethan persuade you otherwise."

"Right. We should have the new structure up in a few weeks." Luke grabbed the shovel and leaned on it. "Then a few weeks more to enclose it against the elements."

"That's amazing." Evelyn glanced at each man, surprise coursing through her. "How do you intend to finish in such a short amount of time?"

Ethan tapped one finger on his temple. "We've got a few pals we can press into service to expedite the raising of the structure."

"We're fortunate to have young Tom Elfe to assist with the woodwork." Luke rested his arms on the handle of the shovel. "You may remember his father, Thomas Elfe, who was known for his fine cabinetry and furniture."

"The elder man died a few years back, at the start of the war." Ethan shifted his weight to rest on his other hip. "Just as well, given his loyalist views."

"His son inherited all of the man's tools so he can carry on the business." Luke straightened and pulled the blade out of the earth. "We're fortunate he's almost as talented as his father."

"I cannot afford to pay more men, especially expert artisans." Evelyn's hope dimmed. Dare she borrow more from her father? What other conditions might he demand? "My funds are limited."

"These friends owe us a favor or two." Ethan winked at her, a conspiratorial gesture. "They'll help without needing any recompense."

Optimism returned to Evelyn's chest, freeing the weight of uncertainty and dread. "You're certain of the schedule?"

Ethan nodded as he motioned to his brothers. "We're going to complete a quality job as efficiently as possible."

"The design you proposed may need a few adjustments to make a sound building." Luke gripped the tool in one hand and shifted the brim of his hat with the other, allowing a cascade of water to fall to the ground.

"Adjustments?" Evelyn frowned, trying to understand what might need to change.

"I'd like to modify the overall size of the house, so it's not such a long center passage." Luke straightened away from the tool and demonstrated with his hands a squat recumbent "I" shape. "With the hall like this, the breeze will be channeled more strongly through it. Making the house cooler in the summer, and when it's closed up in the winter will keep the warmth inside."

"Brilliant." Evelyn beamed at him. "I'm pleased with the idea. Proceed."

"In the meanspace, we're getting soaked standing out in the rain all this time." Bill shook water from the brim of his hat with a shiver.

"At least it's eased off." Peggy switched hands holding the protective umbrella above the two women. "But we all have work to do, I'd venture."

The men bobbed their heads in unison, rain water dripping from their hats onto their shoulders. Evelyn regarded each of them, appreciating their enthusiasm even more than their talents. Soon, faster than she'd imagined possible, she'd have a real home to call her own.

"Let's get to work." Evelyn glanced at Peggy, a silent request to follow her inside. "We'll see to dinner and a fresh pot of tea."

"Aye, miss." Peggy pursed her lips for a moment, then

relaxed them into a line. "I will see what is in the makeshift kitchen. Between that and what we brought with us, we'll soon have a hot meal for you men."

"Will two hours be enough time to work your magic, Miss McKinley?" Bill's sea blue eyes focused on the woman's face, his lips seeming to fight forming into a smile.

"It will do." Peggy tilted her head. "By then you'll be needing a bit of warming."

Bill smiled, his entire visage showing pleasure at her words. He gripped the crown of his hat, lifting and replacing it in one brief motion. "Until then."

As the men drifted in their separate directions, Peggy escorted Evelyn to the door, the umbrella a welcome protection. Peggy folded the delicate item with care, while Evelyn opened the door and stepped out of the mist into the warmth. Peggy slipped inside and pushed the door closed.

Removing her cloak, she hung it on a peg, her servant following suit. Jemma had settled Jim on his little bed of straw, swaddled to keep him warm and secure. The black woman moved about the room, rubbing a rag over the mismatched pieces of furniture. Peggy paused beside Evelyn long enough to determine the whereabouts of the kitchen. She strode away to begin her magic.

Her temporary home felt more real and loving than her former permanent one ever could have attained. Happiness mingled with the anticipation of her new life. One filled with family and friends and plenty of love for all. In her mind's eye, she envisioned Nat as part of her family, the core that would bind the whole. A presence to buffer and perhaps chase away the lingering memory of terror and tragedy. As their relationship evolved, she dwelled more and more on his character and personality. She would proceed with due caution, but the path appeared clear. Finally, her future seemed secure.

Chapter Seven

*J*ingo covered the rough road with easy grace, his hooves falling in a steady three-beat rhythm. Nathaniel had not been able to escape the print shop in more than a week. Desperate to see Lyn, he pressed his horse into a gallop at the bend in the road turning toward her property.

The first time he'd approached the estate at the edge of the woods, the house seemed to loom over the surrounding landscape. He'd been part of the foraging detail searching for anything the troops could eat, to keep them alive and able to fight. He hadn't expected to find much, given the frequent raids of the homes and plantations by both sides in the war. At that time, he'd been surprised to discover the young woman, clearly with child, and her overbearing husband. The man hadn't even tried to protect his property, merely stood by glowering as Nathaniel and several other soldiers ransacked his home. Of course, Nathaniel had told him not to resist, but to not even protest made him appear a coward. Nathaniel had been pressed into foraging among the civilian homes out of sheer desperation. The war would not be lost for want of sustenance. His mission had been vital to achieving the peace they all now enjoyed.

He slowed and then turned Jingo up the lane toward the estate. Three white tents gleamed in the sunlight, nestled under a cluster of maples a short distance from the barn. The statue of the winged horse drew his attention to the new framed building on its stone foundation. A kiln had been built to one side of the work site and two men labored on making bricks from clay dug from along the river bank. Several others worked on raising the rest of the building, dragging planks from the lumber piled nearby. Stacks of finished brick waited to be added to the exterior of the structure. The brothers had said they'd accomplish the reconstruction as rapidly as humanly possible, but they'd done more than he'd thought they could even since his last visit. They had much more to do, of course, but before long the house would be fully enclosed against the weather, if not entirely finished.

Lyn would move in and settle down to enjoy her new home. Surrounded by her slaves and servants. Enjoy visits from friends and family, but she'd be on her own in reality. Alone among people forced to wait on her. What kind of life would that be?

One he'd never endure.

In fact, with each passing week, he wished he'd never made the promise to stay six months. He'd stayed four but the remaining two seemed as though they'd never end. His heart urged him to seek a place of his own where he could choose how to make his own fortune. Not be at any person's beck and call in order to earn a living.

Why hadn't he found a way to break his oath and move on? One simple reason: Evelyn.

He slowed Jingo to a trot, the dogs greeting him with their usual vociferous barking. The door to the carriage house swung open, and Evelyn stepped into the dappled sunshine, a smile in her eyes and on her lips. Lips he hadn't tasted in too long. She hurried toward him, her long skirts caught up in her hands, as he dropped to the ground and strode to meet her halfway across the barnyard. Jingo trailed behind him, bumping his nose into his shoulder when he stopped abruptly. Catching his balance, he tossed a reproving glance at his horse, before clasping Evelyn's hands in his and drawing her close enough to kiss her. A quick survey of the area revealed they were alone. For a moment or two, at least. Time for a quick kiss. He dipped his head to make good on his idea.

The taste of her—sweet and spicy and warm—soothed the agitation in his chest. He'd been away too long, separated from her and the affection they shared. He folded her into his arms, hugging her tight, with his chin resting on the top of her hair. "I've missed you, my sweet."

"You've been remiss in not visiting as you'd said you would." She pulled away from his chest to lift her damp eyes to meet his.

He touched a finger to the corner of one eye, a drop sliding on the tip. He looked at the tear as though he'd never seen one before. "Why are you crying?"

She smiled and shook her head. "I'm simply pleased to see you. It's been a long while between visits."

The dogs milled around the couple, and Nathaniel realized they now had an audience. Ethan and Bill stood by the barn door wearing work aprons hung with hammers, pliers, screwdrivers, and smoothing files. Ethan's frown did not bode well, his jealousy evident. Luke strode up from behind the house where he'd apparently been working. Standing in the open door to the carriage house, Peggy dried her hands on a towel.

He peered at Evelyn as he reluctantly released her hands and stepped back. He could no longer keep his intention to leave to himself. Her expression showed him how attached she was becoming. "I'll meet you inside. We need to talk."

She raised her brows, eyes widening. "About what, pray tell?"

"Give me a minute to tend to Jingo, and then you'll know." He needed a few minutes to soothe the chaos reverberating in his chest. To sort his arguments. She must go with him. To leave her behind just might kill him.

"Very well." She kissed him, lingering for the time it took for her heart to beat twice. "I'll wait with a fresh pot of tea, but not patiently."

He led Jingo to the barn, past the glowering countenance of Ethan, and inside where several horses stood munching in individual stalls. The horses nickered at him and Jingo as they stepped into the aisle. The interior of the structure had also undergone a kind of transformation in his absence. The sweet aroma of hay replaced the musty smell of dirty straw. New boards had been added to the stall walls, the lighter wood a stark contrast to the darkly stained older ones. Bits of dust and hay floated in the shafts of sunlight falling through the open windows onto the freshly raked dirt floor. With a sense of regret for disturbing the pretty scene, he led Jingo into an empty stall near the front of the building.

He planned to stay over, sleeping in the hay loft as he'd done on his other visits. No more tempting the fates by allowing himself the luxury of sleeping beside Lyn. Holding her, feeling and hearing her heart beat, smelling her sweet essence. The thought of their first night together continued to stir a reaction entirely inappropriate to their situation. Perhaps if they became betrothed he'd end his personal vow to refrain from lying with his woman. But not until he'd proven himself worthy of her love.

Stepping to Jingo's side, he tugged the girth loose. A swallow streaked through the barn, flitting in and out of the sunlight on its way from one door to the other. Everything about the place welcomed him, whispering enticements for him to stay and settle. While a small part of him longed to follow the siren's call, the greater part pushed at him to move on. To remove himself from the known to explore the unknowns tempting him. He needed to satisfy the wanderlust clawing at his gut before he could build not merely a house, but a home.

He flung the girth strap over the saddle seat and lifted it off the horse's back. He carried it to the tack room, his thoughts spinning nearly as much as his emotions. If only she would say yes when he asked her to journey with him, to merge their lives into a single unit. Eventually, if he proved himself suitable in her esteem, to marry him. He couldn't and wouldn't ask for her hand until he had established himself so he could support a wife and children. He didn't want to tie any one to his future until he had some idea of what it held. But would she go with him if they weren't married? Dare he even ask?

He returned to the stall, and rubbed the roan's inquiring nose. "You'll go with me, that's for certain."

Jingo bobbed his head, and Nathaniel laughed. He patted his mount's neck and then started removing the bridle. On a sigh, he loosened the cheek strap. Jingo shook his head to ward off a fly, the leather flapping into Nathaniel's face. Nathaniel smacked the horse's neck to communicate his displeasure with his actions and then rubbed his own cheek to quiet the sting. "Stand still, Jingo. It's just a fly."

The horse, uncaring of his chastisement, tossed his head again, but this time Nathaniel stepped back, clear of the swinging strap. He quickly finished removing the bridle and hung it on a hook by the stall door until he finished rubbing down his mount. He grabbed a brush and ran it over the horse's neck and coat, then down each leg. The mindless activity freed his thoughts, permitting them to form a whirling tumult in his brain.

Lyn's new house neared completion, ready for her, Jim, and her servants to occupy. She'd settle in, set up housekeeping and a daily routine. Comfortable. Safe. Secure.

Confining. Deadening.

The concerns raised earlier in conversation with his friends drifted through his mind. Each had a valid point for him to ponder. She'd give up the very aspects of life she enjoyed most in her current situation. He tried to view the trip through Evelyn's eyes, to consider what reservations she'd hold. He found many, likely too many for her to wish to make the journey with him.

The rhythmic thud of boots on dirt warned him of a man approaching. He glanced at the wide opening of the barn. Ethan strode toward him, a smirk on his lips and trouble in his eyes. Nathaniel continued cleaning his horse, his grip tightening on the brush.

"What's this I hear about your imminent departure?" Ethan rested his brawny arms on the top of the stall wall, glaring and frowning at Nathaniel.

Pausing in swiping the bristles over Jingo's rump, Nathaniel considered his retort. "Why is it any of your concern?"

"In a word, Evelyn. You're wooing her, yet you plan to leave." Pointing a finger at him, Ethan jabbed at him in rhythm to his words. "I won't permit you to break her heart."

Nathaniel resumed brushing the horse, his thoughts a jumble even as anger simmered in his chest. But anger aimed at whom? Ethan or himself? "Again, I do not believe it's any of your business what I do."

Ethan pushed away from the wood wall to step inside the stall. Nathaniel turned to face him and, though tall himself, had to look up to meet his eyes. Standing this close to the man proved intimidating indeed. But he'd never backed down from a fight in his life and he wouldn't start at this juncture. Still, discretion could prove to be the better aspect of valor.

Poking the tip of one index finger into Nathaniel's chest, Ethan held Nathaniel's attention as he spoke. "She's my cousin, my family. I have more right to protect her than you because you are nothing more than an outsider trying to hurt my family with your deceptions and false promises."

"I do not want to hurt her, nor break her heart." He had to admit the truth behind Ethan's lecture. His indecision most certainly could result in his inadvertently causing his love unnecessary grief. He loved her too much to hold onto her under the pretenses he'd remain with her. He sighed, letting the breath out over several beats of his own breaking heart. "I will make a point of staying away from her from here on. Will that suffice?"

Surprise flared in Ethan's eyes as he nodded. "Starting this moment. You may as well mount your horse and ride out of here. Delaying will only make it worse."

"She's waiting for me to come talk to her." Nathaniel shook his head and applied the brush to Jingo's side. "I'll think of something to tell her, to explain."

"I don't like that you're hanging around her, like a dog after a bone." Ethan crossed his arms, creating a formidable barrier between Nathaniel and the open stall door. "You're not to wait upon her after this day. Do I make myself clear?"

Moving to brush the other side, Nathaniel managed to put some distance between himself and the belligerent man. He caught his eye and held it for a moment before focusing on the task at hand. "I believe Lyn may have a say in the matter, but I vow to do all in my power to guard her feelings. I can do nothing more."

"If you do, you'll answer to me." Ethan spun on his heel and marched out of the stall, pausing with a hand resting on the half door. "I promise you'll never forget it if I have to make good on my warning."

Slapping the wood with his massive hand, Ethan strode

out of the barn without a backward glance. Nathaniel sighed and returned to his work, well aware of the terrible choice he faced between expressing his love for Lyn and walking away for her own good.

Straightening from brushing the last fetlock, Nathaniel tossed the brush into the bucket outside the stall reserved for the purpose. Then he turned back to stroke Jingo's neck as his thoughts finally settled into the depressing realization he couldn't ask the woman he loved to give up her home to follow him on a dangerous adventure into the unknown frontier lands. He didn't know how he'd survive without her, but he'd try. For her sake, not for his.

His next steps were clear. He'd talk to Evelyn about her plans, her future, while he planned his own. To save her the worry and anguish, he'd keep his intent to himself until closer to when he would leave to travel west, inland, away from the ocean and from her. After he left, nursing an anticipated broken heart, she would have her family to console her. He loved her too much to force her to sacrifice every person she cared for in exchange for him. In the meanspace, he'd enjoy each moment he managed to spend in her company, knowing soon he would never see her again.

Evelyn's decision to have Peggy bake buns earlier in the day had proven fortunate. While she held a tradition of making hot cross buns for Good Friday, the notion had popped into her mind to indulge the whim. Along with steaming cups of chamomile tea they served to satisfy their hunger. Her newly assembled family sat in the modified carriage house, chatting and poking fun at each other. Little Jim had fallen asleep on the folded quilt beside her chair. Arrayed before her sat Jemma and Peggy, with Nat to her right. Everyone had expressed delight at the unusual treat.

"Remember to hang one of the buns in your new kitchen." Peggy bit into the warm bread with a cross made with strips of unleavened pastry dough.

Evelyn shrugged as she tilted her head to one side. "Why would we do such a silly thing?"

Peggy leaned forward, an impish grin lighting her eyes. "Some believe hanging a hot cross bun in your kitchen prevents fires and ensures all the other loaves of bread bake properly."

Nat laughed as he crossed his ankles, relaxing against the chair back. "Sounds like superstition to me."

"Aye." Peggy cackled as she rose to her feet to stir the cook fire. "It is a bit of whimsy indeed. But none of the kitchens in our town in Ireland ever had a fire they didn't want."

"I'd say that's merely a coincidence." Nat selected another bun and waved it in the air to punctuate his observation. "My parents' home never had a kitchen catch fire either and they didn't adhere to such nonsense."

Jemma started the rocking chair in motion, her gaze flitting from one person to another. "Will you make them for Easter as well? Seein' as how you made 'em today."

"I believe so since it's not until the twentieth of next month." Evelyn picked up a bit of sewing she'd started and planned to display in her new house. "I'll make enough to share with everyone as part of the day's celebration."

"Between us, we can turn out a fair number." Peggy nodded as she resumed her seat.

Sipping her tea, Evelyn glanced up to find Nat's gaze resting upon her. His guarded expression started a worm of unease inching through her veins. She set her cup and saucer on the side table. "What did you wish to speak to me about?"

He waved off her question and then pressed his palms to his knees. "Nothing of any consequence."

"Come now, you've held me in suspense for hours." She smiled encouragement as he blinked slowly several times. "Tell me what's on your mind."

He cleared his throat and flicked his gaze to Peggy before addressing Evelyn. "I wondered about your, um, intent as to your school's curriculum." He nodded to himself. "Yes, that's it."

His hesitant answer only served to make her more curious as to the true question he had meant to ask but lost the nerve to submit to her. His fondness seemed to increase each time they met. Maybe he wanted to elevate the level of their relationship, an event which she'd at one time dismissed but no longer. Now she'd consider his question if he broached the subject.

"I've decided on an appropriate number of proper subjects for young ladies to learn." She lifted her tea and sipped. "You needn't worry about such triviality."

"But—" His comment died as the door swung open.

Ethan filled the open space for a second before stepping inside and closing the door with a bang. "May I join you?"

Evelyn smiled and nodded to gather her thoughts, surprised by his unexpected presence. "We've a drop of tea and some buns left you may share with us."

Ethan picked up a chair from the corner and set it down on Evelyn's left side. Evelyn poured while Peggy handed the man a small plate. He picked up a bun with his large hands and bit it in half. His jaw worked in the most intriguing way to masticate the soft bread, leaving her enthralled by the powerful muscles moving along his throat when he swallowed. She'd never thought of her cousin as anything more than a relative. Yet at the moment she had become entirely aware of him as a man. With broad shoulders and massive muscles on his arms. His trousers stretched over thighs the size of her waist. He'd make some lady a fine life companion.

Nat cleared his throat again, drawing her attention. "I'll need to leave for town before much longer, unless you prefer for me to stay."

She glanced out the window to see the sunlight dimming beyond. "It's growing close to dusk. Mayhap you should remain the night and ride in the morning."

A grin stretched his mouth. "As you wish."

"I believe you have time to make the trip to your home this evening." Ethan smacked a hand onto his thigh. He focused his gaze on Nat. "If you depart immediately."

"Do not listen to him, Nat." Evelyn shooed Ethan into silence with a flick of her left hand. "The matter is settled. You may sleep in here or in the barn with Jingo. Your choice."

Ethan muttered an oath as he retrieved another bun. Taking a bite, he glared at Nat. Evelyn sensed the tension stretching between the two men as they took each other's measure. She needed to find a way to diffuse the animosity apparent in their demeanor.

Peggy solved the matter with a quick movement. She rose to her feet, breaking the silence by snapping her fingers. "There's still work to be done before night falls. So up and out with you both. Make use of the time to good advantage."

"You want me to work with Ethan?" Nat's confusion disturbed his normal complacent expression.

"Aye, and why not?" Peggy's fists rested on each hip as she smiled a challenge at the two beefy men. "We most definitely have plenty to be done."

Nat gained his feet and pinned his gaze on Evelyn. "You desire this as well?"

She looked between the two men's glowering visages. The time spent together may prove worth while, if they'd develop an understanding of where they stood with each other. "I do indeed."

He lifted his eyes to stare at the ceiling before lowering his chin again. "As you wish."

Ethan stood, shaking his head with wry mirth in his eyes. "Let's go, man. Daylight's a-wasting."

After they left, Evelyn caught Jemma's grin as Peggy guffawed. "The next few hours will prove interesting indeed."

"Almost makes me want to go out there and help." Peggy moved toward the fireplace. "I'll start pulling together something for our supper."

"I'll sew until Jim awakens." Evelyn examined the partially finished embroidery sampler in her hands. "Then I'll help you, if you need me."

"Jemma can assist me in the event." Peggy glanced at the woman in question. "Isn't that right?"

"I don't mind, if you don't." Jemma smiled, revealing her teeth. "I enjoy making meals."

Evelyn mulled over the exchange between Ethan and Nat while she pulled her floss through the fabric with a sharp needle. In the weeks of the demolition and clearing, Ethan had rarely invited himself into her abode. Why might he have done so on this occasion? The conversation along with their posture suggested one did not trust the other. Ah. Perhaps Ethan sincerely had developed some kind of interest in her and resented Nat's increasing presence. But why? She'd never given her cousin reason to believe she harbored feelings for him.

She recalled the sharp look Nat shot at Ethan upon his entrance. One filled with surprise and a subtle alarm. As though he struggled to stay seated and not leap to challenge an adversary. Much like Frank had dueled with the loyalist officer back in October, and fortunately lived after the smoke cleared. But Nat and Ethan couldn't think she'd permit them to even consider such extreme measures. Still, she chuckled to herself at the image of the two fighting over her attentions.

Would they choose pistols or swords if their jealousy progressed?

On the other hand, she did enjoy being with Ethan. He had been part of her life for as long as she could remember. They'd learned to dance together when the tutor had visited their homes, and understood each other's sense of humor. Nat remained an outsider, though one readily accepted by her family and friends. She shared no past with him, prior to January and the triple wedding. She knew next to nothing of his past, his ancestry, or even much about what he did before arriving in town. Other than his fighting in the militia and raiding her pantry. And yet she admitted to having feelings for him. With doubt on his side as well, might he be concerned about her possibly developing an attachment to her cousin?

A foolish notion she would dispel from his thoughts at the first opportunity. She rather enjoyed the exploration of another's background, discovering favorite foods and songs, as well as the entire process of becoming better acquainted. She had much to share of her own family and what she hoped to achieve in years to come. Wouldn't it be grand to do so with Nat?

Nathaniel entered the cozy lodgings, Ethan close behind him. They'd spent the past two hours securing wood moldings around the windows on the back side of the house. Before ten minutes had elapsed, he'd sorted for himself what kind of man worked beside him. They'd formed a good yet grumpy team until the light had faded with the setting sun and they were forced back inside.

The domestic scene which greeted him released the tension from the time spent with Ethan. He counted himself lucky to be included in Lyn's family. She rocked her son by the cheery blaze in the fireplace. Peggy glanced at him before returning her attention to stirring the steaming kettle suspended over the flames. Jemma carried a stack of bowls to the cloth-covered table, setting them out, ready to receive the savory stew. A vase filled with flowers commanded the center of the small surface.

"Something smells delicious." Nathaniel closed the door after Ethan had passed through. "I could eat if it's ready."

"I hope we came in time." Ethan wiped his hands on his trousers and dragged a chair over to the table. Standing behind it, he rested his hands on the back. "If you don't mind, Evelyn?"

She raised a brow but nodded her invitation. "What about Luke and Bill?"

"They'll be in before much longer." Sitting down, Ethan laid his hands on the table. "They needed to clean up first."

Nathaniel counted the chairs and came up short. "We'll need a couple more seats when they arrive."

Ethan pressed his palms onto the table. "They can make do on the floor. It'll test their mettle."

Laughing, Lyn settled a sleepy Jim on the quilt by her chair, tucking one end over him to encourage him to drift off to his baby dreams. "See if you can locate a bucket or barrel we can employ as a temporary place for them to sit."

Ethan acted as if he intended to remain glued to his seat rather than offering to do as Evelyn requested. If Nathaniel went outside in search of a makeshift chair, Ethan would likely attempt to woo Lyn away from him. Then again, maybe he should encourage the relationship to ensure when he left she would have someone and thus wouldn't miss him. His heart rebelled at the concept of any other man, especially Ethan, making love to his woman. Holding her hand, or bussing her lips. Torn between his desire and his decision, he hesitated to act.

Stomping boots on the outside porch preceded the door swinging open. Luke strode in with a rush of cool night air. "Hello. Ethan suggested we should join the party for dinner."

"Welcome, Luke." Lyn rose from the rocking chair and moved to stand by the table. "Is Bill coming as well?"

"He's right behind me." Luke sauntered in and stopped beside Nathaniel. "Anything I can do to help?"

"Could you locate a couple chairs or something to serve as seats?" Nathaniel couldn't believe his good fortune. Relief flooded Nathaniel's heart at the offer of help. One decision he didn't need make.

"Most certainly. I know exactly where to find them." Luke strode back out the door just as Bill stepped onto the porch.

After Luke disappeared into the twilight, Bill entered the room. His gaze searched out and found Peggy, then he glanced at Lyn. "Thank you for inviting us to supper this evening."

"You and your brothers are always welcome at my table." She grinned at him before turning to retrieve utensils to place by the bowls.

Nathaniel sank onto a hard seat and rested against the back. He draped his arms across his legs and kept a watchful eye on Lyn and her interaction with her cousin. Soon a definite choice must be made, but not tonight. Tonight he'd observe Ethan and Lyn together, poking into whether she'd be better off with him than with Nathaniel. Then he'd weigh the evidence and proceed with whatever the findings suggested as the best course.

Luke returned within a few minutes carrying two large buckets which he flipped to place open end down and positioned by the table. Jemima snared a couple of pillows and placed them on the buckets with a shy smile at the robust men. Lyn indicated where everyone should sit by pointing from one person to a place and then another. Using a fold of her apron to lift the kettle from its hook, Peggy carried it to the table.

"Bill, hold your bowl over here." Peggy dipped the ladle into the bubbling kettle and then poured the stew into his raised bowl.

"Did you make this?" Bill set his bowl at his place and lifted a spoon poised for his first bite.

"I did." Peggy smiled at him, and he grinned in return. "Luke, you're next."

"What are we eating?" He held his bowl as requested and then set it in front of him.

"Rabbit stew with carrots and potatoes." Peggy stirred the contents and then looked to Lyn. "Miss?"

Lyn slid her bowl across the table to receive her portion. "You've spoiled me with your skills in the kitchen, Peggy."

"Wait until I have a proper kitchen. You'll be even more impressed." She grinned at Lyn as she continued dishing out the servings.

As they ate, Nathaniel detected his rival attempting to steer the conversation to topics which focused on a shared history between the cousins. Reminding Lyn about past antics and family gatherings, as well as the common opinions between them. The similarities indeed proved immense. His hopes for a future with her sank as the evening progressed and he came to realize she wouldn't be alone when he left. She probably wouldn't even miss him.

"Nathaniel, what's the news from town?" Luke spooned up a piece of meat and potato and held it ready to consume. "We've lost touch with the comings and goings."

Dabbing his mouth with a napkin, Nathaniel cleared his throat. "The biggest news is that Benjamin Geurard was elected as the new governor to replace Governor Matthews."

"Isn't he a Huguenot?" Ethan appeared aghast at the news.

"We've never had a man with that religious inclination as governor before."

"That's true." Nathaniel regarded Ethan with forced calm. "He's a lawyer as well. Do you take issue with him leading our state?"

"Not as long as he doesn't instill his beliefs onto his official duties and decisions." Ethan dragged the napkin over his mouth and laid it on the table. "What else should we know?"

"There's gossip about the Confederate Congress not making good on their promise of back pay to the soldiers." Nathaniel looked at each of the three muscular men at the table, all soldiers who had reportedly fought with distinction during their enlistment. "Nor to providing the promised half-salary pension for life."

"Dastardly news if proven true." Ethan scowled at Nathaniel as he slammed his fist on the table, making the vase of flowers jump. He shot a worried look to each of his brothers. "We were counting on what is owed us to start the stable. What will we do?"

Bill stretched his back from sitting so long without a proper chair. Pinning his gaze on Ethan, he shook his head. "They owe us for all of our sacrifices on their behalf. They can't get away with not paying us for our efforts."

"If they have no funds, then they have no means with which to fulfill their promises." Nathaniel clutched the spoon hovering over the table. Congress owed him a great amount of money, which he probably would never realize. "Their deficiency impacts every man who served, including me."

"What of the present soldiers stationed on James Island and elsewhere in our state? Are they still unpaid?" Lyn raised her glass of garnet wine to sip as she waited for the response.

"Yes, but I understand the General Assembly is considering other measures to relieve their distress for supplies and food." He regarded Lyn for several seconds, inspecting her features for how she felt about the political aspect of the discourse. Interest lit her eyes as she smiled at him. "At least they managed to provide adequate clothing for them."

"I'm sure they were pleased to have warm attire over the past winter." Luke reached for the ladle and added stew to his bowl. "Peggy, you're a wonderful cook."

"I'm happy you are enjoying the meal, sir." She inclined her head in acknowledgement of his compliment.

"I thought I heard about some farmers experimenting with cotton." Bill glanced at Ethan and then Luke. "Might we try our hand at it to export? Maybe we could generate enough revenue to proceed with our breeding plans."

Luke lifted his shoulders along with the palms of his hands in a brief gesture. "Why not? Though we'd need land enough to sow in a sufficient crop and field hands to work it. Perhaps Father can assist with slaves?"

"He might be willing." Ethan shook his head and sighed. "But it's really not the direction we'd chosen."

Nathaniel commiserated with the brothers and their dilemma. His own plans had changed many times, and those pesky decisions proved aggravating. Each time he shifted his aim, he'd had to alter the steps necessary to progress down the new course. His present path seemed the best of the ones he'd lit upon, and yet the most difficult choice he'd ever had to make loomed on the horizon.

Ethan tapped a finger on the table, attracting Lyn's attention. "Would you consider allowing us to try our hand at such an endeavor? What are you planning to use the surrounding acreage for?"

Lyn raised both brows in response to the suggestion, obviously taken aback by the prospect. "I was not planning to establish a farm from my estate." She laid her spoon in her bowl, and wiped her mouth with a napkin. "I expect my girls will enjoy their studies out of doors whenever the weather permits."

"Of course." Ethan inclined his head though kept his gaze on her. "My apologies. I'd forgotten your intention to start a school."

How could he possibly forget? The man built the house for the purpose. Why would he lie? Perhaps to back out of the proposition he apparently had been about to suggest. That was likely. He'd recognized her reaction for what it was, a denial of permitting any other person to be part of her endeavor without her invitation. She demonstrated a savvy interpretation of the people around her with her nuanced response. Smart lady.

Lyn pushed back her chair and stood, resting the tips of her fingers on the table. "I believe it is time to disperse for the night."

Nathaniel rose to his feet and glanced at Ethan. "I'll walk out with you and your brothers."

Ethan grinned, understanding bright in his eyes. "Very well."

Bill stood and handed his pillow to Jemma. "Thanks for the thoughtful gesture."

"Yes, Jemma. Thank you." Standing up, Luke also gave the girl the pillow. He glanced at Lyn where she stood beside Nathaniel. "Thank you for supper."

"You're welcome." Lyn smiled softly at the group of men. "Sleep well."

"I hope you sleep well, sweetheart." Nathaniel gazed down upon her face, memorizing each feature to recall later when he was alone. "I'll see you in the morning."

"Where will you sleep?" She gazed up at him, her lips slightly apart.

The temptation to kiss her, despite the crowd of onlookers, overcame his senses. He should restrain from following through on his desires, but the urge built so fast he could no longer deny it. He pressed his mouth to hers for a quick buss. "Good-night."

"Good-night."

"Let's go, Nathaniel," Ethan grumbled by the door he held open. Luke and Bill stood on the porch, grinning at the scene. "Time to remove ourselves so the ladies may prepare for bed."

"I'm merely wishing our hostess a pleasant night's sleep." He smiled at her, acknowledging silently how much more he wanted to do. "I'm coming now."

With a last glance at the bemused expression on Lyn's face, Nathaniel crossed the threshold and stepped into the ink black night, lit only by the distant twinkling of stars.

Chapter Eight

*B*elle and Rufus started barking before dawn. Evelyn opened her eyes, and flung an arm over her face. Too early. Or she'd gone to sleep too late the night before. Jim squirmed in his swaddling, the first murmurs of his desire for breakfast. Whether or not she longed to stay abed, his needs outweighed her own. Tossing the quilt aside, she scrambled to her feet and picked up her baby as the barking outside continued. The racket roused Jemma and Peggy, who clambered from their beds.

"What's the fuss about?" Peggy ran a hand through her long hair, detangling it with her fingers.

Evelyn retrieved the light blanket from the foot of her bed and crossed to the fireplace. "The men will determine what the dogs are upset over. Would you start a pot of tea, please, Peggy?"

"Right away." Peggy wound her hair into a loose bun, then began the morning ritual of making breakfast.

"The men will likely join us again." She sat on the rocking chair and prepared to feed Jim, tossing the blanket over one shoulder to ensure her modesty. "Jemma, please assist Peggy with eggs and bacon. Don't forget to add flapjacks as well."

The two women worked together as if they'd done so for years instead of days. Within minutes, the aroma of frying bacon made Evelyn's mouth water. She stared at the pressed glass window, wishing she could see clearly through it to what was happening outside. At least the dogs had stopped their rumpus.

The door opened and Nat walked inside, followed by Enoch Mercer. "Good day, ladies. Lyn, Mr. Mercer wanted to give his regards to you."

"Thank you, sir." Evelyn tucked the blanket more securely in place, uncomfortable with the situation in many ways. "What brings you over so early?"

"My apologies for interrupting your morning, Mrs. Hamilton." He doffed his hat, and held it in both hands. "I'd given my word to your young man that I'd come visit to ensure you were safe."

"As you can see, all is well here." She put the chair into motion to hide her agitation. It was one thing for Nat, or even her cousins, to witness her nursing her son. But to have the neighbor do so proved disturbing. He needed to be on his way. "Thank you for your concern."

She conveyed with her eyes to Nat her distress, which he acknowledged with a nod.

"Let's step outside and continue our conversation." Nat opened the door and escorted the man onto the porch, the door closing with a soft thud behind them.

"How uncomfortable." She sighed and lifted the blanket to peer at her darling son. "The man can be rather rude, can't he?"

"His manners are sorely lacking for dropping in without warning at such an hour." Pausing in the process of ladling batter onto a griddle, Peggy regarded Evelyn. "You finessed his behavior much better than I could."

"Nat helped."

"He shouldn't have brought the neighbor in." Peggy shook the ladle in the air.

"He didn't know I'd be nursing Jim." Evelyn felt she needed to defend Nat from her servant's ill opinion of his actions. "I'm usually awake and ready to receive visitors by this time in the morning. Today is an exception after staying up so late last night."

"I'll take your word for it." Resuming stirring the batter, Peggy glanced over her shoulder at Evelyn. "I wouldn't tolerate such interruptions myself."

"We're living in extraordinary circumstances until the house is completed." She smoothed the blanket over her suckling baby. "When we move, we'll have the appropriate spaces to retire to when necessary."

Nat returned a few minutes later. The rush of chilly air cooled the cozy room until he fastened the door. She studied him as he removed his cloak, the shoulders glistening with rain, and hung it on a peg. He crossed to the table and pulled out a chair to sit.

"What did Enoch really want?" Evelyn asked.

Raking a hand through damp hair, Nat aimed eyes laden with concern her way. "He'd heard some fearful news that has every man on alert."

Gripping the arm of the chair, Evelyn peered at him. His expression sparked alarm in her heart. "What has happened?"

"General Greene has informed the Assembly that if the Congress does not address the deficiencies in paying the soldiers their due, the army may mutiny and turn against the government." He stared at her, his lips pressed into a line, leaning forward to rest his elbows on his knees.

"They wouldn't!" Evelyn could not believe any person would condone such action against the American Congress.

"I do not know, but that is the gossip spreading across the state." Pushing to his feet, Nathaniel paced between the table and where Evelyn sat. "I thought the fighting had ended."

"The threat does not equal the return of conflict." Evelyn stilled the chair to hand Jim to Jemma, then refastened her clothing and removed the blanket. Folding it over her arm, she stood and went to pause Nat's agitated tour of the room by halting in front of him. "Surely the general is merely trying to draw attention to the possibility in order to avoid the event."

"I hope you're correct, but I am deeply troubled by these events. Come to me."

He gripped her upper arms for a moment before pulling her into an embrace. She sensed his deep concern. He rested his chin on her head, and she slipped a hand inside his coat to lay over his pounding heart. She stroked her fingers back and forth across his shirt as he held on to her, trying to calm him. Slowly, he eased away far enough to regard her for a moment before he pressed his lips to hers.

The contact swept a charged current of desire crashing through her. He deepened the kiss, exploring the inner regions of her mouth with a playful flick of his tongue. She wrapped her arms around his neck to draw him closer. Part of her chastised herself for the impropriety of her actions in front of her servants, but she ignored the voice of reason and chose to listen to the voice of passion. Teasing his tongue with flicks of her own. Enjoying the splay of his hand on her lower back, pressing her to his hard frame. He'd awakened a need she'd never experienced prior to his first touch of her hand. A response she could easily become dependent upon.

Nat ended the kiss after several moments, pecking her mouth a few times before pulling away. She reluctantly let him go, embarrassment replacing the passion when she spied her maids watching with shock and a dash of envy.

"With this news, I'm afraid I must leave for town immediately." He studied her for a second and then dropped a kiss on her lips.

"I understand." She squeezed his hands and smiled up at him. "I'll be here when you come back, waiting."

"Fare thee well, my sweet." He pecked her lips again and then hurried out the door.

Her lips tingled from his attentions and she raised her finger to rest upon them to calm the sensation. Staring at the door for several seconds, she hoped he'd come back and kiss her again before disappearing for untold days. The door remained shut and finally she blinked and pivoted to address her maids.

"You want to go after him, don't you?" Peggy winked at her.

Evelyn lifted Jim, squealing, into her arms. "I don't need to because I know he'll come back to me."

Several weeks passed before Evelyn stopped waiting for Nat to return. She tried to excuse his absence, making up reasons for why he had not ventured out to her estate. In truth, although she no longer watched the door or listened for the sound of his horse's hooves coming up her lane, her heart still waited to be reawakened by his presence.

The afternoon had turned stormy, driving every one under shelter in the carriage house. Lightning flashed and thunder shook her composure. Hail had littered the barnyard earlier but had since melted into the puddles stretching across the area between the buildings. Evelyn rocked in the chair by the fire, contemplating the flames while pondering fate and destiny.

Perhaps she was destined to live alone, to never have a loving, kind man in her life. Sure, she'd have her son, and of course her servants, to keep her company. People to bestow her love and care upon. Additionally, she'd have students to shower her attention on and help mature. Such love as she garnered from her family and friends may have to be enough.

"Would you care for a cup of tea or coffee?" Peggy paused by the chair, Jim on one hip with his arms around her neck. "We could make it for you, this little one and me."

She gazed up at her son and then her maid. "I've had enough tea to float a boat."

"You should do something to occupy your hands and thus your mind." The maid joggled the boy for a moment before turning away. "Waiting is difficult when you're bored."

She was right, but Evelyn had no interest in doing much of anything. Especially with the three cousins lounging around the room, sprawled on beds or reclined in chairs, dozing during the unexpected break in their work. She'd not wake them, naturally. With all the hard work they'd labored to accomplish, they'd earned a rest.

Each day they came in and gave her a progress report. The rain delayed the raising of the walls, but only for an afternoon. On the morrow, they would resume their effort to rebuild her home. Moving from the constraints of the carriage house to the much larger space couldn't come soon enough to bring peace to her heart. She liked her companions, and of course loved Jim, but she wanted more privacy than afforded by the small building.

Restless, she gripped the chair arms and pushed to her feet. Peggy glanced at her but didn't comment when Evelyn put a finger to her lips and started toward the door. She needed air, to escape the four walls surrounding and protecting her, despite the storm. She felt as though she couldn't breathe. Something lying in wait for her to lower her guard. Grabbing her shawl from its peg, she wrapped it around her and stepped outside.

She stayed close to the outer wall, protected under the roof extending over the porch. The cool rain-scented air washed her cheeks. Drawing in a long breath, she surveyed her estate, noting the framing of the new building shimmering and patient. The three white tents appeared much like mushrooms springing from the wet ground beneath the trees in the distance. She pulled the shawl tighter about her shoulders and sighed. All around her stood the elements of her life. Was it fate that had brought her to live on this piece of property? Was this estate where she would spend the rest of her life in peace? She hugged herself, hoping she had done the right thing for her and her precious child.

The door opened beside her, and she glanced to see Ethan emerge and close it behind him. Her cousin had behaved in an odd manner ever since Nat departed weeks before. She rarely went anywhere without him appearing at her side. Smiling and offering his assistance at every turn. Such as at the moment when all she craved was to be left alone for a brief period of time.

"You okay?" He leaned against the wall on her left side. "I thought you didn't like thunderstorms."

She shrugged, unsure how to respond without revealing too much of her inner soul.

"Anything I can help you with?" Ethan angled his body to close the gap between them. "You need only to ask."

If she asked him to go inside, would he comply? Most likely not. Unless she became ugly and angry, and thus rude. A state which she would never become on purpose. "I'm content as I am, but I appreciate your offer."

He pushed away from the wall to stand square, his hands by his sides. "I've known you a very long time, Evelyn."

"Yes, you have. What about it?"

"You cannot hide your feelings from me. I can read you like a book."

"I see." She lifted a doubting brow. "What am I feeling now?"

He folded his arms across his impressive chest. "You're lonely and desire a man's attentions."

She raised both brows and regarded him for several moments. He hit upon the right answer on the first guess. Perhaps she exhibited too much of her inner self. "How could I be lonely surrounded by so many people?"

"Being lonely has nothing to do with being alone, but more about wanting to be with someone in particular." He dropped his hands to clasp one of hers. "Someone like me."

She studied him in silence as she adjusted the soft knitted garment draping open and hanging from her shoulders. She tried to control a laugh and compose a polite response to the ludicrous suggestion. While they were cousins, and thus permitted to marry, she did not have any attraction to him. She well understood what role a woman played as a man's wife. Ethan had always been like a brother to her. She couldn't simply turn those feelings into something more appropriate for a life companion to harbor.

"Ethan, I believe you've mistaken my demeanor." She pulled her hand from his grasp and wrapped the shawl around her again. "I am not desirous of a relationship with you."

"You're not?" He frowned as he gazed down at her. "My apologies. I had thought we had the potential for a respectful marriage."

"A marriage barren of love."

"Pshaw." Ethan waggled a hand in the air. "Love is not a requirement for a man and woman to merge their fortunes and futures."

"Mayhap." She shook her head at him. "But I've survived one such marriage, and I shall not submit to another."

He regarded her for several breaths, then looked away to

the puddles merging into a shallow lake. "I'd not heard about your husband treating you with disrespect."

"Nor would I hope many people have learned of the truth." Evelyn followed his gaze, noting the lessening of the heavy rain to showers. "I care for you, Ethan, as my cousin and my friend. Isn't that enough?"

He swung his head around to nod. "I will respect your wishes. I'll make no further attempt to persuade you in a different direction but support you in your true desires."

She inclined her head in acceptance of his apology. "Thank you. For that I am grateful."

"It's Nathaniel, isn't it?"

"Yes." A lot of good it had done her to admit as much. "I hope we can work it out, in time."

"If it's meant to be, nothing will stop you from being together." He leaned down to kiss her cheek. "I believe in destiny."

"But the Fates have a way of writing their own surprising ending to a person's story." She could only hope they agreed with her version and not interfere.

⌇

The arm of the press stuck midway, and Nathaniel struggled to release the jam. He retrieved a screwdriver to attempt to loosen the tension on the mechanism. Frank strode out of the back room, carrying a stack of blank books.

"This thing is not working correctly." Nathaniel finished making the adjustment just as the front door opened.

He glanced up as Emily strolled in out of the cold rain falling outside. She closed the door with a quick push and shivered.

"What are you doing here?" Frank deposited the stack on a shelf by the door. "I thought I was to meet you at home?"

"I needed to bring this essay for the next edition."

She pulled a set of pages from her pocket and handed them to Frank.

"It couldn't wait until later?" Frank perused the pages, a frown appearing on his brow. "Freedom of choice?"

"Exactly." She smiled at him with confidence. "It's time people realize that we should each be able to make decisions and choices based on our own needs and hopes."

Nathaniel tested the lever, and the arm slid smoothly up and then down. He listened to the discussion with interest, but did not interfere between the husband and his wife. Her argument would likely fall on deaf ears, however. Men made the choices for their women. Like they had forever. He didn't see a reason for the practice to change, either.

"Em, you know if I put this in the next paper, you'll receive more upsetting notes and may even be snubbed when you venture out." Frank regarded her for a long moment. "Are you certain?"

Folding her arms, she blinked at him several times and then sighed. "We have an agreement. Are you suggesting you wish to renege on it?"

"I'll put it in, but you'll need to face the consequences."

She smiled at him. "I will be happy to have discourse with any person who wants to engage in a serious debate on the subject."

Frank shook his head as he pivoted to lay the paper on the work table to be composed using the small metal letters and punctuation. He caught Nathaniel's attention with a quick movement of his hand. "So what do you think?"

"About what?" Nathaniel laid down the tool and strode over to the high table separating the customer area from the work space.

"Her claim that every person should have free choice." Frank tossed a smile toward Emily, who waited for Nathaniel's answer.

"I believe women do not always have the knowledge with which to make an informed decision. They do fine with household choices about what to have for dinner or what bauble to purchase." He contemplated Emily's lowering expression with his every word, but continued to press home his point. "Therefore, I think men should make the important decisions."

Emily bristled with indignation. She dropped her arms to clasp her hands together as she shook her head in disbelief. "Here I thought you were more enlightened than that."

"I beg your pardon, but I do not see what you are upset about." What had he said to provoke such a response? Nathaniel went over his explanation and found no flaw with the logic. "Everyone knows what I said is true."

"Your reasoning is faulty." Emily sighed, a sound conveying her dismay at his lack of sanity. "Women are fully capable of choosing for themselves what is in their best interest."

Glancing at Frank, Nathaniel contemplated her statement. What if she spoke the truth? But did she? He studied Emily's earnest expression, espying a wary hope that she could sway his opinion. "What kinds of choices?"

Frank broke in before Emily could respond. His sudden smirk warned of his intent before he spoke a word. "Whether to move from one town to another, perhaps?"

Emily nodded, glancing between them with a question in her eyes. "Most definitely."

"That's too big of a choice for a woman to make." How would she know about land values and locating fertile soil? Or where to find work to support a family? "I think such a decision is beyond any woman's ability to comprehend."

"Perhaps you should find out." Frank crossed his arms over his chest with a laugh. "Ask Evelyn."

Nathaniel drew in a sharp breath and shook his head. "Why would you, of all people, suggest I ask her?"

Emily cocked her head at her husband with a slight frown. "Do tell."

Frank chortled at Nathaniel. "Because it's only right to permit her to decide for herself whether she'd deign to throw her fortunes in with yours or remain here when you move on."

"Move on?" Emily regarded him with shock in her eyes. "You're leaving town?"

"Not for a bit." Nathaniel grimaced at Frank. Why did he spill those beans? "But when I do, I'll go alone because that is in her best interest."

"Does she know this?" Emily continued to frown at him, her hands landing on her hips. "Does she have any idea of your plans?"

He shook his head slowly, agitated by the censure in her gaze. "She won't, either."

Emily wagged a finger at him. "You should put the question to her. She may well surprise you."

"Do you truly believe I should ask Lyn to travel with me into dangerous lands when we are not even officially courting, let alone betrothed?"

"Absolutely."

"What do you say, Frank?" He couldn't believe his ears. Nor could he fathom why he was considering following her advice.

"What would it hurt to find out her feelings on the matter?" Frank crossed to clap him on the back. "I'll even give you the time off to do so."

He glanced between them, feeling as though they'd managed to set him on yet another path. What should he do? Resist or follow?

Chapter Nine

A dusting of snow transformed the countryside into a fairy world. Snow rarely paid a visit to the state, and then only a brief one as the temperatures warmed quickly during the day and melted the white coating into mud. Bundled in his warmest hat and cloak, Nathaniel rode toward Evelyn's house as fast as Jingo could safely traverse the slippery and rutted road. Frank had made good on his word and gave him the afternoon off from the print shop after working days without a break other than to sleep.

Tensions in town and, indeed, across the region remained high. General Greene continued to posture and threaten to use the army to force the people to supply the soldiers. Heated letters had been exchanged and then printed in the paper for dissemination to the public. The uproar that ensued had yet to quiet. Of course, the general hadn't helped matters by his curious approach to communicating with Brigadier General Daniel Morgan by chasing after him in person. Riding one hundred and twenty-five miles into North Carolina with only a guide, an aide, and a sergeant's guard of cavalry seemed foolhardy at best. Doing so had left his army with inferior leadership and exposed their commander to unnecessary danger. Despite the fact he succeeded in catching up to his quarry and thus joining forces with his division, most everyone subsequently questioned his military judgment.

Added to the lack of faith in his leadership was the audacity he demonstrated when he rode into Charlestown, the victorious general, as the British embarked their ships for England December past, but had not invited or included any other state officer in the grand parade through the center of town. Naturally, Major General William Moultrie, the same officer who had defended the town against the Britons' first attack, had marched with the Continental Line, but he was the only other officer to take part in the happy occasion.

The political enmity flowing through the town had heightened every citizen's awareness of the rampant uncertainty within its boundaries. Indeed, within the entire country. The peace treaty had not yet been signed, or at least no word had been received to that effect. Until the war officially ended and the army disbanded, such idealistic skirmishes would most assuredly occur. Which all kept him inundated with type to set for a bevy of announcements and broadsides as well as pamphlets and formal invitations to gatherings.

As he turned Jingo toward the manor and Lyn, he could see the structure rising up against the woods behind the new walls and bare roof. He urged his mount to a canter on the firmer lane leading across the estate. Before long, she would move into her new home, about the same time he moved on. A thrill of uncertainty shivered down his back. How he longed to take her with him. If only he could determine the reasons or the means with which to convince her to take such a daring chance. Despite the assurances of Frank and Emily as to Lyn's willingness to choose to go with him, he quavered at the thought of asking her. Besides, who was he fooling?

She'd never agree to go, and he couldn't stay. But he found himself wanting her to remember him fondly even as she married someone else. A stab of pain somewhere in the vicinity of his soul stole his breath.

Halting Jingo in the barnyard, he dismounted from the saddle, his heavy cloak swirling about his calves as he landed on the ground. Jack hurried out of the barn, wiping his hands on his trousers as he strode toward Nathaniel. The young black man appeared strong and intelligent, as well as sincerely desiring to be of assistance to those he worked for, good characteristics in any man, but most unusual for a slave. He studied Jack as he waited for him to take Jingo. The man deserved to seek out his own future, but of course Nathaniel had no ability to grant any slave their freedom. Indeed, the state government remained the sole entity which could manumit a slave, and they refused to do so except under extreme circumstances. He'd heard of several gentlemen who had pleaded for particular slaves to be freed, but fear prevented the state government from granting the requests. A slave would need to travel to other states that frowned upon the institution to have any hope of freedom.

"G'day, sir." Jack took the reins from Nathaniel with a nod. "Will you be staying the night?"

"Not this time." As much as he'd enjoy waiting upon Lyn for a longer span, he must be at work at first light on the morrow. "If you'll loosen the girth and give him some water, he'll be fine for the short time I'll be here."

"Very good, sir." Jack led the roan toward the barn.

Nathaniel headed for the carriage house with long strides. He knocked on the door and glanced across the yard at the fine house rising from the ashes of the former dwelling. A sturdy, grand place for his lady to call home. More than he could ever give her with his current prospects. He sighed and faced the door as it swung open.

"Nat!" Lyn flung herself at him.

He wrapped her up in an embrace and kissed her with all the pent up passion within him. Then he eased away and drank in the beautiful features of her face. "It's so fine to see you again."

"Come in." She stepped farther into the room, pulling him in with one hand. "It's cold out there."

"I hadn't noticed in my haste to reach you." He handed his cloak to Jemma and then greeted Peggy with the lift of his hat as he removed it. "How have you fared?"

Lyn led him to a chair and sank onto one beside it. "We've been keeping very busy with making curtains and such. Why have you not come sooner?"

He hung his hat on the back of the chair before sitting down. He pressed his palms on his knees to prevent himself from reaching out and touching her. If he touched her, he may never let her go. "The print shop has been very busy with work. It's all so complicated, but let's just say the town folk are up in arms about the army encamped on James Island and General Greene's recent actions."

"Oh dear." She smoothed her skirts and moistened her lips. "I'd hoped peace had come to our fair state with the departure of the Britons."

"We all had the same expectation." After the actual fighting had ended, he'd done all he could to put the animosity behind him. To move forward to a new and better life. "Perhaps in time, we'll enjoy the peace we fought for."

"Give folks a chance to sort out what the next steps must be." She grasped his hand, sending a shaft of desire and longing into his heart.

He looked at their joined hands, studying the way their fingers twined together. Relishing the contact. He moved his thumb over hers and fixed his gaze on her face. "Will you take a walk with me?"

She squeezed his hand before pulling hers away to sit back. "I doubt it has warmed much out there in the last few minutes we've been inside. Why would you wish to venture out of doors?"

"I'd like to spend time with you." Gripping his knees, he leaned forward to wink at her. "Only you."

She glanced at Peggy and Jemma, then to where her son played with several toys near the fireplace and its warmth. "I don't know…"

Her hesitation suggested his idea tempted her to accept. All she needed was a reason to succumb. "I have a little something for you, but I'd like to give it to you in private."

Her gaze flew to meet his, surprise evident in her wide smile. "I'll get my cloak and bonnet."

Minutes later, they strolled hand in hand down the lane toward a merry little creek flowing across the front of the property. Along the banks, a variety of trees provided shade in the summer, but stood stark against the wintery sky. A flock of geese honked as they flew in their V formation in the distance. They came to a clearing in the trees overlooking the sparkling water. He stopped, drawing her around to stand before him.

"Lyn, I care about you, and I want you to know that I'll never forget you."

A slight frown clouded her eyes. "I'll never forget you either. Though I don't know why you'd think I wouldn't remember you."

Should he tell her what he desired more than anything? Do as his friends had encouraged him to do? He searched her troubled gaze, imagining her reaction and dreading what he envisioned. "I have a gift for you."

Her expression cleared with the advent of a smile. "You have no need to give me a present."

"But you'll accept it, won't you?" He slipped his hand into

his breeches pocket and withdrew a felt pouch. Keeping it hidden in his fist, he waited for her answer.

Laughing in delight, she nodded. "If you insist."

He placed the packet in her hand, pressing it against her palm for a moment. "My pleasure."

She opened the small flap and reached inside with her thumb and forefinger. Easing a gold chain from the felt pocket, she gasped and grinned, until a pendant emerged to rest on her palm. She pressed the tiny latch on the side of the gold filigreed locket to reveal a small picture. "Oh, Nat, it's beautiful."

"I'm pleased you like the miniature." He'd had it made by a local painter who had a fair hand with the likeness of Nathaniel's profile. "Would you like to wear it?"

"Please." She offered the necklace to him and then turned her back when he picked it up.

He opened the clasp and, holding the necklace in one hand, stepped close behind her. She pulled her hair off her neck, making his task easier. He reached around her with both hands, grasping each end of the chain and then pulling it to the nape of her neck to fasten the clasp again. All the while, she filled his senses and stirred the desire coursing through him. He placed a kiss on the delicate skin before grasping her shoulders to spin her so he could inspect the result. The locket lay at the base of her throat, gleaming in the pale light.

"Thank you, Nat." She fingered the pendant, viewing the gold surface from various angles. "It's truly a beautiful gift."

"Think of me whenever you wear it."

"I will wear it always." She raised happy eyes to smile at him.

He studied her features, committing them to memory. He hoped she'd keep her word and wear it. Especially after he'd gone.

Evelyn's Promise

Sunlight fell through the windows onto the pine floor in the new manor house. Over the last week, the men had worked a minor miracle. Evelyn stood in what would be the parlor, a smile of joy firmly in place. Dust motes flitted in and out of view in the light. White-washed plaster walls and a barren room surrounded her. Using her imagination, she placed furniture and furnishings, candlesticks and vases of fresh flowers from her own expansive gardens. Indeed, she fully intended to have the garden slave be very busy with the many flower beds she envisioned.

Before many more days passed, the three brothers would finish the building. They'd made great strides, the three brawny men. They'd bartered help from their friends and family to accelerate the work. She'd also paid them in coin and meals as they worked raising the house. Built in the shape of a recumbent I, two stories tall, the façade was impressive yet welcoming. The set of brick steps leading up to the central doors added to the air of importance intended in the design. Before too long, she'd send word to her uncle to deliver the furniture and other items he'd been acquiring on her behalf.

Peggy appeared in the open door of the parlor, hesitating before striding in to stand by Evelyn. She'd been a happy addition in more ways than Evelyn had anticipated or expected. Smart and quick, the woman had proved her willingness and capability to assist Evelyn on multiple fronts. Including having the intelligence necessary to assist with educating the students.

"I've put Jim down for his nap." Peggy perused the empty room, one foot tapping to a beat only she could hear. "He's a sleeper, isn't he?"

Evelyn nodded as she strode into the wide central hall, Peggy shadowing her steps. "I'm grateful for his cooperation while we rebuild our home."

Peggy chuckled and matched Evelyn's pace. "Ethan said they'd finished shingling the roof, so it's closed against inclement weather."

"Wonderful news." Evelyn paused to peek into the dining room which would double as a school room. "We'll need to start cleaning everything, ceiling to floors, so we can begin bringing in the furniture."

"Very well, Miss." Peggy peered at Evelyn for a moment before propping her hands on her hips. "Where would you like me to start?"

"Upstairs, so that you're knocking the dust down through the house." Evelyn glanced at Peggy, pleased yet again to have such a skilled lady as her maid and helper. "I'll speak with the men about their next steps and then come help with the cleaning."

"I'll start right away." Peggy folded her arms and gazed at Evelyn. "This will be a wonderful place for the girls to live in and learn."

"I believe so, too." Evelyn looked down the hall to the front double doors, shut against the March winds. In warmer weather, however, they'd stand wide open along with the rear doors at the far end of the hall. The cross draft would provide relief from the summer heat. For the moment, the barrier retained the warmth from the fires burning in the fireboxes for the comfort of the workers. "Before long, I'll need to begin advertising for students."

"First things first." Peggy pivoted to walk away with measured strides. "I'll gather my supplies and begin."

Evelyn nodded to herself as the maid disappeared through the rear door, heading toward the carriage house where their supplies were stored. Over the past days, many changes had occurred, not least of which the relationship she shared with a certain handsome gentleman. She sauntered through the house, pride blending with anticipation as she moved from room to room, and then upstairs to the bedchambers. The girls would have the upstairs of the foot of the I-shaped building, separated into two bedchambers. Evelyn and her family would sleep in the top of the "I." The upstairs passage connecting the two would be set aside for music and dancing, play acting and recitals.

Her dream, her vision, had become reality. How could she not be happy? She may never frown again, such elation lifted her soul.

She stepped into her bedchamber, the one facing the front yard. Crossing to the dirty window, she gazed out over the view she'd awaken to every morning. She'd had flowering bushes planted around the base of the Pegasus statue, ones hinting at buds preparing to blossom. She identified with the tiny points of red and yellow gathering their strength and their beauty to share with the world. She had Nathaniel to thank for his support and encouragement, as well as his loving attentions. The heady combination over the last few weeks had bolstered her confidence in herself and her prospects. Her hand went to the locket with his image inside, its constant presence reassuring.

Beginning with the night they'd spent in the carriage house, Nat had become more and more important in her life. He was never far from her thoughts, even as she continued to work on building her future while he worked on his in town. The distance didn't matter because he would come out to visit as much as possible. In time, she hoped they'd marry and live at her home. Surely he'd enjoy living in the country more than in town, especially since it meant they would be together.

Turning from the window, she crossed to the door and hurried down to find the men. She followed the sound of hammering and finally located the brothers at the rear of the house, tacking on the last of the door framing.

"Evelyn." Ethan straightened from laying down his hammer. "You're looking beautiful, as always."

"Thank you, Ethan. You've all made amazing progress. I appreciate it more than I can say. I understand the roof is done, and it looks like the framing is completed. What else is left?"

Luke braced his fists at his waist and angled his head to one side. "Some finishing touches inside, such as the newel posts on the main stairs and some frieze work over the fireplaces."

"We still need to finish the back steps here. They're not level." Bill studied the stone slabs nestled onto wooden supports. "I think we may need to switch the stone out for brick like the front."

"That will take another day or two to accomplish." Luke regarded Evelyn for a moment before a smile crept onto his lips. "You'll have to put up with our camping out yonder for a little while longer, I suppose."

"I'd think we could move inside as soon as we clear out the dust and debris." Evelyn folded her hands in front of her apron. "Or you can take over the carriage house, if you'd prefer."

Ethan huffed a laugh. "The tents are enough for the short time we have left to work here."

"Very well."

The sound of a galloping horse drifted to her ears and brought warmth to her cheeks. She fought to keep the smile from her face but lost the battle. "Who might that be?"

Luke guffawed. "One guess."

"Hush now. I'll go greet our visitor."

"You do that, cousin. He'll appreciate your efforts." Ethan chuckled as he turned back to the work at hand.

Heat flared in her cheeks as she strode toward the front of the house, dust kicking up around her with each step. Ethan's teasing about her courtship by Nat tended to remind her of his own interest in her. He'd kept his word and had not pursued a relationship, but she remained aware of his former bid for her attentions. A bid which subtly changed how they interacted.

She hurried around the corner and saw the lone figure approaching. Thanks to Frank hiring two more men, Nat no longer worked all day. Every afternoon he rode out to be with her. They'd have dinner and take a stroll, holding hands and talking about their activities and observations. At the farthest point of their walk, he'd kiss her with such ardor she couldn't refuse him. The grin she'd worn all day widened when he galloped into the yard and dismounted in the twinkling of an eye.

"Lyn, my dearest, how fare you?" He clasped her hands, pulling her to him.

"All is well, my darling." She gazed up at the man she'd come to love. "Why were you in such a hurry today?"

He pressed his lips to her mouth in a lingering kiss. "I admit I'm uneasy with you living out here alone, except for a few servants."

"My cousins remain here still." She cocked her head and studied his reaction. A grin tugged at the corners of her mouth. "I see. You're jealous."

He chuckled as he shrugged, a quick lift and fall of his shoulders. "I cannot help but be jealous of their continuing proximity to my love."

Her heart swelled with his sudden declaration. "You love me?"

"With all I am. Yet I know I shouldn't say anything about how I feel for you." He kissed her again, lingering for several seconds before drawing away to peer at her. "I would like nothing better than to spend the rest of my life with you, if that were only possible."

"I would like that, as well." Evelyn thrilled to his words, his sentiments. "I love you."

He sucked in a breath as his lips formed a hesitant smile. "I've longed to hear you say how you feel about me."

"I've only recently recognized what my feelings meant." She kissed his mouth lightly and then stood back to study his expression. "I'm so very happy to have you in my life."

"I love being with you." He squeezed her hands, a shadow of some emotion passing over his features. "I shouldn't have confessed my love to you, Lyn. It's not fair to you."

"What? What do you mean?"

He released her hands and gripped her shoulders to pull her closer, reducing the space between them to inches. "Despite everything, I have no means or prospects worthy of your affections, let alone your love."

She relaxed with his explanation. "I'm not worried about your potential, Nat. I am confident that you will find a way to make a living."

Nat searched her expression, his gaze flicking from her eyes to her mouth and all around her face. "I don't deserve someone as wonderful and beautiful as you."

"Yes, you do." She kissed him, pressing her mouth to his for several moments. "Come, I'll show you the interior of my new home."

She led him inside for a tour all the while thrumming with joy. All of her desires had been fulfilled on a gusty day in March. Her home rebuilt and almost ready to occupy. Her son cared for by an intelligent and loving maid. Her handsome yet humble man confessing his love for her. She beamed as they strolled from room to room. Her life was perfect. What could possibly go wrong?

The coming of April ushered in warmer air, further encouraging the arrival of spring with its flowers and bright blue skies. Evelyn had been living in the house for several weeks, the delight of her new home still fresh. Only once in a while did an echo of unease disturb her, but surely the feeling would pass with time. At least, that's what she reassured herself when the shadow of memory raised specters in her mind. She'd look to the future, to the flow of positivity she intended to surround herself with. On a fine morning in the middle of the month, she cleared her throat to make a long awaited announcement.

"After breakfast, Peggy, it'll be time to gather what we need for our planned three-day visit to my parents." Buttering a corn muffin, Evelyn glanced at her maid before taking a small bite. The warm bread, with its blend of bacon fat and butter complementing the ground corn, tasted better than any other in her experience. Swallowing, she grinned at Peggy. "You're a fabulous cook."

"My ma is an even better one." A shadow passed over the girl's features. "I wonder if I'll ever see her again."

"You're very brave to have ventured so far from all you know and every person you love, to a place you've only read about in the paper." She couldn't imagine never seeing her family or friends. What if her life had meant she had to leave behind every one she cared about? No state of affairs could ever force her to make such a sacrifice. "It must be terribly hard."

"At first, I cried every night." Placing her fork on the plate, Peggy shrugged. Her casual movement belied the sadness haunting her eyes. "I'm fortunate to have landed in this position. You've helped me to make a new start for my life. For the first time in years, I have hope. Thank you."

"I am pleased you're here as well." She laid a hand over Peggy's and squeezed once. "Before long, you'll have worked off the debt and then may choose where you go in this shiny new country."

Peggy retrieved her fork to pierce a bite of egg. "When do you want to leave for town?"

"This afternoon. We have plenty of time to pull together the few items we'll need for such a short visit." Lifting her cup, she sipped hot tea with honey. "After breakfast, we'll pack what we need, then have an early dinner and be off before midafternoon so we arrive before supper."

"Very well. Will you be wanting Jemma to go along?"

"I don't believe I'll need her talents this time." Evelyn dabbed her napkin on her lips and then laid it on the table. "She can stay and keep an eye on things here."

Later, as the sun began its descent, Evelyn drove the phaeton into the rear yard of her parents' home. The weather had not cooperated during the trip, the wind whipping up into a storm that threatened to inundate them the entire way. As a result, Evelyn's skirts as well as Peggy's dress had become soaked. Little Jim remained safe and secure, if a bit wet, on Peggy's lap. The mares were black with rain, glistening in the light of the overcast sky. Two blacks ran out of the barn to care for the team while Evelyn and Peggy with Jim scurried across the yard and into the house.

"My gracious, give me the little one." Lucille hurried down the hall to take Jim into her arms. "You're soaked through. Go on up to your room, and I'll have your trunk brought up immediately."

Evelyn removed her wet cloak and hung it on a peg, water running down the sides to pool on the wood floor. "I'd adore some hot tea to chase away the chill we've endured."

The back door swung open, and one of the black men pushed through carrying the heavy trunk. "Where you want this, Mrs. Abernathy?"

"I'll show you." Evelyn folded her arms around her waist, trying to warm herself. "Peggy, come with us."

"Meet me in the parlor when you've changed. Jim and I are going to see about tea." Lucille sauntered down the hall, talking to her grandson.

Evelyn led the party upstairs and into the bedroom at the back of the house, overlooking the stable yard. In all her life, the space had not seen significant change. Sure, the quilt on the stuffed mattress changed with time and wear, but the bedframe itself had not. The same writing desk and chair, as well as a marble topped table holding an urn and basin. A few small rugs lay by the bed and in front of the rocking chair by the window. Her room had been her haven from the cares of her youth. She and Amy were very fortunate to have the luxury of having individual rooms. Unlike families with many children, like their cousin Emily's, who all piled into one or two bedrooms, often four or five sharing one bed.

"Put it by the window, please." She waved a hand in the direction she intended.

The man did as requested and then, with a nod, left the room to go back to his other duties. After he'd clomped down the stairs, Evelyn pushed the door closed and went to the trunk, unfastening her clothing as she crossed the floor.

"Help me out of this, will you?" Evelyn shivered as she struggled with the soaked laces stubbornly clinging together.

"Of course. I can't wait to get into something dry." Peggy made quick work of helping Evelyn out of her wet things.

Once again in dry attire, Evelyn went downstairs and into the parlor. She'd left Peggy with the task of drying out their travel clothes. Since they'd brought a limited number of gowns, the task became imperative. Lucille sat on the settee with Jim on her lap, a wooden spinning top with red and blue stripes in his hands.

The familiar furnishings and furniture in the parlor rushed a feeling of serenity through her as she strode across the room. Cherry wood tables with marble tops displayed a variety of miniature statuary of famous sculptures and sketches of world cities on easels. Ornate wallpaper and heavy drapes at the windows hinted at the social rank her father enjoyed. A sideboard on the far wall glistened with crystal decanters filled with an array of colorful liquors and wines.

"I'm pleased you're here." Lucille caught Evelyn's attention with a smile. "The ball promises to be a grand affair."

"Who will open the ball?" She sank onto a chair by the fireplace, grateful for the orange and red flames snapping and popping as it consumed the logs and worked on removing the chill from her skin. The smell of wood burning evoked a sense of comfort she always associated with home.

"The governor and his wife, I believe. They usually do, in any event." The toy fell out of Jim's hands. Lucille held him firm on her lap as she retrieved the toy.

"Have you decided what you'll wear?" Lifting the tea pot from the silver tray on the table between them, Evelyn poured the steaming liquid into two cups. As she stirred in a small spoonful of honey, she glanced at her mother. "Your gowns always cause quite a reaction."

"They're jealous of my fabulous taste." Chuckling, Lucille set Jim on the floor with his prize before picking up her beverage. "I'll decide to-morrow, but I am favoring the daffodil yellow with an embroidered stomacher. Will you wear the gown you recently made?"

"Yes. For the first time. Did you see how beautifully Emily adorned the bodice?" Emily had left the finished gown with Lucille, knowing of Evelyn's intent to stay with her parents for the dance. She'd longed to wear the garment for what seemed like a very long span. "Her skill with a needle improved upon my inferior talents."

Lucille waved off Evelyn's attempt at modesty. "I saw the quality of your stitches, so do not try to denigrate your ability."

She sipped her tea, resting the cup in the saucer as she swallowed. She loved her mother, especially the banter they shared with ease. Peggy's comment about her decision to immigrate to America echoed in her mind. To not see her mother, or her father, let alone Amy, was unimaginable. She fingered her gift from Nat, pondering the emotions Peggy must have experienced as she traveled alone and far from home.

"Where did you get such a beautiful locket?" Her mother leaned closer to view the gold pendant.

"From Nat." She let it fall back to lay against her skin. "It contains his miniature."

"Is he becoming serious?"

She bobbed her head. "We have declared our love for one another, yes."

Lucille sipped her tea and set the cup on the saucer with a clatter. "Perhaps your father should have a chat with him."

"No, please don't send Father to discuss anything with Nat about our relationship. We haven't had the conversation ourselves yet."

"If you're certain?" She lifted a brow as she selected a tea cake from the plate next to the tea pot.

"I am. But there's something else I'd like to talk over with you." Evelyn rested her cup and saucer on her lap.

Lucille swallowed as she peered at her. "I'm listening."

"My maid shared how much she misses her homeland and her parents." Setting the cup and saucer on the table, she relaxed against the chair, relishing the warmth in her stomach. "I do not think I'd be brave enough to leave for a place so far away that I'd not be able to visit with my family and friends."

"You're a strong woman, Evelyn." Setting her cup on the table, Lucille gathered the boy onto her lap. "I believe you'd do what you had to if presented with a situation requiring such extreme measures."

"Thank you for your confidence in me." Evelyn leaned forward to pin her gaze on her mother. "I harbor only a small amount, but enough to adhere to my plan."

"What you must remember is plans can change, and often do." Her mother bounced her grandson on her lap, cooing at him for a few seconds. Returning her attention to Evelyn, she raised both brows and pressed her lips together. "Don't make the mistake of thinking we have absolute control over what befalls us. Sometimes events happen in such a way as to modify our view of the world and our role in it."

Evelyn drew in a deep breath and slowly let it escape. "I don't want my plans changed. I like the direction I'm heading."

"That's well and good, but be prepared for whatever comes next." Lucille smiled at her, all her love and experience in life shining on Evelyn.

She pasted a smile on her face. "With you and Amy here to support and encourage me, I am ready to face whatever may come."

Chapter Ten

The fiddler struck up a merry tune, accompanied by a flute player, as the couples performed a reel. Nathaniel stayed out of their way, a cup of punch in hand. His eyes drifted to the door yet again. Where was Lyn? She had not been ready when the time came for him to meet his friends at the ball, so she'd urged him to go without her and she'd follow with the rest of the ladies. Half an hour had passed and still no sign of her.

All around him, people laughed and conversed. The dancers spun and turned, bowing and curtsying at the appropriate moment. The Spring Ball was in full swing. The celebration brought out the best in everyone as the first festivities after the city had regained its autonomy. Cloth covered tables stood in the corners of the upstairs meeting room in the Exchange, the traditional place for town dances and gatherings.

He turned away from observing the dancers to gaze out the window overlooking Broad Street. The sun had set, the sky a deep blue fading to black sky beyond the buildings of the town. Carriages drawn by teams of horses paused at the steps of the Exchange to disgorge elegantly dressed passengers. A group of ladies emerged from the latest conveyance to stop in the street. He peered closer as they alighted. No, not her. *Damnation.*

"There you are, my friend."

Nathaniel turned to find Benjamin, resplendent in his evening attire, grinning at him. "Have you been seeking me out for a purpose?"

"Indeed." Benjamin folded his arms and regarded Nathaniel for a moment. "Amy asked me to tell you Evelyn has been detained but should arrive soon, along with her parents."

"I see." Another delay in her appearance at the dance. "But where is your lovely wife?"

Benjamin glanced over his shoulder toward the long buffet table loaded with tempting treats and confections. "She stopped to speak with Emily about ruffles and buttons or some other such feminine talk."

Following the direction of his gaze, Nathaniel espied the pair in a lively conversation. "Whatever they are discussing appears quite animating to them. I do hope Lyn arrives before much longer so she'll have time to spend with her friends."

Benjamin chuckled and peered at Nathaniel. "Have you been pining for her over here by yourself?"

Yes, but he wouldn't admit such. He had tried to set aside his feelings, to dampen the desire he experienced at the thought of her, but to no avail. He glanced at the door as another couple arrived. Stifling a sigh, he addressed his friend and lifted his cup in salute. "I'm enjoying the refreshments and the music."

"Come join the gentlemen over by the punch bowl." Benjamin waved in the general direction of the immense fireplace, cold on this mild spring night. "We're having quite a debate."

"Regarding?" Nathaniel followed Benjamin around the

edge of the space allocated for dancing, wending toward the group of men in question.

"Yazoo Lands."

"I'm not acquainted with them." He'd never heard the word before. It sounded foreign and intriguing. For the first time in days, perhaps weeks, his curiosity was piqued.

Benjamin guffawed at Nathaniel as they joined the discussion. "It's more rumor than fact at this point, but what a great opportunity for those willing to take the risks involved."

Frank and Captain Sullivan were in deep conversation with several other men Nathaniel had not had the pleasure of meeting. Their attire suggested they worked as merchants and artisans, much like Benjamin and himself. An influx of new residents came along with the ending of the town's occupation by the enemy. As a result, many new faces appeared among the crowded ballroom.

"The Treaty of Paris guarantees the new western border." Captain Sullivan spoke with confidence ringing through his bass voice.

"But it has not been signed by all parties, and thus cannot be counted on." Frank sipped from a crystal glass containing dark red wine.

Benjamin shrugged and then crossed his arms, regarding each man in turn. "In the event, until the treaties are ratified between the Americans and the British, as well as the French and Spanish with the British, it's all smoke easily dissipated."

"Tell me about the Yazoo lands." Nathaniel glanced from one countenance to the next. "Where are they?"

Benjamin dropped his arms to his sides. "The proposed western border of Georgia is the Mississippi river."

"The Yazoo are a tribe of Indians who live on the river of the same name." Joshua shifted his weight to one leg. "Beyond America's current border with the territory Spain claimed from Britain in recent years."

A thrill of pleasure and anticipation raced through Nathaniel. New lands to be settled by adventurous men such as himself. His small savings to date would not afford him his dream. He'd have to work harder to earn the money needed to move west when the time arrived.

"The problem, of course," Frank said, "is that while the British are granting the area to us the Spanish claim possession of it."

Nathaniel frowned. "How can the Britons cede land to us they don't own?"

"Indeed." Benjamin glanced behind Nathaniel and smiled. "Your lady has arrived."

Another thrill slipped through Nathaniel as he looked in the direction Benjamin had indicated and spied Lyn. She paused at the threshold of the ball room, her gaze skimming over the crowd. He'd never seen a more beautiful woman in his life, and she'd declared her love for him. She wore an elegant azure gown with silver threads that winked and sparkled with each stride. Gold glinted at her earlobes and his locket hung about her graceful neck. When she spotted him, she smiled and started around the dancing couples to join him.

"If you'll excuse me, gentlemen." Nathaniel stepped away from the group.

"Go." Frank chuckled behind him. "We know your priorities."

The path to his lady became obstructed by a dancing couple, so he sidled to the right to avoid a collision. Then Dr. Trent and Samantha walked up to him, blocking his way. While he'd prefer to move on, manners prevented him from immediately continuing his journey.

"You're looking fine this evening," Samantha said. "Your suit is very becoming."

Inclining his head, Nathaniel smiled. "Your compliment

is much appreciated. If you'll please excuse me, Lyn has only this moment arrived, and I am anxious to speak with her."

"We understand entirely." Trent took Samantha's arm, preparing to step aside. "We shall speak with you later then. Enjoy the dance."

"I intend to." Nathaniel smiled after them as the couple strolled away to mingle with the other guests.

"Good evening, Nathaniel." Evelyn stopped in front of him. "You are very handsome this evening."

"Thank you, my dear Evelyn." He inclined his head in appreciation of the comment. He'd toiled longer than normal on ensuring he did not embarrass his love. "But I'm not nearly as beautiful as you are, my sweet."

A blush rose up her neck to stain her cheeks. "You're too kind."

"I can be nothing but kind to the lady I love." The heavens above knew how much he loved the woman standing before him.

But could he ever claim her as his? The problem, or rather dilemma, he faced could not be resolved in a single decision. He had to take steps toward his final choice. Steps which seemed to require his sacrifice of his love for her. The more he considered the matter, the more he dreaded having to let her go. But it would not happen tonight. He'd enjoy every remaining moment with her.

"Would you care to dance?" He'd pay money to dance with her, to hold her in his arms and breathe in her scent. His palms turned clammy and he rubbed them together to dry them.

"I'd be delighted."

Soon they had joined the couples preparing to dance to an English country tune. He couldn't help but smile as the set of four couples formed a circle, moving first one direction then the other, patting hands together, followed by a pirouette in place, before clapping and resuming the large circle. With each tap and spin, his precious Lyn smiled and laughed with him. The flush on her cheeks emphasized the color of her eyes, making them appear even more intense than usual. Captivatingly so.

The whirl and bustle of the jig made them breathless as they laughed and moved through the steps. Several strands of her hair worked loose from the intricate bun on top of her head. He couldn't avert his gaze from her alluring features, the fine sheen of perspiration on her face, and happy expression upon her most tempting lips. The tune ended with a flourish, the dancers executing farewell bows and curtseys. Lyn clapped her hands in delight as she rose from her curtsey. Nathaniel took her hand and led her back toward the punch bowl for some refreshment.

"Dancing jigs is such fun." She took the cup of red liquid with a nod and drank half of its contents. "I didn't realize how thirsty I was."

Nathaniel swallowed a gulp of his punch. "All that circling made me dizzy."

Or dizzy because of his companion? Inspecting the woman beside him, he found only perfection, even where slight imperfections existed. Like the sprinkling of freckles across her nose and cheeks from spending time in the sun. He wouldn't change one aspect of his woman. He paused on the last thought. What right did he have to consider her as his? The question plagued him. Smothering a sigh, he gulped down the rest of his drink. He wrestled in his mind as to whether to confide in her his need to travel. Part of him wanted to stay, and he had pondered over many long nights if he should remain in the state or leave. The indecision drove him to keep his own counsel. What purpose did it serve to upset her before he'd settled on a definitive objective?

Frank motioned for Nathaniel to join the men's group, but

he hesitated before nodding agreement. Turning to focus on Lyn, he tilted his head in Frank's direction. "We're wanted over there."

She glanced to where he'd indicated and then shrugged. "You go ahead. I'd rather catch up with Samantha and Emily."

"Very well. I'll seek you out in a while." He squeezed her hand before releasing her to walk away.

A heated discussion was in progress when he reached the men clustered by the fireplace.

"The word is General Washington himself quelled the conspiracy in Newburgh," Frank said. "He appealed to the officers' sensibilities, reminding the men of his own sacrifice for the country. The mention of his failing eyesight and graying hair drove the point home that everyone has paid a price to win independence."

"A conspiracy?" Nathaniel stood beside Benjamin cradling his punch cup in one palm. "What happened?"

"Apparently, several officers of the Continental Army threatened to organize a coup against the Continental Congress." Frank shifted his grip on the glass cup. "There's a lot of anger in the ranks about the soldiers not being paid for the last several years."

"Well founded anger." Nathaniel shook his head slowly. "I've been told we won't ever be paid."

"Then I have some good news for you." Frank speared Nathaniel with his gaze and a grin. "Congress has authorized five years full salary for every soldier."

"What form of money?" Benjamin asked. "I thought the congress had no funds?"

"Very true, but Robert Morris has financed the payments with his own money in the form of notes." Frank set his cup on the table beside him. "We should receive ours with the next ship from Philadelphia."

"Wait, I don't think it applies to you, Frank." Trent frowned as he glanced from man to man. "Not for the last three or four years at least."

Nathaniel listened intently to the discourse. If true about the monies due, his back pay along with the salary earned from his job might be enough for his plan to move west.

Benjamin sighed. "I see where you're going with your reasoning."

"Clear up your direction for the rest of us." Frank tapped a finger against the glass in his hand. "I'm baffled."

"Consider the fact of the British occupation interrupting our state's autonomy for those three or four years." Trent crossed his arms as he addressed the rapt audience. "Then think about how no one ever created muster rolls for the men who turned out to fight."

"So? We know we fought." Frank's frown deepened, and he tapped the cup harder in apparent frustration.

"True, but no one can prove any one's word with written evidence." Trent shook his head sadly. "You all were considered volunteers, my friends."

"Volunteers?" Frank fumbled the glass and spilled several drops of the punch before he caught it in his hands. "We dedicated our lives to the cause with no expectation of recompense?"

"That cannot be true." Nathaniel shook with suppressed anger. "While I had not counted on receiving any amount, surely they cannot deny all our state's soldiers payment for their service."

His heart had dropped into his feet at Trent's revelation. He'd begun to hope to depart soon, to begin anew. The potential for expansion of the country's borders opened promising possibilities. Opportunities he'd happily explore. Mountains of trees and wildlife as well as prairies of wildflowers and grasses lured him inland to be traversed and mapped for others to settle. Without a doubt, he wanted to begin the adventure. With the unwelcome news from his friend, he would need yet another means to his goal.

"My apologies for sharing such distressing intelligence on such a festive evening." Trent's mirthless grin aimed at each of them in turn. "Perhaps our state officers will determine some other form of recompense."

"I, personally, shall not be waiting for any government action to meliorate the situation." Nathaniel shrugged and squared his shoulders. "I've never found much support from that sector in the past."

"Enough politics and military talk, gentlemen." Benjamin's countenance split into a grin as Amy approached the group. "My wife wishes to dance, and who am I to decline such a lovely offer? If you'll excuse me."

Benjamin broke through the circle of men to join Amy on the dance floor for the next reel. His departure prompted the others to drift off in different directions to locate their companions or other diversions. Nathaniel paused and searched the crowd of people in their finery, talking, laughing, dancing, until he found Lyn in a merry discourse with her friends on the far side of the room.

While he'd realized how anxious he'd become about moving on, one huge question hung over him like an ominous cloud.

Could he face making such a momentous move without her?

The buds on the bushes surrounding Pegasus transformed into open flowers in the days following the ball. Summer lurked in the warming days, waiting its turn. Evelyn kept busy, cleaning and furnishing her home. Several wagon loads of furniture had accompanied her when she'd returned from town.

Uncle Joshua's efforts had yielded quite a lovely collection of furnishings for the house. Each time she placed a chair or positioned a table, she did so with a mix of joy and anticipation. What exactly she expected to happen she couldn't say. Despite the sense of expectation, or perhaps dread, she'd make the house a home replete with love and welcome.

The rattle of a carriage and jingle of harness drew her to the parlor window. A smile lifted her lips at the sight of Nat driving the light vehicle pulled by a single horse. She'd missed seeing him since they'd both been too busy to make the trip either into town or out to the manor. So many decisions and adjustments had been needed and only she could make them. She spun, her long cotton skirts belling out, and hurried to the front door. Curiosity propelled her steps. Why was he in a carriage and not riding Jingo?

Peggy met her in the hall, Jim propped on one hip, his happy gaze fixed on his mother. "Who is it?"

"Nat." She moved to kiss her son on the cheek. The boy had begun scooting around the floor on his bottom, preparing to start crawling in another month or so. "My little Jim is so handsome, isn't he?"

"Yes, of course." Peggy played with one of Jim's hands for a moment before smiling at Evelyn. "Run along and see your man. I know you're anxious to."

With a nod, Evelyn opened the door and passed through to stand in the warmth of the late morning sunshine. She grinned at the handsome devil reining to a halt. "It's about time."

"I agree." Nat chuckled from his seat, the horse shifting its feet and rocking the phaeton. He grasped both traces in one hand and tapped the lid of a picnic hamper on the seat beside him. "Will you join me for a picnic?"

She hesitated for only a second before nodding. "I'll get my wrap."

Rushing inside, she snared her shawl from the peg by the door. "Peggy, I'm going out for a while. Take care of things here for me, please?"

"Of course." Peggy made a shooing motion with her hand. "Enjoy your outing."

In moments, she'd mounted the open conveyance and sat beside Nathaniel, the basket on her lap. "Where did you have in mind?"

He leaned over to kiss her, one arm wrapping around her shoulders as he pressed his lips to hers. She sank against him, savoring the feel, the smell, and the taste of her man. When she'd accepted her father's condition to marry, she'd intended to convince him at a later time to rescind the request. But the more she'd fallen in love with Nat, the less onerous the condition had become. Sensations and emotions combined to make her eyes smart, tears leaking out from her closed lashes.

Nathaniel eased away to peer at her face. "Why are you crying, sweetheart? Is something wrong?"

She shook her head, swiping her cheeks dry as she chuckled. "Tears of happiness."

Nathaniel sighed with relief though his expression remained inscrutable. "I'm glad to know you're happy with me."

"I am. So, where shall we go?" Something in his eyes sent a shiver of apprehension down her spine. Then his expression cleared as though nothing adverse had crossed his mind. She shrugged off the sensation as her imaginings.

"The hill overlooking the river? There's a live oak to provide a bit of shade and a nice breeze."

"Perfect."

As they bounced and bumped down the rutted road, heading south, she started singing. She couldn't help but share her happiness with the world, as it overflowed her heart and soul. If she could bottle the emotions filling her and sell it, she'd make her own fortune. The silly notion added to the sense of giddiness, making her voice stronger as she sang. Never had she expected to feel such joy merely by being with a man.

All the years she'd lived under the domination of her husband, she'd forgotten the initial love shared with Walter. Over the course of the war against Britain, her husband had undergone a dark metamorphosis. Each passing day, he had seemed to grow more bitter and more cynical. She'd retreated behind a façade of her own making, where she pretended to be docile and meek in order to reduce the number of slaps and pushes by his broad hand. She had no way to fight back with strength, so her weapon of choice had been to hide her true nature from him.

The overall effect of her façade made her cower when she considered the weaker version of herself. When Nat came to be with her, she needn't be afraid. She needn't worry he'd hurt or harm her in any way with purpose. His gentle demeanor lifted her heart and soul to new heights.

Nat made her feel good about herself. As if she were worthy of being loved and cherished. When she spoke, he listened with such a keen interest upon his countenance that she often revealed more than she intended. Even then, he expressed his appreciation for her, her son, and all she strived to accomplish. She couldn't envision her future without him.

As they drove along, sitting side by side, her thigh rested close to but not touching his with each jounce of the carriage. She could almost anticipate the sensation of allowing their limbs to make contact, the surge of pleasure sure to follow. She gripped the handle of the hamper to keep from touching him, distracting him from navigating the rough road. The effort took all her concentration and focus to not succumb to the delicious temptation.

Before long they reached their destination. Nat jumped out of the carriage, striding around the horse with a quick rub of the mare's nose. He took the hamper from her and helped her step to the ground. She reached into the back of the carriage and lifted the lap blanket from its home in a side compartment. They walked together over to the immense oak and stopped to locate the perfect spot.

"Here under the tree?" Nathaniel pointed to a different area closer to the creek. "Or over there in the sunshine?"

"Here looks more comfortable." Shaking out the blanket, she spread it on the grassy spot. Kneeling, she sat back on her heels and gazed up at Nat. "Set that here, and let's see what we have for our luncheon."

"Your mother insisted on preparing our meal." He put the basket in front of her before folding his legs and sitting down. "I know it made me hungry the entire trip out here."

Laughing, she opened the lid and peeked inside, well aware of his proximity and perusal. Glancing up at him, she caught another bemused look flow across his features which fled when he noticed her contemplation of him. Something worried him. What was he pondering? A slight frown pulled her brows as she returned to inspect the contents.

Smoked ham. Roasted chicken legs. Several hard-cooked eggs. Two kinds of hard cheeses. A crock of cool apple cider. Iced tea cakes. A feast indeed.

"Cook has outdone herself on our behalf." Resting her hands on the open hamper, she considered her companion. "Mother must think we eat like the hogs."

"I'm hungry as one." Nat rubbed his belly as demonstration of his appetite. "Can we eat now?"

"Hold on a minute, and I'll satisfy your request." She portioned everything onto plates and handed him one.

He winked at her as a smirk settled into place. "All of them?"

"What are you asking?" She lifted an egg and took a bite, revealing the pale yellow center.

"I have many needs." He picked up a chicken leg and eagerly bit into it. He swallowed and grinned at her. "Will you satisfy all of them?"

She chuckled and shook her head. "Only those within my power."

He laughed and took another bite, chewing slowly as he regarded her. "I believe you have the ability to meet them."

"I am happy to make the attempt in any case." She finished her egg and dabbed her lips with a napkin.

"And I am glad to hear you say as much." He popped an egg into his mouth and chewed.

They ate for several minutes in companionable silence. Birds darted among the branches above them, calling to one another from the uppermost reaches of the tree. Cerulean skies provided a contrast for the wispy white clouds drifting by. Beside her, the man of her dreams shared not only a pleasant meal but also frequent glances filled with love and inquiry. The day couldn't be more enjoyable.

She poured cider into cups and handed him one. The brush of his fingers against her hand sent a wave of yearning through her. She longed for another kiss to arouse her senses. They'd had infrequent opportunities to be together of late, thus she'd missed his busses and attentions. Nat had sent notes via one of her cousins as messenger which explained his absence. He'd had his hands full, apparently, both at the print shop and with some other pressing personal business. Mayhap the mysterious business troubled him, causing the flashes of worry she'd noticed.

"Tell me about your week." She sipped her drink and set it aside. "You've been busy, I understand."

"Extremely, which seems to be the way of it for as far into the future as Frank can determine." Nat polished off a tea cake, licking the remains of icing from his fingers before wiping his hands with a napkin.

"Frank must be pleased with his revenue as a result."

"He has no complaints with his cash flow, of that I am certain."

"In time, perhaps the number of jobs will abate."

His smile flattened into lips pressed together. He stared at her for a long moment, his regard both sending sparks through her veins and making her shiver with worry. The questioning look returned. Finally, he drew in a breath and released it on a huff.

"I've exciting news to share with you, sweetheart." Nathaniel placed his plate on the blanket before bracing his hands on his knees. "Or at least, I believe it is such."

She detected deep happiness and a touch of worry of his own, whatever he was about to reveal. If it made him happy, his news must be good even if a bit scary. She straightened her back, clasping her hands together to keep them from trembling. "Tell me."

"I've decided where I want to live."

A shiver raced down her spine, distracting her for a moment from the intense expression on his face. "I can tell you're keen. Where have you decided to live?"

She imagined him taking a house in Charlestown, or even better wanting to marry and move in with her. The vision she cherished, of them as a family, running her girls' school and raising their children, floated in her mind. She couldn't stop the wide smile any more than she could stop loving him. She held her breath, waiting for him to confirm what she hoped with all her wishes to come true.

"West, on the new frontier, along the Tennessee river in the Yazoo lands." He grinned and slapped his knees. His eyes displayed the extent of his happiness but also a hint of concern as he studied her, waiting for her response to his purportedly good news.

Her heart sank. He couldn't. The sunlight dimmed around her, the day losing its pleasure. "Where exactly are these lands you speak of?"

He waved toward the west with one hand. "I'm not certain, but it must be several hundred miles in that direction."

So far away? She sighed and shook her head as a cleft formed in her joy, her heart. Why? How could he consider leaving? She couldn't fathom his reasons for wanting to put so much distance between them. "What about us?"

He grasped her closer hand and squeezed. "Come with me. We can start fresh in a new land. Start our own farm, maybe even an apple orchard. What do you say?"

She pulled her hand free and glared at him. Shock flashed in her chest, a pain to her heart. No mention of marriage. No thought for her safety or well-being, nor for her son. No consideration for the life she'd begun to build. "Are you daft?"

Nathaniel reached for her hand, missed when she moved it farther away, and then let his own drop back to his leg. "I had hoped after we'd grown so close over the last few months you'd want to go anywhere I went."

She'd love to be with him, but *here*. Not in some distant place so far from everything and everyone she loved and cared about. And he still hadn't asked for her hand. She'd most definitely not go with him as his mistress. What if they had a rupture in their relationship and he left her on her own, hundreds of miles from her family with only her two hands to support herself and Jim? Oh, and he'd not even mentioned taking her son with them, should she go. Did he expect she'd leave him behind? How would an infant survive such a journey? She had to change his mind, make him want to stay. But how?

"What about your work at the press?"

He shrugged, his eyes searching her face. "It's only for a

month or so. Frank mentioned he'd release me from my promise so I could take advantage of this amazing opportunity. Plenty of time to save my money before making the move. I cannot wait longer than that to realize my dream."

So he'd never really intended to stay in Charlestown, let alone the state. He'd found a dream. His delusion, to her mind. Her dream lay in the school and her son. The property would be Jim's one day, her husband's legacy for his offspring. How could she give up what she'd been working so hard to make happen, to follow Nathaniel to some unseen, unknown wilderness?

The discussion with her mother regarding plans changing came back to haunt her. His plans certainly had modified over the months she'd known him. Not once had he hinted at such a profound diversion in his future from what she'd expected. She was not as brave as Peggy, journeying far from home and family to start anew. Nathaniel assuredly held no reservation with the concept, his eagerness evident in the grin aimed in her direction. Well, he needed to understand the depth of his betrayal.

"You lied to me, Nathaniel. Hid your true plans from me." Tears threatened as she shoved her skirts out of the way to put her feet under her and stand. Glaring down at the blasted man, she fought for her composure. She'd been wrong to fall in love with him. With any one. Her heart cleaved in two and she tossed her head and stamped her foot, frustration and anger warring inside. "Take me home."

"I only ever agreed to work for Frank for six months. That was time I set aside to make a plan." He bounded to his feet, grabbing both her hands in his. "What have I said to make you angry?"

"If you don't know, then there's no point in continuing this relationship." She knew what she had to do, wrenching though it would be. Her heart shattered into shards, slicing her emotions into ragged pieces as she gazed at the man before her. She took a breath and released it as tears slipped down her cheeks. "I do not care to ever see you again."

What was he thinking? He should never have mentioned his decision to her. Rather he should have simply left, leaving her to wonder where he'd gone, but at least she wouldn't be angry with him.

She threw the dishes and food into the hamper and slammed the lid closed. He'd never seen her so upset. She thrust the hapless container at him, which he grabbed before it fell to the ground. Apparently, she didn't want to chance touching him, even accidentally in the transfer of the container from her hands to his. Hell and damnation.

He strode to the carriage to deposit the hamper in the back. Behind him, she snapped the blanket as she shook it out. Before he could turn around, she appeared beside him to shove the wadded blanket beside the hamper. She flashed a glare in his direction, streaks of tears on her cheeks, and then clambered onto the front seat. Staring straight ahead, she took a position as far away from where he'd sit as humanly possible, her hands folded in her lap.

With a weary sigh, he strode to his side of the carriage and stepped up to take his seat. She didn't say a word the entire time he settled on the bench and lifted the traces. She turned her head to look away from him. Damnation but he had bollixed the entire revelation in such a way as to appear irreparable. He slapped the leather reins on the horse's rump and clucked to urge the beast into a walk.

What could he say to make her understand? He drove in silence for several minutes, contemplating possibilities all while drawing closer to her home and reducing the amount of time available to apologize or explain, or both. He mentally kicked himself for his inane attempt to do the one thing he had resisted because he feared her reaction. Rightly so, as it happened.

"Lyn, I didn't mean to hurt your feelings." Steering around a hole in the road, he peeked at her but only saw the back of her bonnet. "Please, talk to me."

She shifted her shoulders, her cloak draping on the seat between them. The lace trim of her hat trembled as she stubbornly maintained her silence and kept her gaze averted. If she continued to refuse to speak with him, how would he ever make amends?

"You don't understand how important this opportunity is to me." Nathaniel glanced at the passing scenery, the leafy trees and greening fields witness to his distress. "Lyn?"

Silence except for the piercing cry of a hawk and the sound of the mare's hooves on the dirt road.

"I cannot live in South Carolina for the rest of my life. It's too painful, and I—"

The reasons sounded lame even to him. She'd not fathom his motivations for making the torturous choice. Even if he could adequately explain them, she had told him she wouldn't go with him. To leave her home and family behind proved impossible. Still, she needed to comprehend the fact that he had not meant to deceive her in any way.

"I do wish you'd talk to me."

She turned to pin him with her blazing gaze. "Mr. Williams, we have nothing to say to one another."

"I think we do." Her use of his proper name stung, but she had reason to be angry with him. He must explain. If she'd let him.

"Only farewell." She turned away again.

He steered the trotting horse onto her lane, the house looming in the short distance. The dogs ran to the front yard, announcing their approach. Before much longer his time to talk with her would end.

"I didn't tell you of my decision before today because I had not settled on my course of action until a few days ago." He regarded the back of her head and the thrust of her jaw for a moment and then sighed. "Won't you accept my apology before I depart?"

She stiffened and clenched her jaw.

"Whether or not you understand why I must go, the fact remains that I will leave before much longer." He steered the horse into the barnyard and pulled on the reins to halt the horse and carriage. He laid a hand on her forearm and squeezed gently. "I'd rather take you with me, but at least let me go without your resentment in my heart and soul."

Chapter Eleven

Nathaniel's hand on her arm threatened to destroy the barricade she'd erected around her emotions. As always, contact between them instilled an urgent desire to increase the sensations racing through her core. She wouldn't let his words sway her because of what he just said. He would leave with or without her. She couldn't go with him. She swept her gaze over the house and outbuildings, the two dogs with their tongues lolling and tails wagging, and then spotted Jack emerging from the barn. She couldn't leave all of this, her home and family, behind.

Pulling her arm from his grasp, she stepped out of the carriage without looking back at the man who had stolen her heart. If she did, she might relent and forgive him, but she'd never forget him. Her hand found the locket at her throat, the fine filigreed surface comforting even as she realized why he'd given it to her. To remember him after he left. She hurried into the house, closing the door with a bang. The jangle of harness told her Nathaniel had driven away from her. For the last time.

Peggy strode into the passage and paused to frown at her. "What's the matter? Did you not enjoy your picnic?"

"No!" The word came out on a wail and she gasped a sob. "He deceived me, Peggy. I cannot believe he'd leave me."

"Where is he going?" Peggy hurried to support Evelyn as she helped her into the parlor and to the settee. "I do not understand what has happened."

Evelyn pulled a kerchief from her pocket and blotted her tears. "He has decided to move far away and never return."

"What of you? Why would he leave you?"

"He asked me to go with him but said nothing of marriage." Evelyn shook her head in dismay. "How could I?"

Peggy sank onto a nearby chair and pressed her hands onto her legs. "You love him. How could you not go with him?"

"Such a long and arduous journey would not be possible for my son." Evelyn couldn't believe Peggy suggested she should have accepted Nathaniel's outrageous offer. "What would I do if he left me once we made it to wherever he's going? If he betrayed me again? I'd be alone to fend for myself and my son in a strange city, without any friends or family to assist."

"You're essentially alone now, relying upon others to help you achieve your aims." Peggy ran her hands over her skirt, smoothing away unseen wrinkles. "You'd survive, Miss. You're strong and braver than you give yourself credit for."

Evelyn leapt to her feet, agitated beyond words. Nathaniel had made his decision without considering her and her situation. He had the flexibility to make a move such as the one he proposed to strike out upon, but she had responsibilities not so easily set aside. Students to teach in a few months. A child to raise. Her servants' welfare to consider. The debt to her father. All of her obligations weighed upon her, but she must deal with them. She couldn't run away.

She paced from one end of the parlor to the other and

then spun to stare at her maid. "You are much more courageous than I am. We've established that fact."

"I disagree with you. If I were in your shoes, I'd accept his offer and go with him for the adventure."

"I cannot. Even if I wanted to, which I don't." Evelyn paced to the fireplace and stared at the flames licking the logs with red and yellow tongues of fire.

Peggy rose and crossed to stand beside her, slipping her arm around Evelyn's shoulders. "Think on it and you may change your mind."

No, she would not. Her heart reverberated in pain mingled with anger from his withholding such devastating admissions. She would not have allowed herself to fall in love if he'd been upfront with her as to his intentions. She fingered the locket for a moment and then took a step closer to the fireplace. She reached behind her neck to unfasten the clasp. With a wail revealing the depth of her anguish, she flung the necklace into the fire.

"Evelyn, no!" Peggy grabbed up the tongs and moved in to retrieve the jewelry.

"Leave it." Evelyn whispered the command. The gift itself belied Nathaniel's claim of having decided days ago, having presented it to her weeks before. She swallowed the tears threatening to fall. "Do not mention his name to me ever again."

Days drifted by filled with endless chores and sadness. Evelyn worked hard every day to clean and polish the house. Peggy wisely refrained from mentioning the destruction of the happy couple, but not talking about Nathaniel did nothing to ease the anguish from the absence of his laugh, his touch, his kiss. Evelyn pushed herself each day in an effort to forget, or at least not dwell on, the handsome man she loved. Correction. Once loved.

She finished shining the newel post of the wide curving staircase leading up to the second floor. One last rub of the rag in her hand and done. What next? She strolled through the house, sunlight illuminating the interior on the eastern side. As she passed from room to room, her delight increased. Every carpet, table, and chair stood ready to serve her family and students. Fresh flowers in vases graced several side tables, a contribution from the extensive gardens surrounding her home.

Each room displayed a theme within the design of the wallpaper. The Chinese room featured silk fans, cherry tree blossoms, and bright, bold colors. The French room depicted *fleur-de-lis* interposed with bunches of grapes and lavender. The British room featured rolling green hills dotted with white sheep on one wall, Stonehenge on another, and a third with the symbols of England: roses, wrens, and oak trees. She envisioned spending time in each room with her girls, teaching them about the different motifs and cultures.

In time, she'd find peace and contentment in her role as a teacher and mother. The routine combined with the ever changing personalities of her students would replace the burning love for Nathaniel. She'd surround herself with young ladies eager to learn, delving into subjects and activities designed to edify and enhance their minds, and thus improve their chances of succeeding in whatever future they may choose. Evelyn would somehow manage to forget Nathaniel, and maybe her heart would mend if she found someone else. Then again, she didn't *want* any other man in her life. She sighed, the pain of loss fresh and deep.

As the last of her breath left her chest, a low growl sounded in the room behind her. She gasped when the deep bass registered as Walter's voice, causing a chill to flash across her skin. She had to be imagining she heard him. He'd died, after all. Wrapping her arms around her waist, she inched toward the door leading into the Chinese room. Drawing closer one hesitant step at a time, she gulped in air without daring to make any noise of her own. She did not believe in ghosts. Yet the hair on her arms stood up, almost as though pulling her into the room. Finally reaching the threshold, she darted a glance around the interior of the chamber.

A grouping of chairs and a couch stood to her left, centered upon the wall and covered with peach colored fabric. A writing desk and chair nestled beside the merrily burning fire in the fireplace, the lid of the desk closed so the blank book she'd placed inside as well as an ink stand and quill pen remained hidden from view. A flash of light to her right made her gasp and spin to seek out the cause. She looked from one spot to another in the room, her gaze halting its frantic pace when she espied what appeared to be her deceased husband leaning casually against the sideboard, one hand hovering over a crystal decanter of brandy. A snarl grew on his mouth as he scowled at her. His expression left no doubt in her mind that he planned to make her life a living hell once again.

She tried to scream but no sound emerged from her horrified throat. Her knees buckled and she collapsed to the floor in a puddle of mussed skirts, staring at him with her mouth gaping open. It couldn't be. Could it? If only Nathaniel might rescue her from the threat of her husband's abuse. But Nathaniel had let her down and she must face her fears alone. Her greatest fear being of her husband returning to continue what he'd started.

She blinked and the shadow of Walter vanished. Her terrified heart thundered in her chest as she searched the room with her eyes. She saw only inanimate objects she had placed around the area herself. Nothing out of the ordinary. She scooted backward and sagged against the wall, dragging deep breaths into her chest to calm her racing heart even as she continued to rake the room with her terrified gaze. He'd gone. If he'd even been there.

What on earth had just happened? Was she losing her sanity? She waited, straining to hear any sound or motion out of place in the room. She also waited for the thudding in her ears to quiet and her breathing to return to normal. After several minutes, she gathered the courage together to move, to stand up and smooth out her rumpled skirts with shaky hands. Heaven protect her but she sincerely hoped to never have another such experience. She didn't know what to make of the memory flashing in her mind of Walter's belligerent demeanor toward her. Maybe she should move out, back to her parents and the safety of their home. She mentally shook herself. She couldn't permit his ghost—if that was indeed what she'd seen—rule her life. She'd grown in confidence since his death and she wouldn't go back to the cowering chit she'd been.

"Miss Evelyn, where are you?"

Evelyn jumped at the sudden interruption to her thoughts, inhaling sharply as she settled her emotions as best she could. She pivoted and moved toward the open door. "In the Chinese room."

Peggy appeared in the passage outside of the room, a paper in her hand. "I've written the advertisement as you asked. Will you read it?"

"Did you remember to add the opening date?" Evelyn tucked the rag into an apron pocket, accepted the sheet, and then perused its contents. "Yes, I see you did. This serves the purpose well."

"Do you want me to carry it to the print shop to include in the paper?" Peggy maintained a calm demeanor despite the weighty question.

Evelyn had long planned to take the advertisement herself, a ready excuse to see her man. With the present situation between her and Nathaniel, how could she? Putting herself in such a position surely would try her soul. She reached for the locket, but her fingers didn't find what they sought. Peggy had insisted upon saving the necklace, which lay in its felt pouch at the bottom of a silver box containing her other bits of jewelry. She'd not wear it again. She sighed. Seeing the man she wanted but could not have seemed silly and painful combined. Torture of her emotions and comportment.

On the other hand, going provided an opportunity to see her family and friends if only for a brief visit. She'd tell them of the opening of her school and receive their congratulations with all due humility. The achievement of her dream and the embarkation of her future surrounded her, all bright and shiny. To succeed in her aim, she must develop the ability to face uncomfortable and difficult situations with grace and confidence. Another lesson she would teach her students.

Besides, what harm would it do to see Nathaniel in a business setting? Nothing intimate or personal would have chance to pass between them in such a place. Mayhap he'd apologize and change his aim. He probably wanted her back, as he'd claimed to be in love with her. But she wouldn't take him. Not since their relationship had been founded upon the quicksand of deception. She'd grown into a confident woman over the last six months, returning to her true nature. She would not hide her feelings and reactions for any man ever again. She could take the advertisement, but then again what if when she faced him, her will weakened? She straightened her back and smiled at her servant.

"Why don't we both go?" Evelyn rattled the paper in her hands. "We'll make a day of it."

"A lovely idea, Miss." Peggy retrieved the paper from Evelyn's trembling fingers. "When do you wish to make the trip?"

"To-morrow. We'll set out early and plan to stay at my parents' house for the evening." Evelyn folded her arms, tapping one hand on her elbow. "I think I'll carry some flowers to them as a gift."

"Excellent. I'll pack the little one's travel bag."

Evelyn dropped her hands to her side. "Very good. I'll have Jack ready the carriage and prepare to accompany us."

The next morning, as the sun peeked over the horizon, they stepped into the phaeton, Evelyn driving while Peggy held Jim. Jack rode a bay gelding, keeping a watchful eye on the ladies. Evelyn had left Jemma to manage the household and feed the brothers as they finished up outside.

They arrived at the print shop shortly before noon. Charlestown bustled with activity, the streets busy with men on horseback, carriages and wagons trundling by, and people in general going about their business. The warm spring air carried the combined scents of their efforts: baking bread, leather, perfume, and the ever present smell of the sea. Dogs barked from somewhere out of sight. An elegantly attired gentleman led a pet deer by a long red leash past her carriage as she climbed down.

"What a sight, that." She shook her head, grinning up at Peggy. "Wait here. I'll only be a moment."

Checking both directions before braving the flowing crowds, she darted toward the shop. Hesitating for a breath, she glanced at her gown, uncomfortably aware she'd chosen the one she'd been wearing when Nathaniel had first expressed a desire to court her. The pale green skirts barely touched the tips of her matching low-heeled shoes. A bodice the color of a freshly sliced lemon had a V-shaped neckline where she had once worn his locket. Today, she wore the miniature her parents presented to her on her twenty-first birthday five years before. Would he notice? Did it matter? Taking a deep breath, she pushed the door open, a bell jingling above her head. Ink, with its tang and bitter aroma, scented the interior, making her cough.

Nathaniel had given her a tour of the shop during one of her previous visits. She trailed her gaze around the space, the memory of the day vivid in her mind. He'd acted so very gallant and obliging, furthering his own aims while pretending to do the exact opposite. Stay versus leave. She sighed at her folly in trusting him as she spied Sawyer working at the press, which occupied the rear of the public room.

To one side stood the two oblong wooden cases divided into compartments to hold each letter of the alphabet. The upper case, mounted at eye level on an angle for easy access—according to Nathaniel—contained the capital letters, small capitals, and accented letters. The lower case, positioned on a flat surface beneath the other one, held the small letters, points of punctuation, spaces for separating words, and quadrats for making blanks in the line of text. She knew more about printing than she'd ever desired to know, but he had been so pleased she'd surprised him with a visit, he wanted to show her everything.

Frank emerged from the back room, stuffing an ink stained rag into a leather apron pocket. "Welcome, Miss Evelyn. To what do I owe the pleasure?"

"I'd like to place this advertisement in your next edition, if you don't mind." She pulled out the paper, unfolded it, and smoothed the page on the hard wood surface. Pride mingled with elation as she pushed the sheet toward Frank. "My school is ready to open."

"Congratulations." He perused the contents and nodded. "Nathaniel is putting the next edition together now. I'll make sure he includes your notice."

The mention of her man's, rather Nathaniel's, name sent a spike of longing and sadness through her heart. She met Frank's knowing gaze and gulped. Nathaniel was here. She knew he would be. Or at least surmised so. But knowing it and being in the same space proved quite different.

"See that he does." She tried a smile but her lips stiffened. "How is he?"

She'd not meant to ask such an imprudent question. She mentally shook herself. She'd been the one to end their courtship. She had no right to inquire as to his state of mind or being.

"Ask me yourself." Nathaniel appeared from the back room, tall and handsome and his gaze locked on her person. Lines spread from the corners of his eyes and a deep groove etched between his brows. Tense and tired, he studied her for a moment, his gaze flicking down and then meeting hers. A slight frown revealed he had indeed noticed she didn't wear his locket. On a sigh, he studied her for a long moment. "I've missed you, Lyn."

She sucked in a breath in a vain attempt to quiet her pulse rate, a direct reaction to his rich bass voice. Lifting her chin a hair, she prepared to defend her heart from the onslaught of desire and confusion consuming her. "I've been very busy, Mr. Williams, as you must imagine, so have not had time to miss any one."

He nodded slowly, once, then again. "I am doing well, thank you for your query on my behalf."

"As am I." She must remain calm despite the thundering in her ears, the perspiration in her palms, and the urge to move into his arms. "Frank has my advertisement for you to work on."

"You're ready to accept students? I'm sure you're very happy."

He didn't congratulate her or even sound as though he genuinely expressed happiness on her behalf. But then why would he? He wanted her to uproot her life and travel into the wilderness without any promise of a future together.

She had to look out for her own interests and those of her family. Even though she'd like nothing better than to feel his arms around her, his kiss on her lips.

Frank cleared his throat, a raised brow indicating his desire to interrupt. "Will there be anything else, Miss Evelyn? I'm afraid I must meet Emily at her shop in a few minutes to make arrangements for our excursion to France next month."

"France? I hadn't heard you'd decided to take your trip abroad." Evelyn focused on Frank, grateful for an excuse to not look at Nathaniel. "Will you travel with Tommy, too?"

Surely not. Such an adventure could prove detrimental to the child's health, perhaps even fatal should he contract some foreign illness while visiting other countries. Many risks abounded in their own country. She saw no purpose in courting ailments from other lands.

Frank shrugged. "We have many questions yet to answer."

"I'd be happy to have him in my home. He's so young and there seems little reason to risk his health on such a dangerous trip." Evelyn loved children, one of the reasons she looked forward to having so many young girls in her household. The idea of risking the baby's life onboard a ship at sea for pleasure had her shaking her head. Between the dangers of storms, pirates, and lack of fresh food, surely it wouldn't be in the child's best interests. "He'd make a companion for my son, as well."

"I'll convey your offer to my wife." Frank nabbed his hat from a peg by the door. "I'll be back, Nathaniel, in about an hour to proof the type."

Nathaniel picked up the paper from the table. "I'll have this done by then."

"Excellent." Frank tipped his hat to Evelyn and then left the office.

Evelyn found herself staring into Nathaniel's eyes. When

he regarded her with such affection, she had a sense of coming home to a warm embrace. Of safety and security unlike any she experienced with any other man.

"Did you need anything else, Lyn?"

She swallowed, stretching the silence further while scrambling for the right words. She needed him. Longed to follow Peggy's advice if only... She couldn't. "No, I do not believe so."

"It's kind of you to offer to care for Tommy in their absence." He fiddled with the paper in his hands, reminding her of how very clever he could be with those strong fingers.

"One more mouth to feed won't make much difference." She forced her gaze away from his, sweeping the room until she spotted Sawyer contemplating them with humor evident in his expression. She stiffened, irritated by the entire situation. "I must go. It was nice to see you."

He inclined his head. "Until next time."

How many more times might she run into him when she came to town? Perhaps she should stay home until he left. Hide from unwanted encounters which could only serve to stir her senses and emotions, and disrupt her carefully laid plans. Only one thing for her to do.

She fled as gracefully as possible.

Several days later, Nathaniel rode Jingo out to pay a spontaneous visit on Lyn. He rehearsed his little speech as his horse trotted over the packed earth. Dust puffed from under Jingo's hooves with each stride. A canvas sack held his peace offering, bouncing against the roan's shoulder and bumping his knee.

After what seemed like hours he reined his mount to a halt in her barnyard. In one sense, the place seemed a home to him. But the fact remained it wasn't the *place* but the *person* who represented his home. Every aspect of Lyn meshed with what he'd hoped for a new helpmate and lover. If only he could reason with her, make her understand his view of the matter. To accept his offer. Jack emerged from the barn and marched toward him, his long stride making quick work of crossing the yard.

"Good day, Jack." Nathaniel dismounted, dropping to the ground with the ease of an accomplished rider. He untied the sack from the ring on the saddle, and patted Jingo's sweaty neck. "Will you see to Jingo for me? He could use some water."

"Yes, sir. I'll take care of him." Jack took the reins in one hand, preparing to lead the animal into the barn. "Will you be staying the night?"

How he'd love to. He held no illusion she'd receive him with open arms. Not after what she considered his lies and betrayal. Memories of previous nights spent together on her property flashed through his mind and he shook his head to clear them away. "No, I'll be heading back in a little while."

Jack nodded and led Jingo away. Nathaniel watched the pair, the tall dark-skinned man and the pale reddish-brown gelding, disappear into the shadows of the aisle. Then he hurried to the manor house and Lyn.

The door swung open as he bounded up the steps. Peggy stood in the open door, grinning like she'd never stop. He whipped his tricorn from his head, and bowed in greeting to the young woman.

"Mr. Williams, you don't need to bow to the likes of me." Peggy's face had flushed a bright pink. "It's not proper."

Nathaniel held his hat in one hand as he studied the embarrassed lady. "I understand why you say so, but to me you are still a lady. I always bow to a lady."

"I'm no lady, sir." Peggy had turned crimson as she shook her head emphatically. "I'm simply a servant girl trying to get by."

"One day, you'll be free from your debt to Miss Evelyn." Nathaniel moved closer to Peggy and the entrance to the house. "Then you will enjoy the privileges of being a woman equal to any other."

She shrugged and stepped back. "Come on in here. Miss Evelyn is in the music room."

He followed her down the passage, elegantly decorated with vases of flowers set out on occasional tables and sturdy chairs spaced along the oriental carpets. She left him at the door to the room where his woman—he couldn't help but think of her as his—sat at the spinet playing a mournful tune. A melody commonly played at funerals. Why would she choose such a depressing piece?

She espied his entrance and jerked her hands from the keyboard, one flying to her throat. "Nathaniel, what brings you all the way out here? Is something amiss?"

He crossed to stand by her, her frame rigid, poised to rise and flee if he said the wrong thing. She dropped her hand and revealed she still didn't have his locket on. A bad sign. He swallowed as he extended a hand, inviting her to come to him.

"The only thing amiss is us." He wiggled his fingers in invitation. "Will you sit with me?"

She glanced at his hand, then at his face, a question evident in her eyes, before placing her hand in his. He tugged her to her feet and her demeanor changed to wariness. He squeezed her fingers and led her to the settee positioned against the wall opposite the door. Silently, she settled on the seat, arranging her long skirts with a trembling hand. He sat beside her, without letting her go. If he had his way, he'd never release her.

"I have a little something I'd like to give you." Nathaniel put the bag on her lap, and opened the neck to reveal a ripe melon. "It's not much, but it symbolizes my caring for you with a sweet fruit. When you eat it, which I trust you will, I hope you'll think of me."

She studied him for a while, finally permitting a smile to grace her lips. "I enjoy melons. Thank you for bringing me such a fine gift."

"I'm pleased you like it." Nathaniel's tension eased with her ready acceptance of his present. "There's something more I'd like to give you."

Tilting her head to one side, she raised a brow. "What might that be?"

"Lyn, I want to apologize to you for not being more forthcoming regarding my plans." He peered at her, hoping he didn't mangle his speech. "When I came here, I had every intention of staying only as long as necessary before finding a place to settle. When I heard of the opportunity that the frontier offered, I realized what an incredible adventure and chance to make my fortune."

"You've said as much before. What does that have to do with me?"

"I will not leave until June, as agreed. When I go, I'd like for you and Jim to accompany me."

She started shaking her head before he'd finished speaking. "We are not destined to be together. You want to travel and start afresh somewhere far away from here. I've just advertised for my school to open, as you know. I cannot abandon my dreams and hopes to pursue yours."

"We do belong together, my love. We're good for each other." He gripped both her hands, trying to share the urgency he felt. "You know you want to be with me, don't you?"

"I do, but here." She waved a hand as though to brush away his idea. "You could stay here with me."

"I would if my heart and soul allowed me to. I feel as though I'll bust if I don't move on."

"Then we have nothing more to say on the matter." She pulled her hands free and folded them in her lap. "We have to accept the reality that you will leave and I will stay."

"This isn't over." Nathaniel noticed tears glistening in her eyes. How could he stand to leave his heart in South Carolina when his soul demanded he continue on his quest? "We're not over. We'll find a way. I promise you."

Chapter Twelve

$\mathcal{T}$ime had a way of slipping by when Evelyn kept busy. Knowing Nathaniel planned to leave in a little more than a month weighed on her heart. In the past week, she had accepted two young girls into her school. She had room for ten. At the present rate, she'd fill her school within a month of opening. The two students anticipated arriving before the start of formal classes in the fall. Until then, she would have to survive using the money she earned from selling her flowers at the market in town.

The distant rumble of thunder alerted her to an approaching storm. She went to the window looking out the front of the house, but only saw a few clouds to the east. Moving through several rooms, she went to the west side of the house, peering out the small parlor window. Charcoal clouds filled the sky, building and roiling. An incandescent flash preceded a ground-shaking boom. She shivered as the air charged with portent. How she despised thunderstorms.

She went in search of her son, peeking into each room as she strode through the house. Climbing the curving stairs, she wandered through the bedrooms. Finally, she located Peggy rocking Jim, crooning a ditty to soothe his fears from the noise outside. If only singing a song would ease her apprehensions.

"It's only a storm." Peggy maintained the motion of the chair as she looked at Evelyn. "Nothing to worry about, really."

"I try not to fret, but the lightning and thunder unnerve me every time." Evelyn crossed her arms, hugging her waist in a futile effort to hold onto her comportment. "I'm always afraid when the worst ones hit."

All her life, she'd dreaded their existence. Ever since she was a child, and a blinding flash of lightning struck the tree she had sheltered under during a sudden storm. She relived the resulting blast of sound and subsequent fire when the tree exploded over her, showering her with bits and pieces of the tall oak and its leaves. She'd been unable to move from where she'd curled up into a ball, hugging her knees and rocking with fear and shock. Her father had run to her from the barn, snatched her up and carried her inside the house. If he hadn't she might have died. Her mother held her for hours, hugging Evelyn on her lap, until she stopped crying and shaking from the ordeal.

"I understand, but we're safe inside." Peggy glanced at Jim's wide eyes then back at Evelyn. "Why don't you ask Jemma to make tea?"

"That's a fine idea." Evelyn brushed away the horrific memory and turned to retrace her steps.

A shudder moved across her back as she went down the stairs and out the back door. She dashed across the small open space before the impending rain arrived and found Jemma in the kitchen. She requested hot tea and scones with butter and jam and then raced back to the main house, slamming the door shut and leaning against it to catch her breath. Thunder rumbled across the sky, a long, menacing growl thrumming through the boards at her back. She broke contact with the vibrating wood, moving farther into the house. She felt somewhat safer but not by much.

A flash of light preceded an enormous boom that shook the house. She shrieked, clasping both hands over her mouth. Too close. She forced a deep breath, striving for calm despite her inner fear and agitation. With good fortune, the storm would pass posthaste. Another flash of lightning and subsequent roll of thunder had her running for the parlor. She'd sit in her favorite chair and work on some sewing and hope to distract herself from the raging tempest outside her walls. Making good on her plan, she tried with little success to focus.

Running footfalls sounded in the passage, and she lowered her work to see Jack in the open door, dripping wet and eyes wide with fear. She jumped to her feet and crossed to address him. "What's the matter?"

"Lightning struck the barn." He panted his message, struggling to force the words out. "It and the carriage house are both on fire."

"Oh no!" Evelyn ran past him, and he followed her flight down the passage to the back door. "We need buckets of water from the well. Hurry!"

Uncaring of the pelting rain, she rushed to ascertain the extent of damage to the outbuildings. She stopped under the shelter of the tool shed, the heat so intense as to prevent drawing any closer. She stood aghast at the sight of both the barn and carriage house engulfed in flames. Jemma soon stood at her side along with Jack and the other slaves.

"I'll grab some pails from the kitchen." Jemma ran back to the brick building without waiting for a response.

"It ain't no use. We can't fight that, Miss." Jack aimed worried eyes at her, rubbing a hand over his chin. "It's too hot."

"You pulled everything away?" Evelyn stared at the flames before trailing her gaze across the barnyard.

The horses and milk cows had fled to the far end of the pasture, the dogs milling around Evelyn with anxious expressions. Everyone seemed safe for the moment. "It will burn itself out as long as we can contain the flames."

"The other boys are keeping it where it is, Miss." Jack grabbed a pail from Jemma upon her return. "You want me to help them?"

"I can't believe this is happening." She shook her head at the devastation. Another fire, this one caused by an act of God instead of man. She looked back at the house, a mere fifty feet from the flames. She wouldn't lose her home. "But we can protect the manor. Take those pails and defend the house. Move!"

They all worked together throwing water on any exposed wood surfaces. Thank goodness they'd built it mostly of brick and stone. Still parts—doors and window frames—were vulnerable to the heat and smoke. The red light from the fire flickered over the exterior of the house. The sight gave her pause, recalling the previous conflagration. Evoking the stunned horror she'd experienced in hearing of her home consumed by the hungry flames.

She worked alongside the servants, frantically fighting new flames and dowsing hot spots with water. Unaccustomed to such strenuous work, she panted as she retrieved a bucket of water from the well and lugged it to a small fire. She poured enough water to put out the flame, and then spun to see where she needed to go next.

All the while, a heart-wrenching certainty built in her chest, expanding to squeeze out every doubt of its reality. She struggled against the idea, the conviction, consuming what had been her dream. It took divine intervention, but she finally recognized the truth of the matter. What she really needed was to feel safe, secure, and most of all loved. The most important aspect of her desires rested on raising her son with the help of a loving husband. Her dream of teaching couldn't interfere with what was truly important.

She didn't belong here. Mother Nature had sent her message twice, and this time Evelyn would heed it. But where would she go? What would happen to the girls intending to arrive in a couple months, eager to learn?

Questions for another day. The first order of business was to save what she could from the fire. The reddish light had lessened, thanks to her servants' labor. Focusing on the scene before her, she heaved a sigh of gratitude when Jack put out the last of the flames. The other two slaves joined him, holding spades they'd used to smother flames with dirt. Jemma stood by the well, leaning on the stone structure as she wiped a sooty hand across her brow. Peggy emerged from the shadow of the house, carrying Jim in a tight grip, fear plain in her eyes. When had they come out? Evelyn hadn't even noticed them.

"Thank you all for your hard work tonight." Evelyn strode into the yard to stand with her soot-covered, weary servants. She commiserated with how tired and sore they must be. The rain had stopped almost as suddenly as it had started, a relief in its own right. She placed her hands on her hips and perused the small group around her. "Without your help, we'd have lost everything."

"Oh, Miss Evelyn, I'm so relieved." Peggy joggled Jim on her hip, holding one of his little hands. "At least everyone is safe."

"Thanks to Jack's quick thinking." Evelyn tossed him a smile and then looked at Jemma as she yawned. "It's late. We'll see what's salvageable to-morrow and start cleaning up this mess."

"We'll tend to them animals before we turn in. G'night." Jack nodded once, rounded up the other two men, and sauntered toward the pasture.

"Not much good about this night." Jemma yawned again. "Do you still want tea before I turn in, Miss Evelyn?"

Evelyn shook her head with a smile. "You go on. I'll manage."

"Come on, you need rest as well." Peggy inclined her head, indicating with a quick lift of her chin for Evelyn to follow her into the house. "Things will look better in daylight."

Evelyn followed her maid through the back door and into the passage. She pushed the door closed, the thump sounding very final to her mind. The ending punctuation to a sentence. She leaned against the wood, watching Peggy and Jim as they continued down the passage to the stairs. When Peggy reached the bottom, she stopped and waited for Evelyn to push away from the door and stroll toward them.

With each step, the home became a house. While mere hours ago the character of the house welcomed her, now her skin itched and prickled with a sense of alienation. She no longer experienced any comfort from her surroundings, the structure itself seeming to rebuff her presence. She glanced into the various themed rooms as she went, saying goodbye to her scheme.

"Are you all right?" Peggy shifted Jim to her other hip before gripping the rail with her free hand. "You look strange, as if you're afraid. What's the matter?"

"I can't stay here." She shivered, though not cold. "What am I to do?"

Peggy frowned as she spun to face Evelyn. Jim squirmed in her arms, reaching out for his mother. Evelyn accepted him with alacrity, hugging him to her. Her son needed her in any event. He held on to her, and in that moment she remembered the most important aspect of her dream was her promise to provide for her son. To ensure he had the education and upbringing to enable him to succeed as an adult.

In fact, she could be a teacher most anywhere. What never truly mattered ended up being the location.

"You're upset by the fire, but you'll sort it all out on the morrow." Peggy folded her arms, regarding Evelyn for a long moment. "That's not it, is it?"

Her promise could be fulfilled in other ways than the one she'd set out upon. Given time, she'd devise a better course of action. For now, she had only one desire.

"I want to go home." Evelyn kissed Jim on the cheek, reveling in his soft skin scented with chamomile. She peered into her son's jade eyes, recognizing that as long as she had him she actually was home. She speared Peggy with a determined look. "I'm moving back to my parents tomorrow."

"What? You're scaring me."

"I expect you and Jemma will accompany me, so pack what you'll need for an extended stay." The plan unfolded in her head as she spoke. "I will seek my parents' guidance as to what to do with the property."

Delight filled her, replacing the perverse sense of dispossession. Now she was on the right path, though she didn't perceive her destination. Other than an abounding desire to go home. There she would again experience the reassuring security and love she'd been missing. She'd simply stay with her parents until she had a firm idea of what her future would hold.

"Why are you scolding me for returning to town?" Evelyn frowned at her sister while she rocked and nursed her son. At eight months, he stretched across her lap, a little hand curved over her exposed breast as he suckled. "Mother and Father both welcomed me without hesitation."

Amy huffed and shook her head. "Of course, they did.

They never wanted you to strike out on your own so far from them."

"So what are you upset about?"

"You gave up, that's what. First on Nathaniel, and then on your school. What is your next move?"

"I do not know yet. I plan to speak to Father on the subject soon." Evelyn switched Jim from one breast to the other, interrupting the heated discussion for several moments. During the break in the conversation, she framed her next contribution to the exchange. "I suppose I should sell the manor and all the property."

"Must you? You'd have to repay Father for his loan, though you satisfied his first condition." Amy regarded her for a second, a sly smile creeping onto her face. "What about the second one? If you were to find a husband, then you'd not have to worry about paying him back."

"I do not want a husband and I must pay the debt, so I don't have much choice." Since Nat no longer featured in her life, then she'd remain unmarried. Her heart couldn't survive another love so strong and yet denied. "So the sale of the property will pay off the debt."

"I'm sad you and Nathaniel couldn't work things out." Amy fingered the pages of the novel on her lap as the smile turned into a grimace. "He seemed to deflate after you stopped him from waiting on you. His poor heart must be broken."

Hers had shattered, so she empathized with the man in question. She'd loved him with every fiber of her person, every breath, every beat of her heart. Yet he had deceived her about his true intentions. Worse, he prepared to depart the state to move into the unknown. She'd probably never see him again. Perhaps she should at least say farewell and good fortune.

Her breath caught as her pulse sped up to pound in her ears. "When does he expect to leave?"

Amy started, eyes widening as she clutched the book until her knuckles turned white. "You didn't know?"

"Know what?" Evelyn stared at her sister, the rush in her head so loud surely Amy could hear the throbbing.

"He left yesterday." Amy raised the book in front of her chest, flexing her fingers in an unsteady rhythm. "I'm sorry you didn't have chance to say farewell."

If her heart had shattered before, then how could it break all over again? Some part of her had expected to see him at the end of his work day. Surprise him by appearing at the dinner table, wearing the dress he liked. She hadn't anticipated the despair and sorrow of losing him all over again. Her future stretched out before her, a bleak barren road.

"He said he wouldn't leave for another few weeks." Evelyn cleared her throat, swallowing to steady her voice. "What about his promise to Frank?"

"Frank released him since he and Emily have postponed their trip again." Amy laid the book on the low table between them. "Benjamin told me Nathaniel simply wanted to get away from the pain of living without you."

"He told me we'd find a way, but that never happened." Evelyn sat Jim up to burp him, holding a rag made from an old shirt to catch any sputum. "What am I to make of him, Amy? Did he deceive me again?"

Amy folded her hands in her lap, relaxing against the chair back. "I believe he decided to accept the fact you would never agree to leave your family, and he couldn't stay. What compromise is possible in the event?"

"I don't know what to do." Evelyn turned Jim to sit more comfortably on her lap, handing him a smooth wooden rattle to occupy his attention. She fastened the front of her dress and lifted her gaze to meet Amy's. Tears pushed onto her cheeks and slid down to her mouth. "I love him so much it's a physical pain to know I'll never see him again. What am I to do?"

Amy lifted a brow, and nodded sagely. "There's only one thing you can do."

Evelyn studied Amy's mirthful countenance, detecting a serious aspect belying the evident humor and lifted brow. "You're right. If you'll excuse me, I have to speak with our parents."

Spring flowers graced every garden in town. Evelyn had hurried from her parents' house to meet them on their way back from visiting friends. She strolled with them along the street at a pace which became more irritating with every step. Why wouldn't they hurry? Lucille and Richard walked arm in arm, greeting passersby with a nod and a kind word. They'd reached the end of the first block before Evelyn found the nerve to broach the burning subject. She fondled the locket Nat had given her, returned to its rightful place around her neck.

"Father, I am in need of your guidance." Would he agree with her intention? Her heart pounded with anxiety and hope.

"I'm always happy to give advice." Richard winked at her and a grin lit his face. "Even when not asked for my sage wisdom."

She chuckled at his small jest and then sobered. "I have changed my mind as well as my plans."

Her mother lifted a brow in question. "So you've taken some of my advice?"

"Change is not a bad thing, I believe." Evelyn drew in a breath and let it out to the count of three. "I'm not going to open the school. Indeed, I do not wish to live in the house my cousins built for me."

Richard stuttered to a stop, pulling Lucille to a halt beside him. They both gaped at her, eyes wide and silent for several moments. Richard recovered first to shake his head.

"You need me to what? Tell you it's okay to have wasted the time and money?" The slow shake of his head emphasized each word. "What will you do?"

She studied her mother's expression, espying a slow dawning of her true intent in the pressed together lips becoming a knowing smile. "I'm going after Nat. But I do not know what to do about the property, since it is my son's inheritance. What do you suggest?"

She'd said it out loud for the first time. The anticipated terror at the prospect before her never surfaced. Instead, she thrilled at the chance to catch up to the man she wanted as her life companion, her helpmate, her lover. Shifting her weight from one foot to another, she practically danced in the street in her anxiety to head out of town, to find Nat and tell him she'd travel with him to the ends of the earth if he so desired.

"Let me consider for a moment. You've rather flustered me with the sudden change to your plans." Her father peered at her, blinking several times in quick succession. "We shall arrange for your cousins to lease the property, to maintain it and improve it as they see fit, for the next... How old is Jim?"

"Eight months." Pressure built in her chest as the demand to hurry and finish the conversation threatened to overcome her. The time couldn't arrive soon enough for her to escape the town to find her man.

"Ah, yes. Your cousins can manage the property then until Jim is twenty years old." Her father glanced at her mother, a silent exchange of agreement flashing between them.

"A brilliant idea, Father. I knew you would have a sound answer to the dilemma." Her son's inheritance would be in fine hands with the financial wizardry associated with her cousins.

"Do you know where Nathaniel is heading?" Lucille asked.

"Benjamin told Amy that Nat planned to head south to Savannah and then west on the road through Georgia." She'd delayed too long already and the urgency in her breast elevated with each passing second. "If you'll handle the matter, then I shall leave immediately."

"But wait." Lucille frowned and shook her head. "Won't you say goodbye to your family and friends first? Go to-morrow at least, so we can have a farewell dinner for you this afternoon."

"I cannot dally or I may never find him." She clasped her hands to her elbows, pressing her arms against her stomach. "I'm leaving Peggy here as she has elected to take on the girls' school in my stead. I've forgiven her indenture. And she and Bill seemed to have taken a liking to one another, so she finds herself reluctant to leave."

"Do you need money?" Richard rooted in his coat pocket and finally pulled a cloth purse from its depths. He dumped some coins into his palm before gazing at her.

"Thank you, Father, but I have sufficient funds thanks to the sale of my flowers at the market. I really must go."

"Surely you do not intend to travel alone?" Richard's jaw hung as he stared at her. "A woman and child alone will not be safe on the rough roads."

"No, I'd like to take Jack and Jemma with me."

"I've given them to you, so do with them as you will." He put the small purse away and patted his pocket.

"I don't like this idea of yours." Lucille contemplated Evelyn, concern evident in her bearing. "I may never see you again."

Evelyn moved to embrace her mother, holding fast as tears sprung to her eyes and sadness closed her throat. Torn between the urgent need to chase after Nat and the love of her family, she dared linger only a minute more. Memories of their past threatened to weaken her resolve, but then she recalled the love she shared with Nat. She had to find him and tell him she'd love him forever. She eased a distance from her mother to hug her father, smiling through her tears.

"I'm sorry I don't have time for an appropriate parting." Something inside insisted she start on the adventure without further delay. "I'll send you word of my progress when I can. For now, Jack and Jemma are packing the carriage so we can be on our way with all haste."

"I'm relieved you're taking Jack as a minimum." Lucille glanced at Richard and then back to Evelyn. "We'll walk back with you and then see you off."

"I'm grateful for all you both have done for me, and I'll always love you no matter where this path takes me."

She quickened her pace, eager to put the town behind her now that she'd made the most important decision in her life. As long as he didn't elect to deviate from his stated route, or perchance dawdle in some out of the way place, eventually she'd catch up to him.

Chapter Thirteen

Thirty minutes after returning to her parents' house, Evelyn climbed aboard the carriage with Jemma holding Jim beside her. Jack rode a sturdy dark brown gelding, leading the way out of town, following instructions from Benjamin as to the direction Nat had planned to take. The urgency continued to build in her chest as they trotted away from town and toward her man.

Time dragged with each passing mile. The hallmarks of the town gave way to gently rolling hills and forests. Immense herds of deer bounded away from the noisy conveyance. Foxes paused to stare at them before darting into the trees. Red-tailed hawks soared high above, their piercing cry sounding like a warning.

Every hour they rested the horses for a few minutes, themselves dismounting and stretching cramped legs and backs. The hard wheels of the carriage did nothing to absorb the shock of ruts and rocks, rattling their bones and teeth with each jolt. Little Jim fussed for the first hour before crying himself to sleep. Thereafter he seemed to have grown accustomed to the monotony. How far behind Nat had they fallen? How many days of the bumpy ride would she have to endure before she could put her arms around him?

Late afternoon found them approaching a small town grown up around where two roads crossed. In truth, the town consisted only of a handful of buildings, including a tavern, millinery, and an apothecary shop.

"I suggest we ascertain whether we can find lodgings in the tavern." Slowing the horses to a walk, Evelyn studied the group of buildings. "If we go on, we may not come across another place to eat or, worse, sleep for hours."

Jemma tried to quiet the fussy boy. "Jim's tired and hungry, so I agree with you."

"Sure enough the safest plan," Jack said.

Steering the horses toward the tavern, Evelyn halted them. Jack dismounted and moved to hold the bridle of one. After climbing down, Evelyn shook out the wrinkles from her skirt. "I'll be back in a jiffy.

She strode around the carriage and through the door to the tavern, the sound of conversation and a musical pipe meeting her ears. She hesitated inside to allow her eyes to adjust to the dim interior. The large room boasted five tables with chairs, a bar running down the left side, and a small stage where a lone piper played. Along the right wall, a set of stairs led up to the second floor.

"Hello, Miss." An elderly woman stumped toward her, a cane banging the floor with every other step. Her dried apple face featured merry blue eyes and a welcoming smile of yellowed teeth. "What can I get you?"

"My friends and I are seeking a hot meal and beds for the night. Can you help us?"

The woman peered over her shoulder toward the entrance. "I don't see any friends."

Evelyn stiffened at the suggestion she might be lying to the woman. "They are waiting outside with the horses."

The woman bobbed her head several times. "I have a room and supper for you. If you've got any of them slaves along with you, you be sure they find a spot in the loft at the livery next door. No room for the likes of them in here."

"My *friends* will be needing supper as well." She'd not reveal Jemma and Jack's status to the woman, especially since it would be modified before much longer. "We'll tend to our mounts and then return. Thank you for your hospitality."

She spun on her heel and marched outside, glad for the cooler air on her heated cheeks. "There's a livery over there where we can put up the horses and carriage for the night. And a hot supper waiting inside."

"Is something ailing you?" Jemma bounced Jim on her leg as Evelyn stepped back up into the carriage and Jack mounted his gelding.

"Some people prove irritating when they treat others with disrespect." She picked up the reins and slapped them on the horses' haunches.

"What happened?" Jack urged his horse to walk along beside the carriage.

"The proprietress made a point of saying slaves are not welcome within her establishment." She parked the vehicle at the open door of the livery as a tall man emerged from the depths of the stable. "But to sleep in the loft here at the livery. I'll not tolerate such treatment of my friends."

"Don't be getting in trouble over Jem and me." Jack swung his leg over the saddle and dropped to the ground. "We be used to how folks don't want to be around us. I'm willing to sleep over here, keep an eye on our horses and such."

"If you want to, that's one thing. After you have some supper, though." Evelyn climbed out of the carriage, retrieved her travel bag, and then walked over to introduce herself to the owner.

He stood a head taller than her, with brawny arms and wide shoulders. "Good evening, Miss. My name's Bert Jameson and I run the place. What can I do for you?"

"Do you have stalls for three horses and a place to park the carriage overnight?"

"Yes'm, I can help you." He started to turn away to go inside.

"I'd like to let Jack handle settling the horses, while I take care of my son, if you don't mind." She could hear Jim making more noise, the beginnings of a crying fit related to his hunger.

"Fine, fine. We'll manage between us. You can run along, Miss…?"

"Mrs. Hamilton."

"Very good. Rest well this evening."

"Come, Jemma. We'll go on to the tavern and retire to our room to feed the boy before we meet Jack for supper."

Evelyn strode next door to the tavern with purpose fueling her pace, Jemma nearly trotting to keep up. She pushed open the door and ushered in her charges, letting the door swing shut behind them. The woman, a frown on her face, thumped over to where Evelyn and Jemma paused.

"I said no slaves, Miss." The woman shook her head, disgust plain on her face.

"Jemma is no slave. She is my maid."

A gasp came from Jemma's mouth before she slapped a hand over it, flashing a look of hope at Evelyn.

The woman lifted gray brows in surprise. "I'm no fool. I have eyes to see what's before me."

"Then you can see this young woman is a free black, who happens to help me take care of my little boy."

The woman wore doubt like a winter coat. "If you tell me you're saying the truth, I'll believe you. But don't be lying to me."

Lifting her chin, she gazed at the woman for several moments. "I do not lie."

"Very well. I'll show you up to your room so you can refresh yourselves before supper."

Following after the woman, Evelyn glanced behind her at Jemma who smiled back, her elation illuminating her entire face. Evelyn chuckled to herself as she climbed the stairs behind the old woman. Now they had something to celebrate over supper. She longed to continue the journey, to lessen the distance separating her from Nat. But darkness forced her to wait until the sun shone on the morrow to press on.

Showers served only to darken his mood. Nathaniel rode Jingo along the puddle strewn road, heading south on the third day toward Savannah, Georgia, where he'd been advised to turn west. With good fortune, he'd find other adventurers to band together for safety and company. The sound of Jingo's hooves as they plodded along the sloppy thoroughfare became as rhythmic as the ticking of a clock, an underlying reminder of the distance increasing between him and his heart, Lyn.

He'd not expected leaving her behind to be easy. Not for a moment. With each hoof beat, though, his heart sank much like sand flowing through an hourglass. In one direction, with no hope of being turned over to begin again. His Monmouth hat channeled the warm rain onto the shoulders of his light cloak, treated to encourage the water to flow off rather than soaking through to wet his coat and shirt. He glanced over his shoulder at the ponied horse, following docilely alongside his mount loaded with his bed roll, tent, and various supplies necessary for the journey.

He approached the bustling city of Savannah, riding slowly along the road leading into the center of town. He passed farms with crops of cotton and rice on his way. Hogs and chickens roamed freely along the streets. Carriages and wagons rattled and jangled through town. The combined scents of the ocean, of unwashed bodies, and of the droppings of the animals nearly gagged him.

Coming to a juncture of two thoroughfares, he halted Jingo and the ponied gelding to one side and contemplated what he should do next. Strangers flowed past him, barely flicking a glance in his direction as they hurried about their business. The steady rain increased, making him decide to find lodgings for the evening. Soon at any event. A quick look around revealed a tavern halfway down the street stretching to his left. If he turned right, he'd be starting on the westward portion of the road to the Yazoo lands and his fresh start. Yet he didn't urge his horse to walk on. He stared glumly up and down the street, undecided and unhappy.

He'd faced the hardest decision in his life mere days before. While he packed his belongings and prepared for the trip west, he'd shoved aside the ache in his chest. He couldn't allow himself to dwell on the shooting pains stabbing his heart whenever Lyn crossed his mind. He'd done the right thing for her. Not for him. He pressed his right hand to his left breast, attempting to ease the discomfort in his heart. Or was it his soul? Either way, he teetered on the brink of despair.

The first two days of the trip had proved uneventful. Dry dusty roads and bright blue skies inviting him to urge Jingo into a ground covering trot. Eager to begin, he smiled at others who traveled the same road, walking, riding, or in various forms of wheeled vehicles. The terrain didn't vary much as he went south along the coastline. He'd hoped the faster he put space between him and Lyn, the sooner he'd begin to recover from his broken heart. He had quickly discovered he'd been very wrong. When he awoke on the third day to find a gentle summer rain falling, his view of the adventure dimmed.

He and Jingo picked their way for six hours in the rain, slipping on the muddy roads. As a result of the effort Jingo and the ponied horse had to make with the sloppy footing sucking at their hooves, Nathaniel made frequent stops to let the horses rest and drink from a rushing stream. Thus, the sun was well on its way to bed for the day when they had arrived in Savannah.

A shudder rocked his shoulders, Jingo flicking an ear back in query of his abnormal behavior. A wash of urgency flushed through him, leaving him shaky. Or perhaps he was hungry? No, not hunger. Then why did the need to go home overtake his senses with a desperate grip?

It was one thing to have a desire to be at home, but a larger question needed to be answered. Where was his home? He'd left two behind in Charleston, the one in town and Lyn's manor.

A chill worked across his back and down his spine. "I know where home is."

Jingo swiveled both ears back at his statement. Then he stamped one hoof, as if in agreement of Nathaniel's realization. The horse shifted its weight, angling to the left as he cocked his right hind leg. Obviously, he'd come to the end of his patience for dithering on the next move and had decided a nap was in order.

Was Jingo onto something, though? All Nathaniel had to do was turn his head around and ride back to Charlestown, back home to Lyn.

He looked right, peering down the long road leading out of town and away from civilization. Away from Lyn. Away from his home.

"Should I go to her, Jingo?"

The horse tossed his head, jangling the bridle and flapping the leather reins in Nathaniel's hands.

Nathaniel barked a laugh, several elderly matrons glancing sharply at his sudden burst of sound. He tipped his hat to them as they hurried along the side of the street.

"Do you think she'll welcome me into her life again?" Nathaniel gathered the reins, making better contact with Jingo's sensitive mouth, preparing to act on his idea.

The roan waggled his head, a fly pestering his ears, but Nathaniel interpreted the action for himself. "I don't know either, Jingo, but we're going to find out."

Tugging on the left rein, Nathaniel urged Jingo to turn back toward Charlestown. If they traveled at a faster rate, they'd reach town all the more quickly. Heading north, Nathaniel pressed Jingo into a trot, mindful of the treacherous footing for both animals, but anxious to close the distance he'd inserted into his relationship with Lyn. The reward for abandoning his dream? Lyn. If she'd have him.

The next morning as the sun neared its zenith the carriage rattled and bounced behind the pair of trotting bays. Evelyn didn't dare go faster on the rough and rutted road though her heart urged her to increase their pace. She must since Nat, mounted on a single horse and ponying another, would make far better time, thus pulling farther and farther away from her party. The rains of the previous day had done nothing but slow their progress, and increase her concern over being too far behind her man.

"I hope we can catch him up before he leaves Savannah." Evelyn glanced at Jemma perched on the hard seat beside her. "Hang on to Jim so he doesn't bounce out of this blasted vehicle."

"I've got him, don't fret." Jemma clasped the young boy on her lap so he faced the horses' haunches. "He's enjoying himself."

Evelyn smiled as her son's little hands patted Jemma's arms. "He's growing so fast. Isn't it amazing to watch children grow into little people?"

"He'll be walking before you know it."

"I appreciate you coming with me, Jemma. You were under no obligation to embark on this adventure." After the incident at the tavern their first night on the road, Evelyn vowed to act as if Jack and Jemma were freed blacks so they'd be treated with more kindness.

"It seemed the right thing for me to do, since I've grown fond of you and the little one." Jemma shifted her grip on the baby. "I'm happy to look forward to being my own person, free to do what I please."

"You've the right to be free." Evelyn slowed the team to a walk, steered the horses around a hole in the road, and then clucked to pick up the trot again. "Father proved very understanding by not only arranging for the Sullivan brothers to oversee the manor but also by giving me you and Jack."

She looked over her shoulder and smiled at the slave as he rode beside the wagon. The powerful man had a kind heart and an even disposition, thus proving to be a good travelling companion. "I'm glad you've come with me, as well, Jack. When we leave the state, I'll keep my promise to free you both. Then you'll have options as to what your future holds."

The lanky young man tipped his black felt hat with a grin. "The new lands hold more potential for me, so I thank you for freeing me and for the opportunity to escort you to your man."

"I agree with all my heart." Jemma grinned. "He'll be surprised to see you chasing after him, if we can catch him."

Failure to find Nat would be devastating. She'd be adrift in an ocean of strangers and strange lands. She'd be faced with the choice of returning to her parents' home where she'd most likely never be allowed to forget her huge mistake. Or worse, left with the dilemma of how to provide for her son in an unfamiliar town. Given the awful possibilities either choice brought to mind, she had only one course of action to pursue.

"We will." Evelyn smacked the traces on the horses' rumps as the road smoothed out for a distance. "Don't you worry. We'll find him eventually."

"What will the brothers do with such a big house?" Jemma asked.

"They'll likely rebuild the barn as a racing stable. I wish them better luck with the place than I ever had."

"They say those men are gifted, so mayhap they will enjoy success in their endeavor." Jemma chuckled and shifted the boy on her lap. "I'm wondering what we'll find as we continue our journey into the unknown lands."

"I want to find Nat and then worry about the rest." Too many facets of the situation came with risk and danger, let alone uncertainties about the best way forward. As long as she remained focused on what needed to happen as events transpired, she had to believe they would survive and thrive no matter where they landed.

"Looks like we're approaching another town." Jack stood up in his stirrups to stretch for a couple strides before resuming his seat. "Might we stop for a while to refresh ourselves?"

"We all need a rest, including the horses. A short one at any rate." The anxiety pulsing through her veins with each beat of her heart wouldn't permit a longer break in their exodus. Evelyn slowed the horses as they entered the small town's limits. Much like every other town they'd passed through, if you could indeed call the small clusters of buildings a town, Milltown featured a tavern, bank, general store, and other necessary businesses. She spied the livery and soon parked the carriage nearby. She wrapped the reins around the brake and stepped down. "Jack, would you see to the horses, please? We'll meet you at that tavern across the way, the Flying Horse."

She grinned to herself at the swinging sign, featuring a flying white horse. Pegasus. The symbol of her own search for freedom from a life stuck in one place. A life without love. Was it a sign of the success of her mission? She shook the whimsy off as superstition and pivoted to wait for Jemma to clamber out of the carriage and join her on the street. The woman took a moment to adjust Jim's baby dress and then her own, causing a rush of impatience to flow through Evelyn.

Jack dismounted in one fluid swing of his right leg over the horse's back before dropping to the ground. He tied the reins of his horse to the hitching rail. "Sure thing. I'll only be a few minutes."

Jemma clutched Jim to her chest and carefully stepped out of the conveyance. "I'm hungry. We'll order our meals, so they are ready when you come in."

Evelyn stifled a vexed sigh, knowing but resenting the necessity of periodic rests, and led Jemma with Jim across the road to the tavern. "I don't want to stop for long or we'll never catch him."

"Yes, but we have to eat and rest the horses." Jemma paused inside the door of the smoky room. "There's a table in the corner."

Evelyn wended through the maze of tables filled with other guests enjoying an ale with their meal. A card game drew a crowd near the fireplace. The reek of stale cigars and ale battled with the overdose of fragrant waters several women had splashed on. She'd hesitate to call them ladies, however, due to the more revealing fashions of their dresses. In addition, they indulged in dark red lipstick and rouge with painted eyes and lashes. She surveyed the boisterous gathering, noting first the clientele did not behave with the same decorum of places in Charlestown. Second, only a few empty tables remained. She spotted a likely table for the four in her party and strode toward it as quickly as possible, given the number of stares and winks she received from the men she past. As she drew closer to the table, anxious to safely escape the attention of the other customers, she noticed a man sitting alone at a small table by the smudged window. He moved his head, candlelight catching the glint of gold in rich milk chocolate brown hair, and she gasped. Could it be?

"What's wrong?" Jemma came up behind her where she'd stopped to gape.

Evelyn couldn't speak for fear the vision would evaporate. She'd longed for four days to see him, and the moment had arrived when perhaps she had found him. Anticipation fueled her rapid pulse as she gripped the back of a chair at a neighboring table.

"Nat?"

He raised his head with a quick movement and spied her staring at him. His rough features blanched as he shot to his feet. "Lyn. My God, what are you doing here?"

Without conscious thought, she rushed to him, his arms wrapping around her as she'd imagined in her dreams. "I came to find you."

He put enough distance between them to look into her eyes. He inspected every feature of her face, finally locking his gaze to hers as his body stilled. "Why?"

This was her moment. The one in which she must convince him of her intentions. "I've dreamed for many years of flying away on the back of Pegasus. But the statue is fixed in place and never changes. I don't want to live stuck in one spot forever."

"What of your school? Your new house?" He searched her eyes, gripping her shoulders with a firm hold as though afraid she'd disappear. He glanced down and smiled when his gaze lit upon the glint of the filigreed locket. Returning his gaze to hers, his smile widened to include his eyes.

"Peggy has remained behind, and she plans to run the school, hiring help as needed and funding permits." She paused, searching the happy glint in his eyes. "I can be a teacher most anywhere."

"But the manor. You said you could never leave it. You said—"

"Hush. I know what I said, but found I couldn't go through with it. I couldn't live without you in my life. So I've left my estate in the very capable hands of my cousins to make it into their stable. When Jim comes of age, then he may decide what to do with the property." She gripped his hands, drawing him closer. "I love you. I want to be with you no matter where you go. We'll find the perfect place to raise a family out west. No matter what else, I know that you're my home."

"Oh, my love. My Lyn." He clutched her, kissing her—to the cheers and jeers of the tavern's patrons—as though they were alone in the privacy of their home. Easing back from their embrace, he searched her eyes. "Are you certain?"

Ignoring the clamor around them she nodded, too dizzy to put words to her happiness. After the trials she'd endured, the opinions of the others in the room would not stay her actions. She pressed her lips to his, savoring the feel and taste of her man.

"Ahem." Jemma chuckled from behind Evelyn. "You're making quite a scene."

"We'll make more than that." Nathaniel pulled her close, clutching their hands together between them. "Marry me, and we'll make a family together."

"I'll marry you," Evelyn whispered, "and we'll make a home together."

The End

&

Thanks so much for reading *Evelyn's Promise*! I hope you enjoyed Lyn and Nat's story.

To find out about new releases and upcoming appearances, please sign up for my newsletter via my website at www.bettybolte.com. I send out a monthly newsletter with book news to share with my readers, upcoming events and signings, and even a few favorite recipes, puzzles, and other doings!

I'd love to hear from you! Feel free to send me an email at betty@bettybolte.com, find me on Facebook at AuthorBettyBolte, follow me on BookBub, or connect with me on Twitter @BettyBolte.

You can always find an updated list of the titles in this series, as well as all of my other books on my website, at www.bettybolte.com/books/.

Thanks again for reading!

Betty Bolté is known for authentic and accurately researched American historical fiction with heart and supernatural romance novels. She has published more than 20 books of fiction and nonfiction topics. She earned a Master's Degree in English in 2008, emphasizing the study of literature and storytelling, and has judged numerous writing contests for both fiction and nonfiction.

www.ingramcontent.com/pod-product-compliance
Lightning Source LLC
Chambersburg PA
CBHW021122110726
47900CB00007B/2302